VALLEY OF OUTLAWS

VALLEY OF OUTLAWS

Max Brand®

CHIVERS

British Library Cataloguing in Publication Data available

This Large Print edition published by BBC Audiobooks Ltd, Bath, 2010.
Published by arrangement with Golden West Literary Agency .

U.K. Hardcover ISBN 978 1 408 45764 1
U.K. Softcover   ISBN 978 1 408 45765 8

Printed and bound in Great Britain by
CPI Antony Rowe, Chippenham and Eastbourne

Acknowledgments

Valley of Outlaws first appeared as 'Outlaw Valley' by Evan Evans, a five-part serial in Street & Smith's *Far West Illustrated* (4/28–8/28). Copyright © 1928 by Street & Smith Publications, Inc. Copyright © renewed 1955 by Dorothy Faust. Copyright © 2009 by Golden West Literary Agency for restored material. Acknowledgment is made to Condé Nast Publications, Inc., for their co-operation.

Chapter One

At first he had no name, and that was not odd, seeing that, when he appeared in the village, he neither spoke nor appeared to possess hearing, nor bore a sign that would tell people how to call him. He was dressed in a good gray suit, such as businessmen the world over are apt to wear. He had in his hand a slender walking stick, and in his pocket there was a wallet of dark, time-polished pigskin that, when opened, gave out only a small handful of dollar bills.

Everything about this man was neat and precise. He was well barbered and well tailored. There was no outdoor tan on his skin, but it was pink-tinted and clear—the skin of an athlete, as if he were one of those thousands who keep fit in city gymnasiums, squash courts, or swimming tanks. He had smooth, regular features; his hair was a dark, glossy brown; his step was as light and swinging; indeed there was little about him to suggest age. One might have picked him to win a tennis match or come in well in front in a golf match. And yet everyone in the town who saw him judged him to be fifty at the least.

Even on that first day he attracted a good deal of attention. The town of Lister is so small that if a strange dog barks within its

1

precincts, every boy and every housewife notes the new noise, and, of course, the appearance of this deaf-mute excited everyone to the utmost. That excitement grew when the list of his purchases was made known.

From his appearance he would have been set down as a rich man on a Western vacation, but his actions were decidedly out of harmony with that idea. He took $5 in his hand and went from one new gun to another in the rack of Bowen's General Merchandise Store, until Bowen himself, in a pet wrote down on a piece of paper in large letters: $5 WON'T BUY SO MUCH AS THE TRIGGER OF ONE OF THESE GUNS!

The stranger seemed shocked to hear this, and young Sandy Larkin suddenly remembered the Winchester Forty-Five that hung on the wall of his father's room. Once it had blown holes through Indians, but now it was good only to be talked about, and it was coated inside and out with rust. Sandy beckoned the stranger to come after him and led the way to his house, where he displayed the gun. The stranger took down the gun, examined it for a long time with the most painful attention, and then gave his $5 for the relic.

When they passed out through the yard of Sandy's house, the deaf-mute was attracted by an axe head that he kicked up out of the dust beside the chopping block. This he examined with almost as much care as he had given to the rifle. It was of an old pattern, made of the stoutest of German steel—when German steel was the best in the world—but it had a fat-bellied bevel, and it was heavy and clumsy to a degree. It seemed to suit the stranger, however. He offered 25¢ for it and got it for 30¢. Also, for $1.25, he secured an old adz hanging at the side of the woodshed. The day of the adz had passed in the town of Lister.

Returning to Bowen's General Merchandise Store, he now looked over the knives and bought the two best blades in the collection, as Bowen afterward declared. They were long in stock, prohibitively priced, and the stranger picked them out quickly enough from the long case where a big assortment of hunting knives was displayed.

'He's been in the steel business,' said Bowen afterward with much confidence. 'Otherwise, how could he have known?'

After this a quantity of powder and a supply of lead was bought, and also a tarpaulin, a blanket, some salt, and a little flour. The stranger made a pack, clumsily enough, walked a mile out of the town, and then he returned.

He took what appeared to be his last coin from his pocket. It was a 25¢ piece, and, when he pointed to a coil of strong rope, Bowen cut off a dollar's worth and gave it to this singular adventurer.

After that he marched away with a long, strong step, and he was last seen headed for the highest mountains.

For two months Lister buzzed about him.

It was Sandy Larkin who brought down the first authoritative word about him. Sandy, on a hunting trip, had become widely separated from his companions on the gulley-riven side of Mount Shannon, and there, in a narrow little valley, he had come upon a newly built cabin whose logs bore the marks of fresh chippings. In front of it he found a stone oven, most crudely built. When he opened the door, he found that, inside, there was nothing but a homemade chair, a rude table, and a pile of pine boughs for a bed in one corner. Also, around the walls, were a number of coyote, lynx, and wolf skins drying on stretchers.

Sandy found a quarter of venison and, being very hungry, he helped himself to it in true mountain style, and built a fire in the stone oven to cook it. In the midst of this process the owner returned, and Sandy recognized him at once as the deaf-mute who had astonished Lister two months before. He was altered, for he was brown now, very thin, and where his gray suit had been torn it had been roughly mended with sinews. His shoes had given out and on his feet were shapeless moccasins of crude design.

He appeared glad to see Sandy and, with a smile and a wave of his hand, offered the boy all the hospitality that the cabin afforded. Then he put down his rifle and went inside to get salt.

While he was gone, Sandy looked at the old gun. It was well cleaned and oiled, and Sandy learned that the stranger had fitted it with hand-made ammunition. He saw many other details of the curious housekeeping of this man, and returned to Lister bursting with news. Before he left, he had written on the back of an envelope: YOU'D BETTER GET OUT OF HERE BEFORE THE SNOW BEGINS. IT WILL BE TERRIBLE COLD HERE!

But the stranger had merely nodded and smiled, and did not seem to understand the meaning of the message.

'He's a half-wit,' reported Sandy.

This report made a sensation in the town, and a party of hunters who were aimed in that direction promised to find the stranger and bring him in. However, what Sandy had done by chance proved very difficult to accomplish by calculation, for Mount Shannon was clothed in virgin forest, and the forest, in turn, was cut across ten thousand times by gullies, rivulets, and great cañons. It was a labyrinth, and the party of hunters nearly lost their own way, to say nothing of finding the object of their search.

For the sake of convenience he came to be known as 'the man on Mount Shannon', or 'the man on Shannon', and in a little while this bulky title was shortened simply to 'Shannon'. So he received a name.

The mountain turned white with winter. For four months people shivered when they looked at its bald head and forest-darkened sides. Then, with the first thaw of spring, Shannon came down from the mountain, bending under a vast load of pelts. He made no less than four separate journeys before he succeeded in carrying down the last of his pelts. These he turned in at Bowen's store and carried back, in exchange, as many loads of flour, sugar, bacon, coffee, spices, and rolls of strong cotton cloth. In addition, he invested in a new gun with a large store of ammunition, as well as a broad-brimmed hat, a neck cloth, heavy boots—in short, he fitted himself out in garb appropriate to his surroundings.

He was surrounded by curious observers every time he appeared in the streets; many questions were written down and given to him, but uniformly he answered all requests for information by shrugging his shoulders and smiling politely. He had bought some books, paper, ink, and pens, and it seemed clear that Shannon was determined to stay for a long time on the side of his difficult mountain.

For a month he was busy making these journeys back and forth between his cabin and the town of Lister, and, on the last of these return journeys toward the mountain, an unexpected adventure happened to Shannon.

He walked bent under a hundred-pound pack that would have broken the back of an ordinary man, but Shannon was powerfully made, and six or eight months of toiling over the mountains had given him legs of iron. So his progress was slow, but it was steady.

On his second day out, as he went up a trail that was bordered by magnificent silver spruce trees, set out as though by hand for the sake of their beauty and their broad shade, Shannon paused to put down his pack and drink from a twinkling rivulet, and, as he straightened again and the dizziness cleared from his head after bending, he saw a horse standing in the shadows nearby.

It was dying on its feet, dying of old age, he thought, when he first saw it, with its ewe neck and pendulous lower lip and dull eyes, for the withers and hip bones thrust sharply upward and between the ribs were deep shadows. Then he went closer and saw that age could be only one reason for its boniness. For on shoulders, flanks, hips, neck, and even across the head ran great welts that a whip had made. And along the ribs great knots stood out where the loaded end of the whip had been used when it was found that even the cutting lash—it had slit the skin like a knife—was not enough to urge the poor creature forward. On either flank was a great crimson place as big as

7

the hand of a man where the terrible rowels had thrust into the bleeding flesh again and again, and from shoulder to hip ran deep abrasions where the rider, with a swinging movement of his leg, had raked his horse.

But all of these tokens were but minor wounds; the main horror was yet to be seen. For on the right loin, just where the flesh sank away from before the hip bone, the skin had been gathered up, twisted into a knot, and then through this knot, as a skewer, a rough splinter of wood had been thrust.

Shannon jerked the splinter out, but the horse was so far spent that not even its ears twitched. One ear hung forward, the other lay back on its neck, and there was not a quiver in them as the splinter was withdrawn.

There was a long catalogue of other ills besetting this poor creature, such as deep girth galls under each elbow and gaping saddle sores on either side of his spine.

Shannon hastily tore up some grass and offered it; it was untouched. He opened the mouth and placed the grass inside. Some of it fell out; the rest stuck where it had been placed.

Chapter Two

He stood a moment to consider.

There is an old saying in the West that after a white man has ridden a horse to a state of exhaustion, a Mexican can extract another day's labor from the failing animal, and after the Mexican has given it up, an Indian can ride the staggering creature for a week. Indian work, Shannon was willing to venture, it had been in this case.

He took his rifle, made sure that the load was in place, and stepped aside to take aim, but, in taking aim, it seemed to him that he was looking at another animal. His narrowed attention shut out the view of that tormented and grotesque body, and the head in itself suggested such a possibility of equine beauty that the hermit lowered the gun in haste.

He opened the mouth of the horse again, and then drew in his breath sharply. Old age had nothing to do with the condition of this animal. Its state was all the work of a masterpiece of human cruelty, for one glance at the teeth told Shannon that the horse was a scant five years old.

He grounded the butt of the rifle with a crash. Old age may be pitied, but it cannot be salvaged. Youth is a different matter.

Then he could remember that he had heard

or read, somewhere, that hard-worked horses can use a certain percentage of animal food. Even raw meat will sustain them. And this reminded Shannon that among the luxuries that composed this last load of supplies, he had allowed himself one prime treat—two pounds of butter secured in a tin.

He opened the pack straightway and took forth the tin. In the meantime the horse made a last great effort and managed to brace its feet a little farther apart. Its head hung still lower, and shudders of weakness shook the legs.

Shannon lifted the helpless head onto his shoulder, opened the mouth, pulled the tongue out on one side, and into the throat he forced two pounds of choicest butter. Then he stepped back to watch results.

There were no results whatever, apparently. The head hung as low as ever, the eyes were as dead, and the weak legs shook.

He brought water, therefore, and tempted the dying thing with it; still there was no response.

He had bought a quart of good brandy as a medicine. Part of this he poured into the empty butter tin; the remaining half he mixed with water and poured down the throat of the horse. Again there was no response.

He sent the remaining pint of brandy after the first. Then several quarts of water. And yet there was no sign of life.

Then, suddenly, when he had stopped his ministrations, there was a sudden groan, and the hindquarters of the horse sank to the ground in an awkward heap. Vainly he strove to keep his forequarters erect, and in that last effort of courage and spirit he pricked his ears as he struggled. But even that effort could not support him, and he slumped suddenly to the ground. His head struck it with a jar.

The end, thought Shannon.

He had actually remade his pack, when, returning to the horse, he found a slight pulse still moving. So Shannon made up his mind quickly. The last investments that we surrender are those that seem made in a lost cause. Where there is no hope, the imagination and the heart fight hardest.

He cut tender young boughs and wedged bedding around the fallen animal. Upon either side of it he built a strong fire, for the night was beginning and it would soon be very cold.

After that Shannon sat under the stars and watched.

Still the horse breathed; still there was a faint and irregular pulse. By firelight, Shannon began to work on those deep spur wounds, on the wide-mouthed saddle sores, on the gouged place where the splinter had been thrust through skin and flesh. It kept him busy. Presently he was aware that the horse either slept, or was dead. He worked on with gentle touches, half convinced that the body upon

11

which his hands worked was turning cold under them.

So at last the stars began to go out; the great night went slowly away toward the west, and the daylight came, cold and dismal and small. With the dawn came a wind, and with the wind came whistling blasts of rain.

Shannon freshened the two fires and put his coat across the back of the horse. For the animal still lived. He opened his eyes as Shannon stood before him, and pricked his ears a little. That to the man was victory.

The rain was coming faster, now, and certainly, in spite of the protection of the coat and the warmth of the two fires, exposure to the cut of the wind and the wet might finish off this poor derelict. Manifestly the cripple could not be moved except through its own power, so Shannon started to urge it up, and at last, with infinite difficulty, lifting the bulk of the weight with his own hands, he managed to heave the forequarters up. Then he went behind and tugged and heaved again.

At last, braced on legs that wavered and shook beneath him, the beast tried to answer the hand of Shannon and go forward. He pricked his ears once more. In his dull eyes came a faint light, as though to indicate that he understood what was wanted and was willing to do his best.

So, a step at a time, as a child moves when it learns to walk, the horse was brought forward under the high shelter of a spruce with dry ground beneath.

All around him, then, Shannon built a deep bed of softest spruce boughs, taken from young saplings. Then he carried water in his hat, and, the instant it was brought, the poor beast buried its nostrils deep in the liquid. He drank and drank again, and, when the man brought handfuls of seed grass, it was eaten slowly but readily enough. So Shannon had his first real hope.

For a week he lived on that spot. On the fifth day the horse could rise with its own unassisted strength, and go slowly out to graze. On the seventh day Shannon went up the trail and the horse followed like a dog.

Seven days of hand-feeding had made little difference in the appearance of the horse, except that the mud and the ingrained dust had been worked out of its coat, which appeared now as a dark bay. But the sores and wounds refused to close, and the belly seemed about as gaunt as when Shannon had forced the first mouthful down its throat.

Their means of progress was the most leisurely imaginable. Shannon would walk a hundred yards ahead, and then sit down while the bay grazed his way to him, and that process was repeated as they gradually drew a bit farther toward the goal.

That goal was made longer by the roundabout trail that the man was forced to follow, for his usual route, up cliffs and down gulches, would have been quite impossible for the horse. For a whole week they wandered on, and at last they came weaving up the mountainside to the cabin. And when Shannon lifted the latch and walked in, the bay walked in behind him.

Acting on that hint Shannon set to work again. For the building of his cabin he had brought in more logs than actually were necessary, and out of these and some new timber he framed and built a little lean-to against one end of his house. He made it quite high, with a rack of poles stretched across it so that the upper portion could be used as a haymow, for certainly hay must be had if the horse were to live through the winter snows.

Then there was the making of the hay itself. Just up the valley was a level stretch, closely surrounded by timber. Possibly it was the bed of a glacial lake that, having filled in time with sediment, was now rich soil, and here grew tall grass, which Shannon felled with a hunting knife. In these days of mowing machines that eat up many acres in a day, scythe work seems ridiculously slow, and a sickle is worse than useless, but many a time Shannon yearned for so much as a sickle. Reaping a handful at a time, he advanced across that meadow with his knife. The little field seemed like a great prairie. He made gradual inroads here and there, cutting paths to what seemed the choicest grass. And every day he brought in the green load of what he had cut.

So he progressed with his haying—the cutting in the meadow and the shocking of the daily cut near the cabin, and then the storing of the sweet, cured grass in the loft of the horse shed. Furthermore, there was much time to be spent on the bay, grooming him, caring for his wounds.

Many a day went by with no change in the horse except a gradual and scarcely perceptible recovery of strength and spirit. But finally all began to alter. In one day a turning point, as it were, was reached, and from that moment the bay took on flesh rapidly and his wounds closed as if by magic.

Whether it was that his thin, starved blood had first needed to be recruited before his body could swell out to its old strength, or that it required all this time before he could assimilate nourishment properly, Shannon could not tell. He only knew that there was a miraculous alteration almost overnight, and then a daily change in the appearance of the bay.

Once the change began, it progressed with wonderful speed. It was almost like the finding of a new horse each morning, and by degrees Shannon could see that he had picked up no common screw.

He could have told that before. A common nag never could have clung to life as this tormented creature had done. The belly grew sleek first of all. The neck arched, then the lips grew firm and the muzzle square, while fire entered the eyes. After that the quarters and the shoulders filled, the loins were arched across with muscles, and, last of all, the saddle began to be lined with new flesh and the staring ridge of the backbone became a sweeping curve.

The attic now was crammed and hand-packed tightly with good hay, and Shannon had hours to spend at his books, or at his writing paper, if he cared to do so. But he rather chose to spend those hours with the horse.

He had invested such a long agony of time and labor in the creature that it was more of a child than a beast of the field to him, and, as a mother pores over a child at play, so Shannon could sit for hours, contented to watch the beautiful young stallion in his comings and in his goings. To see him eat was a pleasure, almost as if the body of the man were being nourished, likewise; when he drank, he thrust in his muzzle above the nostrils and gulped the snow water as though he loved it. Or again the bay galloped through the meadows or raced with a wild recklessness through the trees, dodging them with a cat-like agility. And it was to the man almost as though he himself raced and leaped and swerved and galloped like mad through the woods.

There was no longer need for him to walk the long round of his valley farm. He could ride the bay. There was neither halter nor bridle requireda touch of the hand or pressure of the knee was sufficient. Life in the mountains was becoming easy and joyous, and, when Shannon thought of that, he would bow his trouble-marked forehead and ponder the future with a great dread. We cannot have beauty and joy without some shadow being cast from the brightness—without the fear of change, at least.

Then, late in the fall, what he dreaded, happened, and the bay was lost to him.

Chapter Three

The day had been long, for at the first streaks of dawn, the stallion began to paw, and Shannon went in wrath to chastise it, but when he opened the door of the shed and saw the lifted head and the joyous, fearless eyes of the horse, his heart melted. He put out his hand to the white-starred brow and speech seemed to rise and swell in the throat of Shannon, although never a word he uttered.

He let the bay out to frolic in the pleasant morning. And all the day was filled, from that moment, with work. The traps were crowded. A coyote was in one fall, a rare wolf was in

17

another, and for his scalp the bounty would be anything between $10 and $50—a veritable prize! Then, in a third, he found a mountain lion, such prey as he never had dreamed of winning.

All these were killed, then, and they must be skinned. By patience and much study of the problems involved, he had learned a good deal about skinning, but he never could rival the skill of a trained worker. Therefore, when at last the carcasses were disposed of and the pelts were framed and on the stretchers, Shannon had no interest in food. He took some jerked venison, swallowed a cup of coffee, and sat down in his doorway to watch the stallion in the meadow. The beautiful creature was stalking a crow as though it hoped to catch and eat it. The wise crow was enjoying the game. It fed in the meadow, or pretended to feed there, with back turned until the stallion pounced. Then, with a flirt of the wings, it would flit ahead or sidewise, to settle once more in apparent unconcern.

Shannon rested from the thought of all labor. He lighted his pipe, and through the drifts of pale, fragrant smoke, he watched the sun slip down in white fire behind the western trees. Suddenly the whole arch of the sky flamed into color. The stream that slid down the ravine was purple and pink and gold. And since the crow had flown away, the bay came closer and made only a pre-tense of grazing, while from time to time it raised its head and looked into the face of its master or up to the great flaring vault of the sky as though pondering deeply and wisely on both.

Then suddenly peace became confusion. The stallion leaped suddenly around, and, when Shannon looked in turn, he saw a rider on a foaming, staggering horse break from the edge of the woods and rush down on them. Twice he turned his head and looked behind him at the forest he had just left, then he saw the bay and threw up both hands in a gesture of perfect joy.

'I've got to have him!' shouted the stranger. 'I'll leave this one . . . the best thing you ever threw a leg over. Do you want pay? Here's a hundred.'

There was no answer from the mute lips of Shannon, but when he saw the other leap to the ground, tear saddle and bridle from his beaten mount, and then go toward the bay, rope in hand, Shannon went into the cabin and came out again, rifle in hand.

He saw a game of tag in progress. The stallion was easily winning, but when he saw his master in the doorway, he fled to him as if for protection. In that instant the rope darted snake-like from the hand of the stranger, and the bay was snared. The rifle rose to the shoulder of Shannon, and he drew a steady bead with a hand as strong and quiet as a rock.

He saw down the sights a lean and

handsome young face, sun-browned, tense with anxiety and haste, and such a wealth of life gleaming from the eyes and quivering in the lips that Shannon lowered the rifle again; he could not fire even at a thief.

Like magic, saddle and bridle had been slipped upon the bay and the youth was in the saddle. Again he glanced over his shoulder at the darkness of the trees, while the stallion stood straight up and neighed loudly and swerved toward Shannon in an agony of fear. The cruel spurs went home. It seemed to Shannon that they were driven into his own sides as the stallion leaped away into the woods beyond.

Then, of a sudden, the little ravine was filled with tumult. A dozen sweating, straining, staggering horses, driven on by whip and spur, came out of the trees and swarmed into the open ground.

'There's the horse! He's near!' someone shouted.

And then, one whose hat had been torn off in the race through the woods so that his hair blew about in confusion, said quietly: 'He's changed to a fresh horse. That's Shannon. But how could he have gotten a horse from Shannon? Where did Shannon get one?'

They came to Shannon, who sat in the doorway, his head upon his hands, and deluged him with excited questions. Had the fugitive secured a fresh horse? In any case, in what direction had he gone? Was he wounded?

Yet never a word of reply did they get to a single one of their questions.

'Why do you talk to a deaf-mute?' he of the wind-blown hair said.

And rapidly he scratched on a piece of paper: WE WANT TERENCE SHAWN. IF YOU CAN PUT US ON HIS TRAIL, THERE IS A FAT REWARD FOR YOU.

He placed that paper before Shannon, and still there was no response.

So he took it again and wrote in large letters: ONE THOUSAND FOR YOU!

When Shannon saw this, he raised his head at last, and the sheriff saw such grief and pain written in that face that he stepped back and beckoned his men to him.

'Leave the old chap alone,' said the sheriff, although indeed he was an older man than the hermit. 'We've got to work this trail out ourselves. Scatter, boys, and cut for sign!'

They scattered obediently. Here and there they poured among the trees, and then there was a sudden shout, and the chase streamed away at the point where Terence Shawn had disappeared.

So Shannon was left alone in the darkening evening, with only the beaten turf to tell of what had been there, and in the place of the beloved stallion, a down-headed, beaten horse, with blood-stained flanks, and heaving sides.

He went slowly toward it. Indeed, there was

no kindness or mercy in the heart of Shannon then, but, in order to occupy himself, he began to walk the abandoned horse up and down, cooling it slowly.

The full darkness descended. The horse stumbled and coughed behind him, then by degrees it freshened a little. It no longer pulled back so heavily on the reins, and Shannon led it to the edge of the creek and watched it drink.

It was midnight when he put it in the shed that the stallion had occupied, but it seemed to Shannon that this substitution was worse than none at all. So does one feel who takes an adopted child, in the vain hope that it will ease the pain when a favorite son has died.

However, that worn-out animal gave him occupation of a sort, during the next few days. It was a strongly made bay, with legs that told of good breeding, and a small head, beautifully placed. Shannon, made wise by his work over the stallion, found it child's play to bring the bay around, and in a few days it was full of life again.

However, he had not the heart to labor over it as he had over the chestnut; it would follow him readily enough, come at his whistle, give him a mount when he worked his trap line, but still there was a vast gulf between it and the other.

So life for Shannon settled back to the same emptiness that he had known before he had found and saved the chestnut. And Shannon resolutely pursued his silent way.

To the horse shed he built a small addition that he filled to the top with neatly corded wood. This he had felled and chopped into lengths in the neighboring woods, and then carried in on his back, for he did not make the mistake of improvidently felling the nearest trunks and making a shambles of his own front yard. All his immediate surroundings remained as wild as ever; the little cabin placed between wild meadow and wild woodland was the only sign of man. Otherwise Nature was left to her own free, tremendous ways.

Then Terence Shawn came again.

Chapter Four

That evening the stone oven barely had been fired up and Shannon was busy with his cookery when the bay whinnied. Shannon looked up, and through the flicker and gleam of the flames he saw a horseman coming up the little valley. Soon the stranger drew near, swung down from the saddle, and, stepping into the dim circle of light, revealed himself as that same lean and handsome cavalier whose previous introduction to the hermit had been so precipitous, Terence Shawn.

23

Shannon went past him with a rush, but the horse to which he stretched out his hand threw up its head and went uncertainly back.

It was not the stallion; it was a beautiful gray, now darkened with sweat, and standing slouched, exhausted, as had that other horse of Shawn's.

The latter was already busily examining the bay, and nodding his satisfaction.

'Here's fifty,' said Shawn. 'And if you can remake a horse as fast as this, you'll get money out of me like water out of a well, old-timer. Hand me something to eat . . . I don't care what. I've got to go on.'

Shannon took the $50, entered his cabin, and came out again. Into the hands of Shawn he put not only that last sum, but also $100, which the outlaw had flung that first day on the ground before the shack.

Shawn stood up, so startled that he dropped from his hand the skewer of wood on which he had been toasting a bit of venison. He stared at Shannon, searched for words, and then, realizing that speech was useless, he scratched rapidly on paper: I'VE TAKEN YOUR HORSE AND LEFT YOU ANOTHER WITH PAY. THE STALLION IS A GRAND ONE, BUT NOT GOOD ENOUGH TO RIDE FOREVER. IF $100 WASN'T ENOUGH, WHAT DO YOU WANT?

Gloomily the hermit stared at these words, then passed back the paper with no added

24

word. He went on with his cooking in that same deadly silence.

Terence Shawn sat down where the shadows were thickest, with his back to a boulder, a stone that had rolled down here from the crest of Mount Shannon some forty or fifty millenniums before. Now moss was gathering around its lower sides, and on its cracked and seamed poll, where dust and leaf mold had settled in the rifts, a scattering of hardy grass and dwarfed shrubbery had grown up, never more than a few inches high. How many more thousands or millions of years would elapse, thought Terry Shawn, before time, and the little prying fingers of winter ice would crumble that heavy mass away and the rivers would carry it down to the sea? Now it sat here in the ravine like an eternal stranger. And so it was, he thought, with this mute hermit. He was dressed in the tatters of any mountain vagabond, and he was set here in the midst of the wilderness, but clothes and position changed him hardly more than the moss and the stunted grass changed the mighty boulder. Both were out of place.

It seemed to Shawn that never had he seen so lofty a forehead, so still and gloomy an eye. Neither sickness nor years could have marked a face as this was marked. It might be that the long curse of deafness and silence had thus left its trace, but it seemed to Shawn more the indication of a trouble of the mind.

There was little reverence or awe in the soul of Terence Shawn. But reverence he felt now, and awe, and a growing shame. Most of all, he was bewildered, for this was an experience outside of all his former knowledge of life and men. If he had taken freely from the strong, like some bandit of the old days of romance, he had given as freely to the weak. The banker might well tremble for the safety of his vaults, when he thought of Terence Shawn, but no poor man had ever been troubled. If he took a night's lodging here and a meal there, he paid threefold, and that was why the sheriff and deputy rode vainly on his trail. They encountered only people who 'didn't know', who had failed to see Shawn go by.

But here, it seemed, was a man who could not be paid for his loss with cash. It struck Shawn that the hermit had passed him like a father going to welcome his son, and, when he had not seen the stallion, he had turned back, buried in gloom.

So much Shawn could observe, even if he could not understand the reason for it, and he was increasingly troubled. To him, hard cash had been an unfailing key to all doors. It never had failed before. And now he felt that his pockets were empty, no matter how many closely packed bills of currency were lining them.

He looked back through the shadows toward his mount. He had stripped the saddle and bridle from it, and, after a drink and a roll, the beast was grazing on the verge of the firelight. It was a good horse, sound and fast, well tested for strength and endurance, and surely there was little choice to be made between it and the stallion.

Yet a difference existed. Now, thinking back, Shawn could remember how the chestnut had taken him down from Mount Shannon and left the sheriff and all the sheriff's chosen men and their flying horses floundering hopelessly behind him. If a horse was no more than a tool to Terence Shawn, when he had ridden the stallion he had known, at least, that he was employing a most efficient instrument. And this helped him to realize the truth—that the horse was something more than a brute beast in the eyes of the hermit.

So he fell into a mood of reverie and wonder, as a man will sometimes do when he learns, for instance, that the youth he has held lightly, mocked and jibed at, perhaps, is the hope and the strength and the pride of some honest household. For all human things there is a human place. But this deaf-mute among the mountains and the horse that had been taken from him seemed almost in a class by themselves.

The eyes of Shawn cleared again as he thought of the problem of this man to whom a horse could mean more than money—more than human beings, perhaps. There was no childish, maudlin emotion about this; instead, the outlaw was aware of something profound and grand.

He made no effort to communicate with the hermit again, but, at the first hint of dawn, he was gone once more, riding the first horse that he had brought to the man of the wilderness.

It danced down the valley with him with the utmost lightness and shook out its kinks in five minutes of complicated and whole-hearted bucking. Then away it sped, streaking through the woods and the gullies with such power that Shawn hardly recognized the mount that, not long before, he thought he had wrung dry of all strength forever.

Straight down from the hills went Shawn, flying back on the same course from which he had recently retreated, and he knew that he was flying in the face of danger. He went with what care he could, but he had come into a region that was extremely difficult to traverse with any secrecy during the day. For the hills were open and rolling, there were not many thickets, and the woods were composed of big trees in small groups, so that one could generally look among the trunks of a grove and see the sky on the farther side.

It was dangerous, but, as he had often done in his life, he trusted to luck and to speed to get him past his enemies before they ever knew he was there. While he was cantering past one of these groves, he saw a glimmer of light move in the trees nearest him, and he swung in the saddle, with a Colt poised.

A tall man had already stepped out, with a Winchester thrown into the crook of his arm, and he waved a cheerful greeting.

Shawn swerved rapidly up to him. 'What's up, Joe?' he asked.

'Oh, they're swarmin' again,' said Joe in casual answer. 'You've got 'em stirred up again, just like a hornet's nest. They're swearin' all the things that they'll do to you, kid.'

'They're hot?' queried the outlaw.

'They're nothing but.'

'I don't see why,' said Shawn.

'Maybe they've got no reason,' answered the tall man, as Shawn led his panting horse into the darkest center of the trees and loosened the girths. 'Only the story that I heard was that when Bowen of the General Merchandise Store came home the other night, he found a gent sitting with his daughter on the front porch. Is that right?'

'I don't know,' answered the other noncommittally.

'It had the sound of nothin' else but Terry Shawn,' insisted the mountaineer. 'Bowen says to his girl . . . "Who's that with you, Kitty? I can't see in the dusk, here."

' "I don't know," says Kitty. "This gentleman says that he's waiting for you."

'Then the gent stood up.

29

' "I was waiting for you, Bowen," he says, "because I swore that I'd come to pay a call on you. I swore it the day that Chet Lorrain was railroaded to the gallows by your high-paid lawyers. I swore to Chet, before he died, that I'd call on you and see whether you'd any claim to keep right on living. My name is Terence Shawn," says you.

'This here little announcement made the girl screech, and old man Bowen, he curled up and reached for his gun. But he changed his mind.

' "All right," says you, according to the story, "I ain't going to do what I came down to do. Because, while waitin', I have been able to see that you have a real reason for deservin' to live, understand?"

'And then you said good night to the girl and beat it. Is that the true story, kid?'

'Suppose that it is,' said the outlaw. 'Why should it make people boil over like this? What harm was there in it?'

'Harm?' shouted Joe. 'Man, do you mean to say you don't know that it's better to kill a man and have done with it than to shame him and let him try to get even afterward? Old Bowen is raving around and swearing that he'll make a saddle out of your tanned hide.'

'Is that all that bothers these people?' asked Terence Shawn in real amazement. 'I tell you, Joe, take things, by and large, I can't figure men and their ways. They just naturally have

30

got me beat.'

'Have they?'

'They have,' said Terence gloomily.

'It's because you're such a simple, honest, and lovin' soul,' declared Joe with profound irony. 'Come on to the shack with me and have a snack of something to eat . . . you're always empty. And then you can explain some things to me.'

Chapter Five

There are plenty of ways of preparing beans, as everyone knows, and if you have any doubt as to the methods of serving them, look at any pork-and-beans advertisement. But Shawn's way was unique. He simply sliced away the top of the can and drank off the contents, the can poised in one hand and a formidable and ragged-edged chunk of pone balanced in the other.

He kept silence. Joe was talking excitedly, but Shawn, with the meditative eyes of one who eats, viewed the far horizon.

'Do you hear me?' barked Joe.

'What?'

'I say, whatever has brought you right back into this mess, so soon after you raised it?'

'Well,' said Terry, searching idly for a reason, 'I wanted to see the girl again. I wanted to apologize for swearing in her presence.'

'You lie,' said Joe with a calm surety.

'I've got to be going,' said Terry with a start.

'Wait half an hour, kid. It'll be near dusk then, and you can slide along through the hills as safe as can be.'

Shawn made no answer. He went on out into the open. There he took his horse and drew up the cinches.

'You know that sucker, Dick Glover?' inquired Shawn, still with his mind remote from the situation.

'Went to school with him,' said Joe.

'You're friends?'

'None better. We used to fight only on week-ends. Sundays we rested.'

'I did Dick Glover a good turn the other day,' announced Mr. Shawn.

'How come? I didn't hear him giving you any special praise last time I saw him,' remarked Joe.

'Which was when?'

'This morning.'

'Where?'

'Hereabouts. He was with the posse. All he wants of you is the hide,' was Joe's reassuring reply.

'There's gratitude,' said Terry Shawn, striking a thoughtful attitude. He added, with a sigh: 'You know, Joe, people have got me beat so bad I pretty near give up.'

'What? Liquor?' asked Joe hopefully.

'No, hope,' said Shawn. 'I pretty near give up hope. I've always been saying to myself that one day I'll settle down fine and sober and be a credit to some lucky town. Do you see?'

'Go on,' said Joe, yawning shamelessly, and making no effort to hide it.

'But now that I come to think it over,' he said, 'I don't know that it's worth while. Being bad is easy . . . just live naturally and you're sure to raise a riot. But doing good . . . that's the stickler, and that's what breaks my heart. I'm like a little kid, Joe, I just don't understand.'

'My heart . . . it sure does bleed for you,' said Joe, rubbing his chin with knuckles hard as flint.

'You take Bowen,' explained the outlaw, putting his foot in the stirrup. 'Now that fat sucker comes home and finds a gent waiting all ready to kill him and roll his fat body down into the gully and chuck twenty ton of slip rock down on top of it. I had the place all picked out, Joe,' said Shawn sadly.

'Stop,' said Joe. 'I'm goin' to bust out cryin' when I think what you've given up, kid.'

'But I didn't kill him,' said the outlaw. 'I let him crawl away, the skunk, and I said no more about troubling him.'

'No,' said Joe, 'you never would understand. It's this way. Bowen's a gent that's always been lord and master the minute that he stepped

33

inside his front gate. And along you come and show him up to be a four-flusher. And the one you pick to show it in front of ain't anybody but the person that's nearest and dearest to him. I mean Kitty Bowen! And still you can't understand.'

'*Ah,*' murmured the other. 'Perhaps you're right. You could always cut for sign wonderful, Joe. But the other thing,' went on Terry Shawn, after giving his horse a violent warning to stand still, 'the other thing that cuts me up the most, is about your old friend, Dick Glover.'

'My boyhood chum,' Joe assured him.

'There's a gent,' said Shawn, 'that I was right charitable to the other day.'

'How come, would you mind saying?' asked Joe.

'Why no, I'd as soon tell. I was coming along in the need of a horse, and riding a regular hell-cat on steel. I says to myself . . . "where shall I leave a grand horse like that and take up another? Because, no matter where I go, I'm sure to leave a better horse than I take." Well, I could have drifted over and taken Sim Peters's roan mare, or around to Calway's in the draw and got his brown gelding that talks three languages and runs like thunder. But I happened to think of the nice hardy colt that Dick Glover had, and I said to myself . . . "Dick and me have never been particular good friends, so why not start right in now and put

34

him on the list?"

'Well, I did it, Joe. I dropped over and cut his horse out of the corral and I strapped down my horse and left him in the place of the fresh one. Now, Joe, the next thing I hear is that Dick Glover is on my trail and after my scalp.

'It's hard, Joe,' sighed the outlaw. 'And there's no pleasing men. The best way is just to hold 'em up, rob 'em, and make 'em feel friendly because you took their money and not their hide. Joe, I'm plumb disgusted. I've got half a mind,' he added gloomily, 'to cut loose from these here diggings and strike away in a new direction.'

Joe, during the latter part of this moving speech, had been busy working the corner of a cut of tobacco, and now he bit off a huge section and stowed it with difficulty in one capacious cheek.

'Might it have been a chestnut?' asked Joe at last.

'It was,' said Shawn. 'And I'm not surprised that you know about it, Joe. A horse like that . . . every 'puncher on the range would be breaking his heart for him after a few days.'

'Bones,' said Joe.

'What do you mean?' asked Shawn, confused.

'You said hearts . . . I said bones.'

'What's your drift, Joe?' Shawn was more puzzled than before.

'I said that horse would break more bones than he ever would have a chance to break hearts.'

'You're wrong,' answered the outlaw complacently. 'He's a lamb. I never came across one like him. Went like silk and I never had to touch him with a whip or a spur all the way down from the hills. It was like being tied to wind. Let him go and it was like sailing a kite . . . you just touched the high spots. Slow him up, and he came back as smooth and as soft as your own bandanna handkerchief.' Mr. Shawn cast about him for more eloquent words, for there was the light of disbelief in the eye of Joe.

'You could put that horse,' continued Shawn, 'in a corner and tell him to stand, and he'd stand all day. You could put him outside your door and he'd watch it like a dog. He was a horse that you could have sat down and had your coffee with in the morning. I used to read the newspaper to him,' added Terry Shawn, warming to his story. 'Now what have you got to say to that?'

He sat in his saddle and grinned amiably down upon Joe, who answered with gravity: 'There are gifts that can't be gained by study,' he began. 'You've got to have a talent for 'em. You've got to have a head start, so to speak. And then you've got to keep right on cultivating, to have the sort of gift that you've got, kid. It's rare, kid, and it's beautiful.'

Young Terence Shawn turned his handsome head a little. 'What's that?' he asked expectantly.

'I have seen some grand men in my day,' said Joe. 'Right back in my village there was a world-beater . . . and down in Mexico I met a couple of gents with the real native talent. But I tell you, Terry, that when you open up and get into your stride, there ain't anybody like you at all. You stand away off by yourself.'

'Shut up!' commanded Shawn. 'Stand off for what?'

'For grand, gray-bearded, mossy, granite-faced, cloud-busting lying,' declared Joe. 'I've got a real respect for you, kid. When I hear you open up on one of your yarns, I wish that I could put it down in shorthand. When you die, I'm goin' to get famous repeating things that you've said.'

'Humph,' said Shawn without wrath. 'Go on, you sap. Go on an' get the poison out of you. What's wrong with what I've said? I might draw in my ears about reading the newspaper to him. Nothing else.'

'You know Chuck Marvin?' asked Joe, ignoring Shawn's remarks.

'Don't I?' was Shawn's fervent reply.

'Can he ride?'

'About the best on the range . . . bar one,' said Shawn with a shameless assurance.

Joe could not help a faint smile. 'I was over to see a little party the other day,' said Joe. 'It was Chuck Marvin, who'd come a three-days' journey to take a ride on a chestnut horse that a greaser has got over at Lister.'

'Look here,' said young Shawn. 'I'm talking about a horse that I left with . . .'

'Keep yourself in line,' said Joe, 'and wait for your turn. I say I saw Chuck Marvin workin' and laborin' on that chestnut . . .'

'He's a grand man to rake a horse,' admitted Shawn with some jealousy in his voice.

'Grand?' repeated Joe contemptuously. 'The only use he had for his spurs was to sink 'em into the cinches and wish that they were fish hooks. Chuck, he could hardly keep his head tied onto his neck. First he banged one shoulder and then the other . . . then he tried to sink his chin through his chest, and after that he tried to hit the small of his spine with the back of his head. He kept a good hold on the pommel and the cantle, too. But pretty soon his wrists began to give way. There was a dash of sun-fishing thrown in at the end, but I can tell you with all that the chestnut was just getting warmed up to the work!'

'It's another horse,' insisted Shawn with irritation. 'It couldn't . . .'

'The doctor worked over Chuck for pretty near an hour before he came to,' went on Joe, unperturbed. 'Lucky he wasn't hurt bad . . . only a few ribs and an ankle smashed, as it was. Though I did hear something about

38

concussion of the brain, and a twisted backbone. Otherwise, he was as fine as could be . . . as fine as you'd expect a gent to be after ridin' on a horse that would sit down in a corner like a dog and listen when you read the mornin' paper.'

'What an ornery, mean, low-down, useless critter you are, Joe!' remarked young Mr. Shawn with some irritability. 'I still tell you that I don't know anything about this horse you're talking about.'

'*Aw,*' said the tall man, 'Glover tried to keep the horse, but a greaser in town saw it and claimed it and had ten pals to swear it was stolen from him a couple of months ago. He knew its brand, its name, its bloodlines, and everything else about it, and the judge had to pass the horse on to him before Glover even had a chance to get the pony shod.'

'Pony?' said Shawn with a rising anger.

'No,' said Joe, ignoring the interruption, 'they didn't get him shod. They took him down there and they started. But they only had eight men and ropes to handle him, and he knocked over the anvil, smashed the forge, and spilled the fire everywhere. And while they were putting out the fire, he just took off the rear end of the shop and chucked it out into the pasture, and then he walked off to enjoy the sun. However, the greaser has him now, and he's offering the horse to anybody that can ride him. The only drawback is that you've got to pay five dollars a throw.'

'It beats me,' said Terence Shawn with a good round oath. 'He's the sort that would eat out of the hand of a baby.'

'He still would,' said Joe. 'And you could let him walk over ten babies and he never would touch one of them. And he stands in his pasture there and makes love to everybody that goes by. But if you start to make him do anything . . . that's a little different.'

'*Bah!*' said Shawn. 'I can make that horse . . .'

'You can't,' said Joe firmly. 'You didn't know him. He wasn't grown up the last time you met him. But now he's had experience, and he's changed, and you wouldn't know him. They call him Sky Pilot over in Lister now.'

After a moment of thought, Mr. Shawn changed the conversation. 'When you get to town, get me a side of bacon, will you?' he asked.

'Sure I will.'

'Here's the price,' said Shawn, tossing him a bill.

'I don't need fifty dollars for a side of bacon,' said Joe.

'I've got no change, and I'm in a hurry. I'm goin' to get me the chestnut, Sky Pilot, Joe.'

Joe folded the bill and slipped it into his money belt.

'You go right on, son,' he said. 'I don't think

40

you'll ever come back to bother me for the change.'

Chapter Six

His horse had profited by a thorough breathing spell—the cool of the dusk was beginning—and now the kid galloped briskly away, taking the straight road for Lister. He had not had that goal in his mind when he started, but wherever the horse was, there was his duty.

Duty had forced him to undertake the restoration of the horse to the old man, and he wondered to himself, speculatively, how difficult the task would prove when he approached the town and found the pony.

He would have preferred that the horse should be in the hands of any rancher, no matter how rich or how well he kept the chestnut guarded, for such men could be deceived. But for a fellow of the type he guessed the Mexican to be—that was a different matter. It would be like entering a wolf's den to take away the cubs before the mother's very eyes. A horse that brought in $5 a ride was, to the Mexican no doubt, a veritable treasure, and neither day nor night would the fellow be away from the stallion.

Purposely he had not asked where the

chestnut was kept. That information he wished to draw from another source, and the thought of the coming interview made Terry Shawn tilt his head a bit to one side, with an expression that was close to sheer deviltry.

So he went on toward the town of Lister cheerfully, not allowing his thoughts to roam too far into the future. Indeed, there never was a great deal of time for reflection in the life of Terry Shawn, for he never settled down to a lonely moment without having to listen up and down the wind, like a hunted wolf. And whether he were facing some winter storm in one at the bleak mountain passes, or whether he were passing a month of watchful waiting in the ravines of Mount Shannon, or among its lofty, polished peaks of rock, his soul was usually less employed than his wits, his eyes, and all his senses. He had a natural instinct for trickery, knavery, and fun, and this he allowed full play at all times.

He swung out of the dark at last, above the town of Lister, and he examined it with complacent satisfaction, almost as one might regard a picture one has painted. For he knew Lister so well that each of the lights had a meaning for him, and he could even pick out the dim glimmer of Mrs. Dodge's lamp from the broader and clearer flare of Mrs. Thompson's window across the street. He knew Lister. He had to know it, for Lister was his base of supplies.

So he studied the familiar spot, as I have said, with a perfect content, and then he drifted off to one side. He left the lights of the little town behind him, entered a little valley, and came presently through the trees of the grounds of a considerable ranch house. He listened carefully for a moment, and looked keenly about. Then boldly he rode from covert.

Behind the ranch house, from their own quarters, the cowhands were raising a song; a dog slipped from the shadow of a brush patch, sniffed at the legs of Mr. Shawn's horse and disappeared again, and Terence Shawn went on to the farther corner of the building.

There he stooped from the saddle and looked in through the open kitchen window. A large Negress was waddling about the room, intent, apparently, on repairing the after-supper disorder, evidenced in the heaped pans that strewed the sink. She had a benevolent appearance, did the Negress, although he could not decide whether it was an inner content that made her so cheerful or simply a habitual and fixed expression of joy, which the constantly uptilted corners of her mouth gave her.

'Hello,' he said.

'Where you talkin' from?' said the Negress, lifting her head and surveying the ceiling. 'Has you come down for ol' Aunt Midget, angels?'

'Hello,' said Shawn again.

And now she located him. 'Hello, man,' she said. 'What you want?'

'A great big slice out of that roast ham that you've got there on the warming shelf.'

'Step right inside,' said the cook. 'Step right inside and help yourself! I hope I ain't turned no hungry creature from my door. Nor neither would Missus Bowen be wantin' me to.'

Shawn obeyed the invitation, literally stepping out of the stirrups and through the window.

'You-all has been riding quite a piece,' said Aunt Midget. 'Set down and shove your feet under that table.'

'Everybody gone from home?' asked Shawn.

'Everybody,' said Aunt Midget. 'There ain't scarcely anybody in callin' distance of me except about ten of the boys in the bunkhouse. You hear 'em tunin' up?' She jerked her thumb over her shoulder toward the window, through which poured the strains of hoarse and timeless music from the cowpunchers.

Terence Shawn smiled. He could not help understanding this scarcely concealed reference to the cook's guard so close at hand—in case Terence should turn out a robber.

However, she made no pause for him to speak, but went blandly on in her good-natured, husky voice, informing him that the family had gone into Lister to attend a dance in the town dance and lecture hall.

'And what be your business in this part of the world?' asked Aunt Midget, piling a new heap of chops on the plate before her guest.

'I've been hearing a good deal about a bang-up sort of a horse around here,' he said. 'I mean a horse that some greaser has got . . . a horse that anybody can have who can ride him.'

'You mean Sky Pilot?' she asked. 'I heard about him, too. He's as good as an epidemic to the doctors. He lays up a man a day, regular. And there's nothin' small and mean about him. No cracked ribs and bruises and dislocations, and such. When Sky Pilot gets busy, he finishes up. Busted hips is special with him'—Aunt Midget sighed—'and fractured skulls he is extra fond of doing. But slammin' them on the ground so that there's nothing left of them to patch is his main line. He's a lovely horse, I can tell you. And you'd be comin' down to ride him, young man. Is that it?'

'A man can have a try,' he suggested. 'There's no harm in that, Aunt Midget.'

'There ain't,' she said. 'You can no more than lose your life, and we've all got to die someday. Only it ain't just the sort of a death that I'd be pickin' you out to choose.'

'No?' he said politely, swallowing a great draft of coffee. 'How would you lay me out, Aunt Midget? How would you figure that I'd be trimmed up and put on the shelf?'

She turned and looked down at him with a

degree of penetration that gave her almost a disdainful look. 'Guns,' said Aunt Midget at last.

'Guns?' he cried. And he held up his hands.

She nodded vigorously. 'You've hardly ever seen such things, most likely,' she said, winking broadly.

'I'm a quiet man,' he declared.

'All the bad ones are,' she answered with a perfect assurance. 'A fire that roars ain't the fire that does the work. The fire that just gives a quiet little hiss . . . that's the one that burns the bread in the oven and melts the top off of the stove.' She nodded her head again.

Terence Shawn narrowed his eyes. 'Suppose that you're right?' he suggested. 'What then?'

'Oh, I'm right,' she assured him confidently.

'You don't seem scared, Aunt Midget,' he teased.

'Scared?' she cried. 'Scared of a man?' Her strong bass laughter boomed and flooded through the kitchen until the pans heaped in the sink trembled with the vibration.

'I have swep' out a whole roomful of 'em,' she said. 'I have started forty of the wildest mankillers on the run with one ladle of soup in their faces.' And, as she spoke, she scooped out a dipperful from a great black pot at the rear of the stove and waved it in the air. Shawn shrank away with startled eyes. But she, without spilling so much as a drop, returned the ladle to the pot. She chuckled softly.

46

'Scared?' she said. 'I hope no man is ever goin' to scare Aunt Midget. But, land . . . a little, narrow, wizened-up boy like you . . . !'

Her laughter boomed again and Shawn flushed a little. He had a vague and boyish desire to announce himself in all the splendid dignity of his crimes and his daring deeds, but he restrained the impulse and smiled instead.

'I won't try,' he said. 'I wanted to talk about a horse, and not about guns, Aunt Midget. Where could I find the Mexican?'

'That José? I don't know. You go down and ask for the meanest-lookin' man in town, and the orneriest, and the worst, and that's him. I don't know where he lives.'

'You never saw Sky Pilot bucking?'

'I never saw him pitch one lick,' sighed the fat Negress. 'Fact is, it ain't no easy thing for me to go roamin' around the country. When I tried to get into the buckboard the other day, the dog-gone' step, it busted away under me. Everything, these days, is made for lightweights and skeletons. They don't take no account of folks with a little substance to 'em!'

Meanwhile Terence Shawn had risen to go.

'Here, you!' called the cook. 'Mister Outlaw, Mister Robber, Mister Horse Thief . . . whatever your name might be . . . you come back here and sit down and try some of this pudding. It'll be good for what ails you.'

Chapter Seven

Comfortable, and at rest with himself and the world at large, Terence Shawn at last departed. Only with difficulty had he been able to press $1 into the great, moist hand of Aunt Midget, and now he jogged his refreshed horse softly through the night.

And anyone, seeing into the mind of Shawn, might have had reason to believe that before the morning Aunt Midget might have cause to revise some of her opinions about the harmlessness of men. For an idea had come to Shawn, which, as it developed slowly, pleased him more and more as it stepped from shadow into the light of a fuller understanding and determination.

He had come to Lister to ask about the horse and to hear an answer from a very special pair of lips, and although he had no doubt that he could learn what he wished from the first chance passer-by on the road, still he was inclined to persist in his first determination to take the reply from one only.

And that one was none other than Kitty Bowen.

She had rested in his mind ever since his last meeting with her. She was no classic beauty. Her mouth was too large, except when she smiled and dimpled. Her nose was too short, and it wrinkled absurdly out of sight when she laughed. But she was so finely made, so poised, so clear cut, that one could not but rejoice to look at her. Besides, the sound of her voice attracted one from the first. You learned from it of her splendid womanliness, of the warmth of her heart, and, when you looked at her, you saw, not the slight imperfections, but the glorious whole of her.

Ever since his meeting with her, the image of her had lain in the back of the outlaw's mind. And now he had a foolish desire to hear of Sky Pilot through her, and her alone. He knew that it was a perverse and foolish desire, and yet he could not help being sure that he never would give up the effort to see her until he had fulfilled that desire.

There was nothing in his mind to say to her, except to put the one question. No doubt she would think him as mad as this act deserved to be called, but, for some reason, what she thought of it hardly mattered. He merely wanted to be close enough to see her, to breathe of her presence, to taste the wine of a delightful personality, and then it would be easier to go back to the loneliness, the long rides, the deadly silence of the dark nights among the mountains or on the bare and dangerous face of the plains.

So he came to his decision, although the reasons, as always, were vague, uncertain, unimportant. His resolution had gripped him almost before he knew it. Feeling the truth of that, he was not a little reminded of the ways of the habitual drunkard, drawn down the street by an inexplicable force, until at last the familiar saloon sign flares before him, and he turns with a guilty thrill through the familiar swinging doors and into the aroma of damp sawdust, of smoke, of pungent beer and whiskey. So young Terence Shawn was drawn on by an irresistible fate, knowing that danger lay ahead, yet rather prizing the adventure because of the thrill that was in it. And he went straight to the lecture hall.

He knew all about the place. There had been a time when, with no shadow on his name and fame, he had walked freely into that big barn-like building, had presented his ticket for two, and, idling a moment at the door, had then drifted off into the dance. In those times he had looked all men in the face carelessly, cheerfully. He looked them in the face still, because he dared not do otherwise. He must search every eye to see where danger lurked.

Opposite, and a little down the street, in the mouth of the dark alley that ran between Duncan's Livery Stable and the Lucas Blacksmith Shop, he sat in the saddle and looked across to the dimly lighted doorway of the hall. The familiar knot was there of cowpunchers who had tired of the dance or could not find partners, and who therefore had come out here to look at the stars and guess about the weather and remark on the progress of various love affairs—old and new.

They leaned against the hitching rack on their elbows. They leaned against the wall. They shifted to stare curiously at new arrivals. And suddenly Shawn was glad that he was not one of them. They had their world of people, but he had his world of the mountains.

He looked back at them, dim and gigantic across the stars, and he would not have changed. This cheapness, this paltriness, this humdrum existence.

Almost fiercely, he turned and jogged around the block and tethered his tired horse in the brush just behind the hall.

Two or three young couples were out there, moving slowly, arms entwined, talking in low, tender tones. And even love seemed small, foolish, and petty to him.

He stood in the starlight and considered the matter for another moment. In logic and in common sense, he had seen enough to convince him that the game was not worth the candle. She, after all, was like the rest. She was in there dancing, chattering, nodding, smiling incessantly, while the tired whine of the violins moaned through the air.

No common sense in what he was about to do, either, but, as one who has put his hand to a task, he felt impelled to finish it. The sudden contempt he felt for all these people made him the more confident in going on with the

51

scheme.

So he returned boldly to the front of the building. In the darkness around the first corner he paused, and there he brushed himself carefully. He had only a handkerchief to work with, but then he knew where all the dust wrinkles were, and it was not the first time that he had made himself presentable without light or mirror.

His chaps remained behind, hanging over the saddle horn, and it left him lighter and surer of foot for whatever emergency might occur.

So he went forward and turned in through the doorway. There was only a casual turning of heads, he noted scornfully. Blind creatures not to recognize a danger in their midst.

At the ticket window he was asked: 'How many?'

'One, please.'

'That'll be a dollar . . . You get your supper ticket inside.' And the hands tore off a ticket from the roll without a lift of the head to scan the face of this new patron.

Then, behind him, Shawn heard a quiet voice among the idlers at the door: 'Boys, that was Terence Shawn.'

The ticket seller looked up hastily enough at that. His jaw fell and his eyes grew big. Both his brown, gnarled hands reached for the cash box. One of those brave fools and noble cowards, who die for their sense of duty, was this man.

'It's all right,' said Shawn. 'I'm not on the warpath . . . unless I have to be.'

Chapter Eight

Before entering the building, Shawn turned and looked back, and he noted the narrowness of the passageway that opened upon the street. The single lamp that illumined it gave a dim and smoky light, yet it was decidedly bright enough to shoot by and he knew that, in case of a retreat, he could not come back this way.

He went briskly on up the steps, which widened and opened above upon the spacious reception room in front of the dance hall. Smoking was not allowed here, but certain cleverly surreptitious smokers held their cigarettes in hollows of their hands, touched their lips only now and again with innocent fingers, and yet appeared to be faintly breathing cigarette smoke all the time. He, Terence Shawn, never had been one of these rule breakers, even in the days of his wildest boyhood, for he had scorned such petty misdeeds. That contempt that he had felt surging in him before, now rose and grew into a mastering passion.

There were fully a dozen youths loitering here, and every one of them appeared to know him on sight. They gaped at him and from one set of loosened fingers a cigarette dropped and was allowed to glow, unheeded, upon the floor. But Shawn went on through the wide doorway and entered the dance hall itself.

Two dangerous situations had been met and now lay behind him. Some of those youngsters he had just passed appeared weak and vicious enough to shoot a man through the back, but he dared not turn to glance behind him. What shielded and supported him now, above all, was simply his own calm indifference to the circumstances in which he found himself.

The dance was in full sway; the orchestra on the far platform had not exhausted its first energy; the violinist was profuse with trills, and the cornetist made his instrument tremble with grace notes, and the slide trombone still clowned vigorously through the most raggy passages. The floor throbbed underfoot; the very streamers and cross lines of bunting high above swayed and shook with the music and with the dance. And Terence Shawn looked into his own heart and marveled, for he was not moved.

There had been a time when he had yearned for another sight of the familiar dance floor, more than for diamonds. That time was gone. Lister, from his fortified viewpoint, this evening, appeared no more than an ant hole, and all its people, rich and poor, were like ants, stirring busily here and there, working or playing, never idle—yet still cramped in that dark hole in the ground in spite of all of their activities.

So thought Terence Shawn, as he stood at one side and watched the dancers go by. He thought that they seemed not really happy. Here and there he saw a jolly couple, recently become lovers, perhaps, and enthralled, still, by the marvels of one another. But the majority of the dancers were not happy. They had come because they hoped for a joy that they could not find, and they remained in the weary hope that something rare would happen, some touch of the heavenly fire descend, perhaps, before their eyes and set a human soul on fire.

But presently he saw the two people in whom, for obvious reasons, he was most interested. One was the sheriff, the other was the sheriff's partner, Kitty Bowen.

The regular concentric circles of the dancers began to diverge and fall into disorder now. Many of the couples had stopped dancing. Some hurried toward their chairs, ranged along the four walls; some huddled together in dense groups, the women gravitating to the inside of these groups, and the men remaining on the outer rims. And even those who continued to dance were turning their eyes, more and more, upon that slender young man who stood near the door, one hand upon his hip, only his head moving a little, as he swept the hall with his calm scrutiny.

So, out of the maze, the sheriff suddenly came striding, Kitty Bowen at his side, toward Shawn.

He was a fighting man. His jaw was set, and the muscles at the base of it were bulging, while his eyes glared. He would have come shooting, beyond a doubt, had it not been that Kitty Bowen was trying to keep up with him— and clutched his right arm to keep pace.

'Terry Shawn,' rasped the sheriff, 'I . . .'

'Hello, Sheriff,' interrupted Mr. Shawn pleasantly. 'Now, I call it dog-gone" kind of you to give up your dance to me, Sheriff. See you later, old fellow.'

And he stepped forward and took Kitty Bowen in his arms. The sheriff, dazed, stretched out a detaining hand, but it slipped from the coat of Mr. Shawn, and there the dignitary of the law stood, crimson-faced and motionless. He realized that it must have seemed that when the rider appeared, he, the upholder of the law, had straightway brought a dancing partner to the criminal, and patted him kindly upon the shoulder, as the two danced away together.

What could he do? The sheriff quite forgot his guns. The affair had been shifted to a plane on which he seemed powerless to think or to act.

'Are you going to hold up everybody in the

room?' Kitty Bowen was asking of her new partner.

'Me?' asked the outlaw, in a surprised manner. 'Why, I just came down for a dance and a chat. I've been thinking about you a good deal.'

'The music is getting very bad,' observed Kitty.

'We'll shake 'em up a little,' said the outlaw, and, as they were passing the orchestra stand at that moment, he waved cheerfully at the musicians.

They stood up of one accord, as though a gun had been swung in their direction. The music staggered almost to a close, and then it began again with a fresher and a truer swing than ever, as though those men of art, in appreciation of a brand new situation, were rising to it with all their will and skill.

There were few dancers on the floor, now; the merrymakers were huddled together in the corners. And great was the buzz of excitement that rose, as questions were asked and answers hazarded, about Terry Shawn and his lovely partner.

'I've got about half a minute left,' said Terry Shawn. 'The sheriff is coming to, and he'll have his guns out, pretty soon. I had a question to ask you, Kitty. That's why I came.'

She nodded. Her head was turned to the side and raised a little; she seemed to be looking into the distance with absent eyes. She seemed to Shawn neither frightened, nor embarrassed, nor happy, but merely thoughtful.

'I want to know about Sky Pilot,' he said.

'Sky Pilot?'

'I mean the horse.'

'Oh,' she said.

'Where does he hang out with the Mexican?' asked Shawn.

'José has rented a lot from Jud Makin, and he keeps the chestnut there. What do you want with him, Terry?'

'I've got to make a present to a friend,' he said rather inaccurately.

'Did you have to come into the dance hall to ask that question?' she asked.

'I've sat with you, walked with you, talked with you, Kitty, but I've never danced with you,' he said by way of explanation. 'Besides, I wanted to ask you another question. When can I see you again?'

'I never leave the valley,' she said.

'That's what the dog said to the wolf.'

'Yes, they want you,' she said quietly. 'Will they ever have you, Terry?'

'Someday they'll have me. But I ought to have a few years left before they do.'

'Not if you keep coming to dances,' she warned him.

'It depends on where I have to go to find you.'

'I'm going riding tomorrow,' said Kitty.

'Which way?'

'Up Lawson Creek.'

'What time?'

'Oh, about nine in the morning.'

'That's a funny thing,' he said. 'I was going to go riding up Lawson Creek myself at that same time.'

She turned her eyes straight toward his at that, and looked brightly up to him, then she smiled, and the heart of Terence Shawn contracted and then expanded so wildly that all the hanging lanterns in the hall blurred together before his eyes, and the music was multiplied in his ears as though it were the straining of great martial trumpets.

'You'd better jump,' said the quiet voice of the girl. 'They've blocked the doors, but you could get out of that window, there.'

'How far is it to the ground?'

'Thirty feet, but there's a shed roof just under the window.'

'So long, Kitty. It was a grand dance,' said Shawn joyously.

'So long, Terry. I'm glad you came,' she said as he slipped from her.

The sheriff had endured inaction long enough, and now he was coming for Shawn, his ready guns glimmering wickedly in the lantern light, and everyone was silent except one girl who had begun to scream hysterically.

Terence Shawn dodged through the crowd, and over their heads he tossed a little knot of banknotes into the midst of the musicians. He leaped up, caught the lower sill of the high window, and swung himself up into the gap.

He stood up against the blackness of the outer night and threw one glance before him at the sloping roof of the shed, then one glance behind him, where the sheriff stood with guns poised, shouting to him to surrender.

Fire jetted from the muzzle of one of those guns, a *tinkling* shower of glass fell around Shawn. Then he jumped, struck the roof, rolled forward, head over heels, and barely caught the outer rain gutter in time to check his fall. The nails worked loose. The gutter stripped off the edge of the roof with a noisy *screech*, but Shawn had dropped lightly on his feet to the ground below.

Chapter Nine

When Shawn struck the ground outside, he had no great amount of time left to get away. He had barely located the spot at which he had stationed his horse, when the rear door of the hall was cast open by the sheriff, who was cursing savagely, because of his long and violent efforts to force it. The shaft of light fell fully, in a wide wedge, upon slender Terry Shawn, and the oaths of the sheriff turned to a wild shout of joy.

He should have fired instead, and saved a split part of a second, for, in that precious fraction of time, Shawn leaped to the side into enveloping darkness, with two bullets winging wickedly close to his ears.

Then he sprinted for his horse and leaped into the saddle. A good horse needs no spur, at such a time. The fear and the need of its rider sent a quiver of fright and eagerness through its body. So, the instant that he felt the weight of Shawn in the stirrups, the gelding was running, and fighting for his head.

Straight out from Lister he raced, and not until there was a mile of darkness between them and the confused lights of the town did Shawn at last manage to get his mount in hand. When that happened, he swung around in a sharp curve that brought him, almost in a straight line, back to the village. Trotting his horse softly on, he paused twice in the shelter of brush, and watched rushing bands of riders storm through the night, beating wildly out from Lister. He knew why they rode, and he laughed at their speed. The more of them who mounted and galloped out, the easier would be the task that lay before him.

He knew where the fields of Jud Makin lay, and to them he went. There, at the head of the town, where the houses thinned and changed to infrequent dottings on the landscape, there was a little shack beside the river, and, as Shawn slackened his pace and went on more slowly than before, he heard before him a clear masculine voice, raised in song, and the *tinkling* of a guitar. He bent his head; the voice sang in Spanish. He drew closer—Spanish, to be sure—and learned that the song was a ballad of the incredible exploits of a bold brigand and his lucky adventures with the purses of men and the honor of women.

Down the bank by the edge of the stream, he threw the reins of the horse and went from it toward the shack, pausing again and again, and circling until he made sure that the noise of the musical instrument was coming to him from the farther side of the shack. When he was sure of that, he went forward more confidently, and presently he was creeping along the side of the little shanty.

He found the Mexican sprawled in the doorway, his guitar in his lap, his head against the door-jamb, his black hair falling back from his pale face, which was turned toward the stars.

The song ended. 'And what do you think of it?' asked the voice of José.

Shawn bit his lip. This one rascal was apt to give him plenty of trouble, but if he had a companion, the work might be almost impossible. Say what men will about the courage or the lack of courage of a Mexican, in the night he makes a very efficient fighter, if he is a fighting man at all. And Terry Shawn knew all about the potentialities of the

Mexican who now sat before him. There was no more dangerous man on the southern side of the Rio Grande, and hardly three on the northern side, for that matter.

There was no answer, immediately, to the remark of José, and the latter snarled: 'Tell me, devil, what do you think of it? Answer me.' Still not a voice replied. Then José caught up a blacksnake, and its sinuous body curled and whisked out of sight as he snapped it. 'Speak to me! For you can speak if you wish to. Speak to me, child of the raw north wind and a sandstorm. Ugly soul of tequila, poison heart, witch, will you answer me?'

It turned the blood of the white man cold to hear him. It was hard to imagine that a second man was inside the shack, but it might well be a woman who dared not stand up to this brute.

The fingers of Terry Shawn began to twitch, and he crouched a little in his deep disgust and anger.

'No,' said José in a greater passion than before. 'You will not speak. Not here, not now. You save your words. But when the right day comes, then you will speak. When you think that you can conquer me, devil. But you are wrong . . . always I am your master. I take you in my hand, I bend you, and I make you what I will. *Ha!* Stand over and give more room to my thoughts, in there.' With that, he turned on his elbow and struck savagely into the darkness.

The answer was a snort and a heavy

trampling, and the heart of Shawn was partly relieved and partly thrilled with wonder. It was the horse that lived inside the shanty!

'José,' he said.

The Mexican turned as a cat turns when a dog comes suddenly around a corner upon it. He looked venomously up at Shawn, his lean, ugly face all twined with malice and with terror.

'*Sí, sí,*' he answered, after he had run his eyes over the slender, well-poised form of the outlaw.

'Who are you? I am José, but who are you?'

'There's my card,' said the outlaw, and he dropped a $5 bill into the lap of the Mexican.

The latter clutched it, then he stumbled to his feet. His sullen voice turned to an easy and droning gush of courtesy. 'I understand, *señor,*' he said. 'There are two fortunes for men. There is a fortune by day and there is a fortune by night. *Señor,* perhaps, has tried already by day. Now he wishes to try the other half of his luck. Is it so?' He drew closer, and his laughter bubbled with unhealthy pleasure.

Shawn stepped back. 'Get the horse out,' he said. 'Throw a saddle on him, and let me have my fling. If I ride him, he's mine, eh?'

'*If* you ride him,' repeated the Mexican, disappearing into the shack. Presently he was heard alternately cursing the horse, and chuckling. 'If you ride the horse, he is a present to you. You shall take him and be happy with him, friend,' he said, smiling, as he led the chestnut into the starlight.

Certainly, in the hands of José, Sky Pilot had not deteriorated in condition. He had had the best of food, or else never would his coat have shone in such fashion; he had had a sufficient share of hard exercise, also, given by those who had paid for their chances to ride him, first with dollars, and then with broken bones.

Only in spirit had he altered from the gentle-mouthed and star-eyed creature on which the outlaw had descended like the wind from the mountains. Indeed that very lack of spirit was what had caused Shawn to misjudge the capabilities of the animal. A little more iron in the soul of the stallion, and he would have guessed the value of what he had ridden that other night. But now, with his ears pricking slowly forward or else quivering back, tight against his head, his eyes glittering, and his feet reaching and pawing uncertainly, he looked the very spirit of evil, and treachery, and danger.

'*Amigo,*' said the outlaw, 'tell me why you hate this horse?'

'I have such reasons,' said the other, 'that I have made a song out of them. One day I'll sing it for you, perhaps.'

He stopped suddenly short, but it was not difficult for the white man to get the implication. Perhaps, when he lay, smashed and broken against the ground, long sick and slowly recovering, there would be a chance for him to hear the song of the Mexican, in which the story of Sky Pilot was told at length.

Terry Shawn took thought with some gravity. If, in fact, he were thrown and hurt so badly that he could not get away from the place, the law would soon have him in its arms. He never could trust to this treacherous José to take care of him and nurse him loyally back to health and strength again.

'Stand him out here,' he commanded.

With a half hitch taken cruelly deep and hard in the upper lip of the chestnut, José stood the horse in the required spot, where the starlight shimmered more brightly over him.

'He's a devil,' whispered Shawn to himself.

'He is, *señor*,' said the Mexican eagerly. 'And who would not like to have a devil for a slave? Who would not like, *señor*, to cross mountains and deserts on wings, eh?'

'But you, José, who would love to rule a devil so well, why don't you ride him yourself, then?'

'I *have* ridden him,' said José sadly. 'But cannot give the same life twice. It can only be sold once.'

'Now, what do you mean by that?' asked Shawn, perplexed.

'My meaning is clear. No? Let it go, then, for the important thing is that you should ride the horse, *señor* . . . or else take your fall. Do you see? You have all this field to circle in. That fence is so high that even he cannot jump it, yet. If he does not buck you off, or rub you off against the fence, then it will be well with you, *señor. You* shall have him. Begin, *señor.* Begin!'

'Hold his head, then,' said the outlaw sternly and crisply. 'I'll ride him unless he bucks his jacket off Are those cinches strong?'

'They are, *señor.* Try them.'

'If one of 'em breaks, or a stirrup gives way with me, I'll have a gun on you while I'm falling, José, and I'll send your sneaking yellow soul to the place where it belongs. Hold his head now.'

With a single bound, he was in the saddle and had swept the reins into his hand.

The Mexican, in the meantime, had leaned far forward. Now he threw up his hands with a groan that was half fear and half rage.

'It is *Señor* Shawn!' he cried. 'Oh, devil, now you have met your match!'

Chapter Ten

The exclamation of José seemed, in part, joyous at the thought that the chestnut was now, perhaps, to be mastered, and in part it seemed angry because the end of his money-making seemed in sight.

Shawn had but the slightest glimpse of that play of emotions in the face of the Mexican. The next moment, Sky Pilot took control and went straight forward, not like a horse about to show his paces as a skilled bucker, but rather like a racer off the mark, his head thrust out, his ears flattened close to his head, his quarters sinking with the power and the lengthening of his stride.

But Shawn gathered that trouble was ahead. He settled himself more deeply in the saddle, although the rapid vibrations of a running horse are the most unsettling thing in the world. The temptation is to rise in the stirrups, lean forward, and let the long loin muscles whip freely back and forth as the horse gallops. But Shawn settled deeper and secured his knee-grip by turning in his toes a little, throwing all the power of the thigh muscles inside the leg. He was gripping hard, and yet, like a perfect horseman, he was giving himself to the motion of the run. He sat strongly, but not rigidly, and waited for the shock.

It came, but not exactly as he had expected. The chestnut left the ground in a broad jump, but he twisted himself a little to the side, and then came down with arched back, dropped head, and rigid legs. So mighty was the impact that the hoofs cut through the hard soil like plowshares—so clean was the impact, that Terry Shawn went numb of brain. Even then, he would have stuck in his place, had it not been that the little twist at the end of the leap acted upon him like a fiendish leverage. He was literally peeled from the saddle and hurled violently through the air.

He might have broken his neck from a fall of half that force, but Terry Shawn knew all about the fine art of falling. One should not sprawl, and yet one should be loose. The instinct is to go face down, with fending arms thrust out. But Terry Shawn knew that one must turn the side first, the back if possible, and hit with a roll.

Hard to think of such things when being hurled from a bucking horse. But, after all, if he had not been able to crowd a great deal of thinking into the split part of a second, he never would have been what he was. He struck the ground, rolling, and his fall carried him spinning under the lower bar of the fence.

More than half stunned, his wits reeling, still he was conscious of a shadow leaping after him, of hoofs that beat against the rails, and of a cloud of dust swept over him, and he half stopped his breathing.

It was the chestnut, which had come after him with a tigerish ferocity, and then, realizing that this man could not be reached, went tearing off around the corral, head raised as he eyed the top bar.

But that fence was not only insurmountable, it was beyond all consideration for jumping, and had been built for that reason, especially.

Sometimes a fresh-caught wild horse will try the impossible and hang himself over a rail, but not the most frantic horse in the world would dream of tackling this barrier.

Yet the Mexican, hurrying up, rope in hand, went with an anxious step. He cursed and berated the horse as he advanced, and Shawn, sitting up with staggering brain, heard a speech somewhat as follows: 'Son of a devil, you have won again, but you have not beaten me. I come again, and I bring my rope with me. Listen to it, my beautiful. This is music. You have heard it before. You cannot escape. Dance and pound upon the ground, but you won't smash me. You are afraid, my pretty one, because you see the rope in my hand.'

The eyes of Shawn cleared a little; he staggered to his feet. And now he saw José advancing with outstretched arms, a coil of rope in either hand, feinting first one and then with the other, while the chestnut backed, and pranced, and danced, looking satanically savage, and quite aware of the danger before him.

He plunged suddenly to the right; the left hand of the Mexican feinted. The horse whirled, and instantly José cast from his other hand. But it seemed that the chestnut had nerves of thought, and muscles of rubber, for he spun about again, and, leaping from under the evil whisper of the rope, he galloped off to the farther end of the enclosure.

José, gathering his rope again into his hands, laughed harshly. 'I am coming, nevertheless,' he assured the high-headed stallion. 'Run from me, and you run from your shadow. You cannot escape from me, my beauty. Steady, therefore. Stand patiently. Put out your head for your master.'

So he came up again with the stallion, and this time the horse rushed straight ahead, as though frantic with fear. But when the rope shot out, he braced himself to a halt and swerved away from it.

Shawn had picked the thorns of a cactus out of his shoulder. He shook himself like a dog out of water and found that there were no broken bones. Then he climbed the fence and gave José his aid. So the two of them managed to corner that clever dodger, and the rope of the Mexican went home around the neck of Sky Pilot. The instant he felt the touch of the rope, he stopped and stood, shuddering. Whatever lessons he had learned, plainly he had learned them well.

'Hold his head,' said Terence Shawn.

'You ride again, *señor?*' asked José, a sudden burst of admiration warming his voice.

'I ride again. Hold him steady.'

And a second time Shawn leaped into the saddle.

The story began in the same way. There was a blind rush of speed, a leap into the thin air, a sidewise spin, and shock on stiffened legs. But this time the rider clung to his place; he was prepared.

Sky Pilot, as though disappointed at this result, started on at a soft jog, and Shawn studied the silken ease of that movement. He gritted his teeth. All this had been revealed to him on the very first day he had mounted the animal, and yet he had closed his eyes against the truth. Who could have guessed that this horse, which he had picked up from a hermit among the mountains, would prove to be a gem, a jewel without price?

At any rate, the horse had gone from him into the hands of the Mexican.

These thoughts were interrupted by a sudden burst of fence-rowing, done with a neatness and finish that put to shame every other talented performer at that line of trade within the experience of Terry Shawn. He felt as though he were riding a section of steel cable, flourished and snapped in the air by some malicious, gigantic hand.

And then, suddenly, the chestnut was trotting on again. The Mexican was shrieking with excitement, dancing and waving his hands.

'The whip, *señor!* The spur! Now let him taste a master in the saddle!'

But Shawn had not advanced to that stage of confidence. There was some other trick in the wily brain of this animal. Besides, he wanted a bit of a breathing spell, so that the darkness could depart from his own head. It was as though he had been beaten over the back of the head with a bludgeon.

Then straight into the air plunged the chestnut, and floundered backward. Of all the tricks of man-killing horses, none is so deadly as this, and Shawn barely had time and wit to jerk himself out of the saddle, as the horse fell. Cat-like, the chestnut sprang to his feet again, but, equally quick, Shawn had leaped to his place in the saddle and clung there.

Once more into the air, and down again. Three times the stallion repeated this maneuver, and each time Shawn escaped by a narrower margin.

After that, Sky Pilot went on with his soft jog trot, shaking the bridle, and thinking. It reminded Terry Shawn of a battle in the days of his childhood, when in his home town he had stood up to the son of a blacksmith—a lean, tall, hard-muscled boy with blue eyes, as cold as the eyes of a fish. Twenty times he had rushed that lad, and twenty times he had been received with a new trick, a new cunning shift that baffled him. However, in the end he had managed to come to close quarters, and then a few minutes of hearty punching had laid the stalwart lad on his back, defeated. So it might prove with the stallion.

Barely had he reached that hopeful conclusion, when Sky Pilot began to spin like a humming top. There was no bucking, simply an amazingly rapid revolution, so that he seemed to have been fixed upon a pivot and spun there.

His head reeling, his body wavering, Shawn gritted his teeth and prayed for success. The star points had turned into long, gleaming circles of light, the trees into vast streaks of blackness, and the Mexican had been multiplied by ten and stood at all sides of the corral—ten men gesticulating, leaping, shouting wildly: 'The whip! The whip!'

Then Sky Pilot stopped himself, with a thrust of the forehoofs that buried them fetlock deep in the soil. He began to spin in the opposite direction, and the brain of Shawn crumbled.

He fought against defeat, but his muscles seemed to have turned numb and limp. He was leaning far to the left; somehow he could not seem to pull himself back into the saddle. Neither could his knees get a more secure hold, but began to loosen.

If only he could hang on for ten seconds longer. Ten eternities, as soon. All at once he lost the right stirrup. He felt his right leg crawling up the flank of the spinning horse, and then, all at once, he was cast free and shot into the dust at the feet of José.

Chapter Eleven

There was no question of scrambling or crawling out of the way of another of the stallion's charges. Where the outlaw fell, there he lay, inert, in a crumpled heap, thoroughly stunned. It was pure good fortune that he had dropped at the feet of the Mexican, for the stallion whirled away from the threatening rope in the hand of his master.

Afterward, Terence Shawn got uncertainly to his knees, and wavered there like a pugilist trying to pull himself together after a knock-out blow, that he might continue the fight. But continue, Shawn could not—he was beaten.

When he stood up, all at sea, he managed to keep himself erect by clinging fast to the tall fence until his eyes cleared a little, and then he saw José leading the stallion past him and into the shack.

In time, he was able to follow. He sat down shakily near the door. All his leg muscles were trembling and twitching, turned quite to pulp, and he had to use all his willpower to keep his head erect, otherwise, it would have lopped over to one side like the cut branch of a tree.

Then José sat beside him, smoking.

'It was a bad fall, *señor.* However, you have no broken bones, and I shall tell you this one thing . . . no other man has sat the saddle on him so long as you. I thought for one moment that he had a master. *Ah,* well.' There was a profound sorrow in his voice as he spoke. Then he added slowly: 'If you have failed, *señor,* who is there ever to ride him? The devil must live without a master.'

'My friend,' said the outlaw, beginning to roll a smoke with automatic fingers, 'tell me why you hate this horse so much?'

José laughed savagely, then he asked: 'He is a strong horse, *señor,* is he not?'

'He's a lion, José.'

'He is a beautiful horse, *señor?'* went on José.

'He is. I never have seen a finer.'

'Nor one half so fine. I, to be sure, have lived with good horses all the days of my life. I have raised them and worked them. I have exercised thoroughbreds since I was big enough to sit in the saddle. I never saw one before like him.'

'Then you should be happy. He's your horse,' said Shawn.

'Tell me, *señor!'*

'Yes, José?' prompted Terry Shawn.

'Suppose that was the best horse in the world,' began the Mexican, 'would he take the place of a son?'

'Of course not,' said Shawn.

'Of a daughter, then?'

'Certainly he would not, José.'

'But what of a wife, *señor?'* asked José

76

softly. 'You hesitate. Let me tell you. I don't mean some old, fat squaw, but a pretty young woman with white teeth and big dark eyes. Is the horse worth a wife like that?'

'No, no, José. I don't have to stop to think in order to give you an answer to that question.'

'But then there are other things,' went on José, half closing his eyes. 'A good house for instance . . . a home, *señor,* with a pretty garden in front of it, like that of an *americano.* Vegetables behind that house, perhaps, some good ground . . . enough for the plow, and enough for the pasture land, also. Some good cows and goats, as fine as ever filled a milk can or turned on a spit. Plenty of trees for wood and for shade. A stream running around the corner of the hill, all filled with trout. And over the mountains, deer, and all that a man could care to follow with a dog and a gun. Moreover, plenty of other land to get when one wished, and get cheap. Tell me, *señor,* would that horse be worth such a place?'

'Well,' said Terry Shawn frankly, 'it depends. To a fellow who wants a home . . . no. To a fellow like me, who needs wings, well . . . that's different.'

'Wings. Wings,' said the Mexican, suddenly hoarse with emotion. 'Ah, that's the thing. But consider also that there was a position to be given up. Many kind friends. An employer, out of whose pockets money ran like water out of a spring. "How is it with you today, José?" he would ask. "Alas, *señor,*" I might answer, "I am troubled. My wife sits at home, crying for a new red dress of silk, and I am a poor man." "Well, José, send her up to see the *señora.* She has some things she won't wear again." Or another time . . . "It is a bright morning, José." "Yes, *señor,* bright for those who have sunshine in their hearts already." "Now what is wrong?" "My corn is ready to reap. The wind is shaking the grain out of the heads. All will be lost.'Then go at once to save it. Take Miguel, and Pedro, and Gonzales, and Federigo. Go at once, José. Save your corn. Take two days, or three. Then come again."

'In that manner he would speak,' mused José bitterly. 'Ah, me.' He dropped his head down upon his chest and was silent.

Terry Shawn was silent, also. For his own part, he never could have given way to such violent emotion, but he was determined that he would not interrupt the narrative of the Mexican. Here were more words than one expected from the sullen fellow, but that heroic effort to ride the stallion seemed to have warmed the Mexican's heart and loosened his tongue. The moment of confession was upon him, and presently he continued.

'All the way of life stretched out like a sweet rose, *señor.* A beautiful road that goes neither high nor low, but dips pleasantly into the cool of the trees, and curves beside a river, and pauses on a hill. Children, a kind master, a good wife, a bright house, rich land, plenty of money. But then . . .' He caught his breath and threw up both his hands in a wild gesture. 'Wings! Wings! One day I saw a yearling come in from the higher pastures. The whole herd galloped . . . the yearling slipped out before them with his mane standing and his tail streaming behind as though it were painted on the wind. He turned his lovely head and looked back to the herd as if saying . . . "Let us go faster. Why do you stay behind?"

'I, José, beheld this. I looked at him no more. I looked up. I could not think. I went blindly home. I sat in the darkness. My wife brought me food. I thrust her away. She sent my two children to me. I shouted at them and sent them flying. All night I sat with my thoughts, and what they were, you have said. Wings! Wings! I felt like a kitchen fowl in the yard. Feathers to beat and flutter, had I, but they would not bear me up. But on the back of such a horse . . .' José's eyes flamed with ecstasy, even now, as he thought of the magnificent creature. 'Well, then, in the morning, I was already an old man. I had forgotten how to smile, for the fire was in my heart, and I walked about with my eyes turned upon the ground.

'For a year, I nourished that colt. He had oats each day. He began to feel himself. He was like a stallion of four years. He scorned the earth when he walked upon it . . . the sound of his neigh was louder than ten horns blowing together . . . and his gallop was like the gliding of light over the waters.

'Now I had envy and desire in my heart, but still I was true to my master until a black day came. He had a great friend who came from Mexico City to see the ranch and the horses. He knew horseflesh. He glanced at all the others, but when he came to the red chestnut, there he stopped. On the way in from the pasture, I heard him talking money, and my heart stopped.' José stopped speaking and gulped hastily before he could go on.

'Well, *señor*, I must save words and pain by telling you quickly that the next day, we knew the chestnut was to go, and that that night he was to leave us. When I heard that, I went down to the village church and prayed for strength, but no strength came to me, and in the middle of the night I went into the stable and brought out the colt.

'I did not even think to take one of my own horses to ride. I never had committed any crime before. Only this one. And I said to myself that, if I took this one horse, at least I left behind me my wife, my two children, my house, my lands, and all my old hopes in life. Pile all of them into the scales, weigh them against the horse, and you yourself have said what is the difference.

'Well, *señor*, I know that the lawyers would not have understood what I meant, but I felt that God would understand. So I went out from my old life with empty hands, and only that colt. That was how I began again.' He paused a moment, thinking back to that tumultuous time.

'I went for the high mountains . . . they pursued me . . . I escaped from them. I ran like a deer, and the colt ran beside me. For ten days they hunted us, and the ribs began to stand out through the skin of the chestnut, but at last we escaped. Then for two years I wandered. All men knew what I had done, and all men were against me. Therefore what do I do? I steal, I rob, and I hunt . . . not animals, but men.

'At last every trail is on fire against me, and I cross the river to the northern shore. I am an exile, and my only companion is my horse. And still, *señor*, I am on foot. Why? Because evil has come into the soul of the colt. A petted child is the son of the devil. A petted horse is a spoiled horse. Besides, I had no chance to break him properly, for where I paused was only for the day or the night.

'A hundred times I tried to ride him . . . he learned to pitch me from the saddle, as he pitched you this night. At length I made my heart hard, for I was tortured, having given up my life for the sake of a horse that was a curse to me. I determined that I would conquer him by time and cruelty, and therefore I made up my mind to starve him.'

Chapter Twelve

The excitement of the Mexican had been growing for some time, and now it became so great that his voice trembled, and his words stumbled upon one another.

'I began to see,' he explained, 'that it was no horse but a devil that I had. A devil it had been in the first place, that tempted me away from my happy life, my home, my work, and gave me that madman's desire for wings that would carry me faster than any pursuit could follow . . . that would make me strong enough to strike down my enemies and escape from their vengeance, that would make me free, in spite of the numbers against me. When I began to see this, then I swore that I would conquer him or kill him, or that he should kill me.

'I starved him, then,' said José, 'until he was so weak that I could mount him and he could not buck me off. Then I made him go forward. I was cruel. I think that I would have mastered him, if it had not been that three old enemies from south of the Rio Grande came upon my trail, and rushed after me.

'There was nothing for me to do but to hurry ahead. That horse that was too weak to pitch me from the saddle could gallop still a little, and, as long as he could stagger, he still went faster than the other horses could run.

'At last they persisted no longer. For two days they had followed me, and for two days I had tortured the chestnut . . . then I dismounted and saw that he was no better than a dead horse. He would take neither food nor water, and he had strength only to brace his legs for a few moments before he dropped down. So I left him and carried the saddle back through the trees.

'But not yet am I through with that devil horse, for he came into the wise hands of *Señor* Shawn, who brought him back to life once more. And from *Señor* Shawn the horse was given to another, and from that other I claimed my property. And so here he is again. Once more I may talk with him. Once more he can tempt me and make me miserable.

'*Señor*, I have opened my heart to you. Now tell me why it is that I cannot raise a rifle and put a bullet through his head?' He had shouted out the last words, throwing up his hands and beating them back against his face and his breast; his voice broke almost into a sob of desperation.

Shawn had listened to this story with growing amazement. Now he said: 'You steady down, José. Let me tell you that you're wrong about one thing. I didn't gentle the stallion . . . all I know, I'll tell you. I came through the

83

mountains with twenty men behind me and a dying horse under me. I hit a little valley on the face of Mount Shannon, and there I met an oldish sort of fellow, deaf and dumb, living like a hermit. He had that chestnut before his shack, and I roped and saddled it, and left some money for boot, and then rode like mad.

'I made all the distance from Mount Shannon down through Overbury Cañon, and then out to Clinker and back to Lister. I left the poor sheriff eating out his heart with rage. And I kept on, and the chestnut never said no. Still, José, I didn't know what a treasure he was, and so I swapped him, simply because he was tired at last. If I'd known, he never would have come back to you, José.'

'You are not a believer,' answered José sternly. 'You cannot see that men have nothing to do with this and that God has everything. Only, *señor*, you have not explained one thing. How did you ride my horse down from the mountains? No other man ever dared to sit on his back.'

'I'll be honest, José. I rode him just as I found him. He never looked wrong, once, on the way. He never so much as shied, and he never said no to me, no matter what I asked of him. He went all day, and he was coming up against the bit when I finally got rid of him. That's all I know, José.'

'The hand of God. The hand of God,' said José.

'The hand of the old hermit up on Mount Shannon, I should say,' answered the outlaw. 'If there's a mystery, it's in how that old tenderfoot managed to take that dying horse you talk about and turn him into what we see inside the house here.'

'It is true. That is very strange,' murmured the Mexican, his thoughts turning in this new direction. 'Deaf and dumb, did you say?'

'Yes.'

José nodded, then he continued: 'That is a sign, also. God is upon that man with a curse or with a blessing. All who come into the life of the chestnut are marked men.'

'With the hoofs or otherwise,' said Shawn, grinning, as he rose.

'How long do you stay here, José?' he asked.

'How can I tell?' answered José in a wild and gloomy voice. 'I am but clay, and God or Satan molds me. I stay here until a voice comes, and I know that I shall hear one.' He said that with that firm conviction with which a fanatic pronounces his favorite doctrine.

'Wait only a few days,' said the outlaw. 'I'm coming back again. I'll ride Sky Pilot, or he'll ride me. *Adios,* José!'

There was no answer from José. He had seated himself in the doorway of the shack and had fallen, apparently, into a brown study, so the outlaw moved away and went back to his horse, which he found grazing contentedly on the steep bank of the stream. It tossed its head and pricked its ears to welcome its rider. So Shawn mounted, and, as he walked the horse away, he heard again the *jangling* of a guitar made soft in the distance, and faintly he could make out the singing of José.

He told himself that surely the Mexican must be mad, but, nevertheless, that explanation did not entirely satisfy him. He had his own share of superstitions, picked up along the range, and the solemn narrative of José had turned his blood a little cold.

In the meantime, however, he told himself that he had a more important mission, even, than the discharge of his debt to Shannon, or the acquisition of Sky Pilot, and that was the meeting with the girl the following morning.

It was late, now. His bones were growing sore from the two heavy falls that he had received; therefore he turned aside into the woods, and, in the first convenient little clearing, he made a soft bed of pine boughs and rolled himself in his blanket.

He could not sleep at once, however, but lay on his back, listening to the *crunching* jaws of the horse as it grazed on the long, rich grass, and to the whisperings and sighings of the wind through the trees. Now and again a breeze of added force touched one of the pines, and, far away or near, a bough rubbed against another with a mournful, groaning sound. Above him, the stars shone white and still; he looked up through the strange spaces and through the dark and empty holes where no stars at all were shining, and the mind of Terence Shawn began to grapple with new ideas that troubled him—with thoughts of old Shannon on the mountain, of that madman, José, and of Kitty Bowen, last of all, who was no less wonderful to him than the brightest of those stars in the sky. At last, he turned upon his face, to shut out these disturbing ideas, and he fell into a sound sleep.

When he wakened, it was the first of the dawn. A thin fog had risen during the night. His face and hands were wet, the blanket was damp, and all the trees were dripping softly in the silver gloom. The horse, having found a thick bed of pine needles, still lay asleep, and its breath rose in white puffs that melted instantly into the fog.

When he sat up, his bones ached sadly from his falls of the preceding evening. This world seemed a gloomy place and hard to understand, but at least the mysteries of the Mexican's belief now appeared merest moonshine and nonsense. It was a workaday world once more, made up of men, women, horses, guns, and hard, substantial realities. As for that realm of spirits that obtruded itself upon the Mexican, it was the fancy of a madman.

So thought Terence Shawn, and mechanically he went about the building of a fire and the preparation of his breakfast. Food was tasteless to him, however. For, with a growing excitement, he looked forward to the possible meeting with the girl. He began, like all who are hopeful of great happiness, to discount what she had promised. Certainly girls make promises easily and break them with equal unconcern, so he told himself that there was hardly a chance that she would be there.

The evening before, she had been excited, no doubt, to see him at the dance, defying all the powers of the law so blandly, but now it would be very different, and, when she wakened and saw the world turned gray with this disheartening mist, she would forget the glamour of the night before.

After his morning meal, he looked over his horse with his usual care. The work of the day before had been very exacting, but, nevertheless, the horse had stood up under it well, and, now, with a kindly eye, it sniffed at the bridle and saddle that its master brought toward it. About his mount's condition, therefore, Shawn felt reassured, and he swung into the damp saddle, at last, certain that, if danger came near, he could show it a clean pair of heels, on that day.

He took his bearings, after that, as well as he was able. The fog had not lifted. The weird, pale mist still tangled in the woods and breathed dankly down the draws, but at length he located himself, and he took his way toward that cañon, leading out from Lister, where he had promised that he would meet the girl.

It was well after 8:00 when he entered the cañon. He cursed the haste that had brought him there so much before the time. The long delay would try all his nerves.

He had barely made up his mind to that fact, when he made out the dim outline of a rider traveling just before him, up the valley. He checked his horse to a trot and stole closer, and suddenly he knew that it was no man, but a woman who was showing him the way up the cañon.

Chapter Thirteen

It was Kitty Bowen. She turned her horse when she heard him, and came, smiling toward him through the mist.

'How did you guess,' asked Kitty, 'that I'd be an hour early?'

'I didn't,' he confessed. 'I didn't guess that you'd come at all. But I'm terrible glad you did.'

'I had to tell them that I was starting for town to see Jenny Moran,' she said, 'so of course I had to start early. They suspect me, you know . . . they watch me every minute, now.'

'They watch you?' repeated the outlaw. 'And

who are "they", would you be telling me?'

She paused a moment and watched his lean and handsome face hardening, and his keen eyes narrowing. 'Since you danced with me,' said Kitty Bowen, 'they think that you may come to see me again. They think that I may be the bait, Terry, with which they'll catch the fish.'

'It's the sheriff?' asked Shawn.

'Of course.'

'It's a low thing to do,' observed Shawn bitterly. 'And what do your mother and father say?'

'They're worried, too,' she answered frankly.

'Aye,' said Shawn. 'They wouldn't be having you run about with a man like me . . . a robber, Kitty, and a murderer, and a man of no faith. They've told you that, I've no doubt?'

'Well,' said Kitty, 'how good are you, Terry, and how bad?' Then she added: 'We'd better be drifting up the cañon . . . I think the sun's coming out, Terry.'

They turned their horses up the ravine, accordingly, and, glancing to the east, Shawn saw that the pale disk of the sun was looking more and more brightly through the fog, making one quarter of the heavens a glowing, translucent, pearly white. Still the mist did not clear away, and the black, wet trees dripped mournfully beside them and over them, as they went up the narrowing ravine. It seemed to

Shawn that he could not have chosen a more unlucky moment to see the girl. In a time of bright sun and cool winds, say, the life of an outlawed man might seem joyful enough, but now his existence must appear to the girl very like that of a drowned rat.

'That's a hard thing to be asking a man,' said Terry. 'You'd better ask the others. I'd rather you did.'

'I've asked both kinds,' she said.

'What kinds?'

'Those that hate you, and those that love you.'

'Those that love me?' exclaimed Shawn.

'Old Joe, for instance,' said the girl, smiling a little.

'Him?' cried Terry Shawn. 'I've never had a good word out of him in all my life! Nothing but hard cracks and meanness, confound him. He was joking with you, if he said a good word about me, Kitty.'

Instead of answering, she looked straight up the valley and smiled a little.

'According to Joe,' she said at last, 'you're a saint, and a prince without a princedom, Terry. You've never done any wrong to anyone, but you've been forced to the wall, a few times.'

'*Humph,*' he said.

'The reason you're poor, is that you give your money away. The reason that you have to keep running, is that you've taken money from one man to give it to another. And, after all,

91

Terry, you aren't very rich, I suppose.'

He was silent.

It seemed to Shawn that this girl was bantering him mercilessly, making rather a fool of him, for, all the while she spoke, she turned a faint smile upon him, sometimes a smile of the lips, more often, simply of the eyes. Indeed, she impressed him rather as a keen-minded man than as a woman. He was thrust away at arm's length, and he felt a bit of nervousness mastering him.

'Then,' she continued, as he remained silent and stared at the wet rocks over which they were passing, 'there are the others. They say different things.'

'The sheriff?'

'Yes, and most of the rest.'

'Things such as what?' he urged.

'That you're a thief.'

'Ah,' murmured Shawn.

'And a bank breaker.'

He flinched.

'A horse stealer,' she went on mercilessly.

'I've paid double for every horse I ever took!' he cried.

'After taking them by force,' she answered, looking so straight at him that his head dropped again. 'And,' she went on, 'they tell me that you're a remorseless enemy, and that you never forgive an evil turn.'

'I don't know,' muttered Shawn. 'An eye for an eye . . .'

'That's Old Testament,' she interrupted. 'But they say, too, that you've killed men . . . that you always will keep on killing them . . . that you like to kill . . . that you're a murderer, Terry Shawn.'

Now, as she brought out this indictment, he began to speak in answer at each pause, but, when she had concluded, he sat stiffly in the saddle, pale, lips pressed, hard, together, perspiration beaded on his forehead.

'Is it true?' she asked him.

He tried to answer. At last he found his voice and shouted: 'No, no! I swear it's a lie!'

It was as though he were shouting the words for the whole world to hear. The girl turned her head to one side, and still he thought that there was a faint smile in her eyes as she listened.

'I've never fired at any man,' he said, 'except when I was cornered, except . . .' He paused and looked at her desperately.

'I could understand a lot,' she said with a sudden warmth. 'You go ahead and talk right out to me, Terry, just as if I were a man.' So saying, she let her horse drift a little closer to him.

'Heaven bless you,' said Shawn. 'You're the right stuff. I can talk to you, Kitty, I think. Only it's hard to know where to begin. About the thieving . . . suppose that we begin there.'

'Begin at the end, and not at the beginning,' she suggested. 'I know, somehow, that you never took from a poor fellow who couldn't afford a loss. And I've heard about the Bunyan bank, for instance . . . how you sent back half of what you took, when you heard that they were having to close down because of the loss. It isn't that I'm thinking about. Of course it's bad, but somehow it doesn't bother me much. I suppose you did it more for the fun than for the money, because, as Joe says, you're not rich today. However, the other thing is different, isn't it? How many men, actually, have you killed, Terry?'

He counted them up slowly in his mind. 'Sloan . . . ,' he said, 'Justis . . . Morgantal . . . Devine . . . Ross . . . Perkins . . . and Chicago Jim.' He made a pause between each name.

'That's seven,' she said.

'That's seven,' he said, and he moistened his dry lips and looked sidewise at her for judgment.

'But there are all sorts of people,' said the girl, nodding and frowning. 'Even Dad says that there are some men who need killing.'

He reined his horse closer, and he said fervently: 'Do you mean that, Kitty? Would you listen?'

'Just wouldn't I, though!' exclaimed Kitty Bowen heartily.

'Take Sloan,' he went on, reassured. 'He was a bully from the mines. I was only a kid. Sloan tried to bully me at the Dickins Bar in Phoenix. You know, Kitty, I was afraid. I'd never pulled a gun on anything but rabbit. I had to fight or show yellow. I . . . well, I killed him, Kitty, you see.'

She nodded.

'Justis was a top-lofty Englishman, and a scoundrel . . . he tried to run off with my sister. When I stopped him, he tried to shoot me down, but he was just a mite slow.

'Then there was Morgantal, the gambler. He tried to shoot me from behind. There's the scar across the back of my neck to prove it. But, as I fell, I twisted over backward and shot him over my shoulder, you see.'

Her interruption seemed to him perfectly without reason or sense. 'How old were you then, Terry?'

'Then? Oh, eighteen, I suppose.'

'That was three at eighteen,' said Kitty with her sweetest smile. 'But go on, Terry. It's terribly interesting.'

'You see that it wasn't my fault those three times?' he asked anxiously.

'Of course I see that.'

'Devine was a hired man. He came down from Montana with five hundred dollars in his pocket and another thousand promised if he managed to get me. Well, he missed, and I spent the five hundred on his funeral, which was only the fair thing to do.

'There was Ross and Perkins. Ross came after me because I'd killed Devine. He caught up with me in the Sierras near the edge of a

95

little town. We had it out, hand to hand. He didn't die for a week. Perkins was a great pal of Ross. He took my trail because I'd killed Ross. Two years later we met. It was a fair fight and a fair draw. He had me through the hip and the stomach. He was fast as lightning, but my shot hit him between the eyes. I was six months getting on my feet.'

Kitty had turned very white.

'Chicago Jim was the last. There wasn't any cause for that. There was nothing between us, but he wanted to get a reputation. He was a good game one, and I only wanted to nail him through the hip, but I slipped and it hit him in the body. Well, that makes seven, Kitty.'

'Only seven?' said Kitty, with an odd smile. 'Only seven, Terry?'

He rubbed his hard knuckles across his chin. 'I wasn't counting Mexicans,' said Terry timidly.

Chapter Fourteen

He felt, as he said it, that something was wrong—that it would have been just as well for him if he had avoided making that last statement.

Miss Kitty Bowen looked down at the ground for a time, thoughtful and still, then she drew her horse to a halt.

They had come to a sharp turn in the ravine, where it spread out in a broad, level floor before them, not overshadowed with lofty trees, but broken rather here and there with tufts and patches of foliage. The wind came up this open valley and bore in its arms rapid and thick drifts of the fog that had been growing more and more translucent.

Now the damp wind made the face of Kitty shine, and the wisps of her curling hair were pressed close against her pink cheeks, so that she became a very wet beauty, indeed, as she sat there before the outlaw, tapping the butt of her riding whip nervously against her boot.

She turned and looked straight at Shawn, and he wished that she were looking almost any other place in the world. 'I'd like to know,' said Kitty.

'Well?' murmured Terry Shawn.

'How many Mexicans were there, Terry?'

Woe fell on Terence. He stared at her aghast.

'You wouldn't be counting them, Kitty?' he asked in dismay.

'They're human beings,' declared Kitty, tipping up her chin.

'Maybe they are,' he admitted.

'They've got souls just the same as you or I,' said Kitty.

He was silent, trying to fathom this thought, trying to establish its reality and substance, but he found it a hard task.

'Of course,' she said, 'you don't have to tell me, Terry Shawn. I haven't really any right to know.'

At this danger signal, he started. 'Now that I look at you, Kitty,' he said, 'dog-gone me if you haven't a right to ask me anything that you please. I never saw you look so fine, Kitty, as with the wind in your face and the clear, bright look in your eyes.' He stopped again. Something told him that he had said the wrong thing again. 'But after all,' he went on more soberly, 'is it worthwhile for me to tell you any more, Kitty? You can see the sort of a fellow that I am. I've told you pretty freely. I suppose that you wouldn't be wanting to know me any better after this?'

'Did I say that?' asked Kitty.

'No, you didn't,' Shawn admitted.

'Then tell me. Terry . . . how many Mexicans were there?'

'I don't rightly know,' he said.

'Just try to rough 'em in,' suggested the girl dryly. 'Count 'em by tens, Terry.'

He regarded her reproachfully. 'It's not as bad as that,' said Terence Shawn, watching her face with the utmost anxiety. 'You're terribly hard, Kitty. As a matter of fact, I'll tell you. There were only nine, altogether.'

'That makes sixteen dead men to your credit,' said the girl. 'I'd like to see the notches, Terry.'

'I gave away my old pair of guns,' he

answered gravely, 'but if . . . ' He paused. He began to suspect that there was something behind her apparent cheerfulness.

'How old are you?' she asked.

'Twenty-three,' he said.

'You killed your first man at fifteen?'

'Yes,' he faltered.

'That's eight years. Only two men a year. Why, Terry, you don't kill a man more than once every six months. That's not so bad, is it?'

He protested eagerly: 'It's been more than a year, now. I give you my word!'

'But you're sure that's all?'

'I think so,' he said.

'And you've only shot sixteen men?'

'I didn't say shot,' he corrected her in all honesty. 'I said killed, Kitty. You've got to allow that there's a pretty big difference there. You might nick a man,' he explained, 'and not do him anything but good . . . just let the fever out of him. You understand that, Kitty?'

'I see,' she said, smiling. 'Sort of a doctor, aren't you, Terry. Sort of a wandering physician. And I'll bet that you never charge a penny for a treatment.'

Wisely he was silent.

'Well,' said Kitty, dropping her aloof attitude, 'I suppose it's pretty bad.'

Inspiration made him remain silent.

'There isn't one single speck of remorse in you!' she stormed at him suddenly. 'You're proud and glad that you've done those

shootings and killings. It's what you stand
. . . it gives you your reputation. "There comes
Terry Shawn . . . you'd better look out . . . he's
a terrible killer. Kill a man as soon as look at
him!" You like that. You drink it in. Oh, I
know.'

'You don't though,' he argued with heat.
'You don't know anything about it, Kitty.
Speaking of remorse,' he continued, 'I tell you
that nobody has suffered the way that I have.
Many a night I couldn't sleep. Mind you, I
never forced the fighting. I never looked for
trouble. But to think, in any case, of a man
lying there dead . . . it's a terrible thing. It
haunts me. I've been tortured by it, Kitty,
speaking of remorse.'

'You look it. You look tortured,' said Kitty
ironically. 'Oh, I see you think I'm a regular
soft-head, Terry Shawn. But I'm not. You'd
never give up this life, you love it so well.'

'I live the way that I see a chance to live,' he
insisted. 'But if I saw a chance to do better, I
mean if I had something else to live for . . .
dog-gone it, Kitty, you know what I mean. I'm
wild about you, I mean.'

'I didn't come out here to talk like that,'
said Kitty, growing a brighter pink.

'I know you didn't,' he said. 'But I did,' he
admitted shamelessly. 'I had to tell you.'

'I've got to go back,' said the girl, turning
the head of her horse around.

'No!' exclaimed Mr. Shawn violently, and,

with a prick of the spurs, he lifted his horse fairly across her way.

Kitty turned as white as she had been red before. For, indeed, no one in the world could have been prepared for the sudden change that had occurred in the outlaw. It was like seeing a sword in a showcase, one moment, and to see it, the next, held level with one's eyes by the skilled hand of an enemy.

For one dreadful giddy moment Kitty's heart failed her. Shawn seemed a madman in this wild mood. What desperate move would he next make?

'You knew, too,' said Terence Shawn in a ringing voice. 'Of course you knew that I was so crazy about you when I went into the dance hall last night that I couldn't keep away. You knew when you came out this morning that I'd tell you that I loved you, but you just thought that you'd try the high hand and keep me under. I tell you, you can't. You can have done with me, mighty quick. Say the word and I'll never cross your trail again. But if you want to think me over . . . here I am, and here I'll always be. Kitty, I'd do anything for you. I'd work harder than a beaver for you. I'd build you a house and work in the ground for you. I'd make you happy, or die trying, but I'll not be a slave and a bulldozed sneak, the way it seems you'd like to make me. You knew I was a gunfighter before ever you let me meet you here. Now you know some more facts. Do you

101

want to hear something extra?'

As this torrent of words burst upon the ears of Kitty, the last vestige of her calm smile, her manner of easy superiority, vanished. She shrank smaller in the saddle. She watched him, fascinated, and the—'Yes.'—that fell from her lips was spoken automatically.

'I'll tell you, then,' Shawn went stormily on. 'I lied when I said that I had remorse. I've never gone after a clean decent fellow, and the skunks that I've accounted for, I'm glad of. I love the fighting! I'd rather have a good fight than a million dollars. I like the snarl on the mouth of the other fellow, and the second of quiet before the draw, when his nerves are working on him, and he has to go first for his gun. I love it, do you see? Only, I love one thing better, and that's you. I'd chuck it all for you, quit clean, turn around, and start new, and once I made the new start, I'd never go back on you. Because I just plain love you and want you. Have you got anything to say?'

'I have to go home,' was all the astounded Kitty could think to reply.

'Have you got anything to say?' he repeated savagely.

And, pressing his horse closer, he passed an arm and a hand of iron around Kitty. She was trembling so violently that she could not manage to free herself; her wits were quite confused and no words would come to her.

'Let me go, Terry,' she pleaded.

Instead, he tipped up her face and kissed Kitty Bowen fairly on the lips.

Then he stood on the ground, offering her the hat that had tumbled from her head.

'Your hair will be getting all wet,' said the outlaw.

That voice brought her out of the mists of confusion.

'Yes,' murmured Kitty, but she made no move to put it on, and held it in her hand, staring helplessly before her.

Shawn sat his horse again beside her. 'We'll start on back, now,' he said.

'Yes,' she agreed. But she made no move, and let her horse start on of its own accord, the loose reins hanging on its neck.

Chapter Fifteen

Now Kitty Bowen, as she again drew near her home, found the thought of a ride into Lister a great bore. She wanted at once to be alone among familiar objects, and, above all, to be alone in her own room. So she cast discretion to the winds and, instead of going to town as she had planned, turned back toward the ranch house when she had said good bye to Terry Shawn.

Her head was quite awhirl. Nothing had been as she expected to find it—least of all,

Terry Shawn. When they said good bye, she had feared that he would kiss her again, but, instead, he took off his hat and regarded her gravely and humbly, from a distance. It almost seemed as if, having treated her roughly that one time, she had thereby become a thing sacred to Terry Shawn, and, as she went on toward the house, she knew that for all his lordly declaration of independence he was now in her hands.

She even checked her horse, and, turning in the saddle, looked back toward him, smiling a little, but already he had gone into the woods and was out of sight.

So she came home, unsaddled her horse, and turned it into the corral. Then, having tossed a pitchfork load of hay over the fence for it, she went into the house. On the side verandah, she came straight upon the sheriff. Involuntarily she started back with an exclamation of surprise.

The sheriff did not rise; he maintained his position in the chair, slumped far down on the middle of his spine. Only at sight of her, he began to waggle the upper one of his crossed legs more violently.

'Hello, an' how are you, Kitty?' asked the sheriff. 'And what kind of mischief have you been into now?'

'What a queer thing to ask,' said Kitty, frowning.

This morning she did not like this badinage,

104

to which she usually responded so brightly. The sheriff suddenly appeared to her an unkempt, slovenly, ridiculous, and repulsive person. She had to exercise tremendous self-control to prevent that opinion from shining forth in her face.

The sheriff, however, appeared oblivious of the bad impression that he was making. 'You wouldn't talk to me about it,' he said, with a sly wink. 'But I can guess, honey. I can guess. Dancin' around with gunmen and robbers and murderers in the night, and gallivantin' off in the day to secret meetin's with them. You can't fool me!'

The sheriff was shaking a long forefinger at her in teasing admonishment, when Kitty, flushing with annoyance and confusion, rushed suddenly past him into the house. At this he shrank still lower into his chair, his great, spindling shanks stretched awkwardly out before him.

The clothes were never made that would fit the sheriff accurately, and long since he had given up the effort to find a tidy measure. He would walk into a store and say: 'I want something that'll wear, y'understand? Now show me some good wool, will you?' And when it had been shown to him, he was apt to seize the top coat of the pile. 'This'll do for me.'

'It fits you pretty bad in the arms, Sheriff,' the clerk might suggest.

'I don't like to have no coat hangin' around my hands and botherin' them,' the sheriff would retort, putting down the money for the coat.

He was a caricature. He knew it and had almost forgotten to be hurt by the sneers and the smiles that greeted him on all hands. In a way he knew that his popularity was founded in a large measure upon that same absurd appearance; for who could be jealous of the brave exploits of a man who, in all other respects, was totally absurd?

So the votes were always cast for Lank Heney, and he remained sheriff, smiled at, scoffed at, but trusted implicitly by all of the law-abiding people of the range, and dreaded as ardently by the criminals. So the sheriff had almost forgotten, in the process of time, that his skin, after all, was very thin, that shame and misery were as wife and child to him, and that nothing remained for him in life except to go on existing as a sort of ridiculous hero.

He had forgotten these things until the girl rushed past him with scorn and anger and disappeared into the house. Then, sliding still lower in his chair, he clasped his long, bony face in his long, bony hands and asked himself what he had done.

For suddenly he was sick and weak, as he had not been since his school days, when the little girls had giggled behind his back, or had stood aside and laughed to see him stumble as

106

he passed them. So it was on this morning, suddenly. He found himself as sensitive as he had been in those other, earlier years. And why? When he asked himself that question, the answer that leaped into his mind made him sit up, stiff and straight, and grip his knees in fear and in pain.

He was not more than thirty-five, but the whole world treated him as though he were fifty. He was thirty-five, but Kitty Bowen was twenty. He was a clown; she was everything that was gracious, graceful, and desirable. So the sheriff told himself. And the greater the distance that he struck off between them, the more profoundly he plumbed the abyss, the more bitterly his heart ached.

Looking back to what he had said to Kitty, it seemed to the sheriff that he had uttered no word that should have angered her so seriously. However, all his life he had been unable to understand what pleased and what displeased others; he only knew that ridicule and scorn always were heaped on his head whether he were silent or noisy.

He could hear the girl inside the house, and then the brisk, cheerful voice of her mother: 'Goodness, Kitty, you haven't gone racing all the way to town and back?'

'I didn't go to town at all,' said Kitty sullenly.

'Where *did* you go, then?'

'Oh, I jogged up the valley,' said Kitty. 'It

was too foggy for a long ride to town, so I just had a breath of air and then came back.'

'Kitty,' said her mother, 'really it looks to me as though you're getting a little sense. It's the first time that I ever heard of such a thing as weather stopping you from doing what you wanted to do.'

A door *clicked* shut and the voices could no longer be heard out on the verandah. The sheriff rose slowly from his chair, unlimbered his awkward height with a yawn and stretch, and then walked with a slouching stride down the steps and away.

He did not mount his horse. In fact, intended only to stroll up and down for a short time to try to take his mind off his troubles.

To amuse himself, he followed the fresh sign of the horse on which Kitty had ridden. Just beside it, and weaving now and again across the second trail, was the sign of her going forth, and the active eye of the sheriff noted the differences. Little pebbles and dust grains were still being dislodged from the upper edges and sides of the latter set of tracks and rolling down into the bottoms of the hoof prints. But the earlier tracks, although hardly much more than an hour old, were already settled. Both sets had been made within the last two or three hours, because the fog and misting rain had not yet wet down the tracks nor drenched the cracks where the dry earth showed through.

He regarded these things with a careless and yet a comprehending eye, and presently he turned off from the straight path away from the house and found himself following the trail toward the nearest copse—certainly she had told the truth and had been riding up the valley, and not down it.

In the meantime, it eased the sheriff's mind to have this small employment. He had come out to Bowen's on request, to use the place as headquarters in the hunt for the outlaw, Shawn, and this little encounter with the girl had crossed him like a sudden and blighting shadow.

He advanced, then, toward the trees, following the trail with a mere glance now and then. As he came close to the edge of the woodland, he noticed another set of hoof marks in the grass. Here they came to a pause, turned back, entered the trees. Here they passed straight on down the valley toward Lister. Here the tracks of the girl's horse had turned to the side—and here the other rider had come alongside.

What manner of horse had made those tracks, then? Or might it not be that the second trail had been made at a different time?

Upon his knees, the sheriff examined the tracks and he saw that he was wrong. Just as the grass was erecting itself in one set of hoof hollows, so was it rising once more in the other. And the look of the gravel in one shallow hole was like that in the next.

No, those two had ridden side-by-side, unless the second rider had trailed the first.

No, that was not possible either, for the hoofs of the girl's horse had remained on the narrow bridle path, while the other rider had taken the rough on one side, as a man, say, would do to please a lady.

The heart of the sheriff contracted with pain. A man had been riding with Kitty Bowen up the valley. What manner of man could this be—one who would not call at the house of the Bowens; who made secret appointments in the early morning; who saw the girl, rode with her, and left her suddenly to slip away down the valley once more, while she came on to the house, her face glowing with happiness?

Now, as the sheriff repeated all of these details over to himself, he found himself suddenly in the position of one who has been hopelessly juggling the pieces of a jigsaw puzzle until by chance they suddenly fitted together and made a well-ordered whole. So it was with the sheriff, and as he added up the bits of evidence, he saw, with a pang of wonder and grief, that all of this testimony pointed straight toward some man who dared not call on the girl at her house.

Who, then, could be afraid to come to Bowen's place? One under the shadow of the law, perhaps—such a one as handsome young Terence Shawn, who the very night before had dared to enter the dance hall in the town of Lister, and while there had made a fool of Sheriff Lank Heney in the eyes of everyone.

Chapter Sixteen

When that exciting possibility entered the mind of Sheriff Heney, he became at once the man of action. He cut straight through the rear of the woods to the back of the Bowen place, where he caught up his mustang, whipped and spurred the antics and pitching out of the system of that tough-mouthed little mongrel, and then raced him back to the valley trail.

As he shot past the house, he saw Kitty's face at a window, and he could not tell whether the face was pale through fear or was only blurred to paleness by the speed of his going, but in his heart of hearts he shrewdly suspected that the girl guessed his mission. He wished, then, that he had departed more secretly, but there was such a fire burning in the soul of the sheriff that it drove him recklessly on, until he came to the woods in the ravine.

There he checked his pace a little—not to an easy trot or canter, but to a gallop at which he still could search the trees before him with some degree of thoroughness. He maintained that pace for a considerable distance, and then he saw suddenly what he wanted, startlingly close.

He was riding in a little woodland lane, the floor of which was carpeted with a thick layer of pine needles that deadened the sound of his hoof beats. Looking to the left, he saw another horseman riding down just such another winding lane, and not twenty yards distant. They looked at one another at the same instant; Heney recognized Terry Shawn and reached for his gun, and he saw Shawn grab at his own weapon.

There was this difference between them—the sheriff, as he sighted the foe, steadied his horse and drew it to a stop, so that his marksmanship might be more accurate, whereas Shawn, with a shout and a touch of his knee, turned his mount straight on through the trees. He charged his enemy as he fired!

Never had Lank Heney been so alert as he was on this day, never had his hand been so swift, and the result was that he got in the first shot, firing from the hip. He knew that shot was low to the right; his second was equally high to the left, but before he could get in a third bullet that would split the difference and drop Terry Shawn from the saddle, the latter, charging fiercely, had fired in turn.

A kind providence saved the sheriff. His mus-tang, stopping short, swerved a little to the side and, squatting on its hind legs, threw up its head. Straight through that head went the bullet from the outlaw's gun, and the little mustang pitched over on its side, dead. The sheriff barely managed to shake his feet loose from the stirrups when he was sent spinning head over heels. His head struck a root. He came up staggering, dizzy, his hand empty—he had lost his Colt in his fall—and found Terry Shawn just before him with a gun held lightly in his fingers, ready to drop on the mark.

'Hello,' said Shawn. 'I see you're a popular sort of man, Lank.'

The sheriff said nothing, but blinked his way back to full consciousness.

'Even your horse will die for you,' explained the outlaw with a grin. 'What sent you zooming down the valley on my trail this morning, Sheriff?'

Lank regarded him with a quiet interest. His time to die had come, and he was amazed that the ending troubled him so little.

'A touch of luck,' said the sheriff. 'And a touch of luck beat me.'

'We'll call it luck'—Shawn nodded with great good nature—'after you've missed two shots. Now what'll I do with you?'

'Doesn't it look like a good place for a shooting?' inquired the sheriff.

'What am I to do?' answered the other. 'Drop you in cold blood?'

'You'd hang back on account of that, I suppose,' taunted Lank Heney.

Mr. Shawn grew pink. 'I'm a skunk, then . . . it seems,' he said.

The sheriff regarded him with bright, cold, hostile eyes. Being about to die, he was frank. 'You are,' he said.

'And that's why you've been hunting me so extra hard?'

'To get you out of the way,' declared Lank Heney, 'I would have given a leg or an arm . . . my right arm.'

'How did I ever harm you?' asked the younger man, turning his head curiously to one side.

'How did you ever harm me?' gasped the sheriff. 'Haven't you been making trouble in this county time out of mind?'

'I never took a penny from your pocket,' protested Shawn.

'You've been defyin' the law,' said the sheriff.

'You never made those laws . . . what's the law to you?' asked the boy.

'What it is to everybody,' answered Lank Heney. 'The law's what gives every kid a chance to grow into a man, and every man a chance to keep what he makes. What's the law to me? Why, kid, the law's my uncle, and father, and brother, the same as it is to everybody except the poison-hearted wolves like you. And it's the law that'll get you,

114

Shawn, and hang you up with a rope.'

'Thanks,' said Terence Shawn. 'Dog-gone if I don't think you mean what you say. But look here, Lank . . . who made you the grandpa of the law this way? You ain't making an election speech now, you know.'

The sheriff flushed. 'I never made an election speech in my life,' he said. 'For the rest of it, you're a murderin' thief, Shawn. Drop your gun and finish me.'

'Turn your face to that tree,' said Terence Shawn.

'Not while I'm alive,' said Lank Heney. 'I'll take mine in front.'

'All right,' said the boy. 'You're a nervy fellow, Sheriff. Maybe I could take some sort of a message to your folks for you, eh?'

'I've got no folks,' said Lank.

'Not even a cousin?'

'Not even a cousin.'

'Well, then, you'd want to remember some friend?' suggested Shawn.

'I've got no friend,' said the homely sheriff.

'No folks, no friend?' said the outlaw. 'Nobody to leave your guns to?'

The sheriff pondered this. 'I would sort of like,' he said, 'to have my guns nailed up in the sheriff's office in Lister and to have it written under them that dying didn't bother me none.'

Shawn narrowed his keen eyes and waited for a moment.

'You ain't going to break me down!' shouted

115

the sheriff angrily. 'Go ahead and finish, will you?'

'I've got an idea,' said the outlaw in a curious voice, 'that you're one of the kind of folks that I used to read about in school. One of those people that are sorry that they've got only one life to lay down for their country.'

'You're a skunk, Shawn,' said the sheriff fiercely. 'But what you say don't bother me none.'

'You start thinking on this,' said the outlaw. 'When you're dead and buried, nobody'll ever think twice about what you were or what you've done. You've got no family . . . you've got no friends . . . you've got no one to grieve for you or remember you, Sheriff.'

'I don't need any!' cried poor Lank Heney desperately. 'I know that I've done my duty and ridden hard and played fair, and worked for the law. I've done my job the best that I could . . . and heaven have mercy on my soul. Shoot and have done with it, Shawn.'

Terence Shawn began to rein back his horse.

'I'll take you at long range,' he said. 'The trouble with you, Sheriff, is that you never learned how to shoot. If you was to get another chance at life, you'd ought to settle down and practice a couple of hours a day. Your first shot missed my knee, and your second one shaved my right ear, and I wasn't twenty yards away. That's pretty careless shooting, Sheriff, even if it was a moving target. You might do for a barroom fight, Lank, but out in the open, with a Colt, you ain't much good. You should have stuck to a Winchester . . . it's slower but surer. I tell you what, Lank, don't you go around trying to look like a hare when you was meant to be a tortoise. "Slow and sure" ought to have been your motto. Steady now.'

The sheriff made a single step forward and raised himself to his full height. He saw the glimmer of light on the short barrel of the revolver, a steady, shining streak that would let immortality into his soul. Then he closed his eyes and thought of the sweet face of Kitty Bowen. Never had it seemed lovelier, more appealing.

He steadied himself; his nerves were as taut as the strings of a violin. Yet no shot came. Then fury seized the sheriff. This man was playing with him, taunting him, and waiting for his strength of will to break down.

'You yellow-hearted scoundrel!' cried the sheriff, and he opened his eyes. He looked around him then and he saw with utter amazement that there was no rider before him, and no threatening revolver leveled. He stared wildly about him—and saw that he was alone in the woods. Then, out of the distance, he thought that he heard laughter. He dropped on one knee and listened, and he made out, with certainty, the soft pounding of departing hoofs. After that he stood up slowly. His head was whirling. In his heart there was rooted a fixed and immovable measure of reverence, but now the sheriff could not decide whether heaven or Terence Shawn were most to be thanked for the life that had not been taken from him on this day.

Chapter Seventeen

There was a day to be idled away, and the first part of it the outlaw spent in drifting slowly across country until he came to the shack of his friend, Joe. That amiable and shiftless cowpuncher should have been at work, riding herd on his small band of cattle, for they needed his attention, but, when Shawn looked in upon him, the man was employed in garnishing a saddle with some intricate carved designs.

When the shadow of Shawn fell upon him, Joe did not look up.

'Where did you learn to do that work?' asked Shawn.

'Stand out of my light,' said Joe. 'You know little about me, kid, and what I can do. I ain't spent all my life on the range.'

'It ain't a true thing they tell of you, either,' suggested Shawn.

'What ain't true?' asked the artist, bending

118

more closely over his work.

'That you were a tout on a racetrack down at New Orleans?'

'Will you back up and give me air?' cried the angry artist.

'Or that you sailed before the mast,' went on Shawn innocently, 'and used to live on hardtack and kicks all the way around the Horn?'

'It's a lie!' yelled Joe, now looking up.

'I see that your arm's tattooed, though,' said the observer. 'Why did you have it done?'

'Why would you think?' asked the other dryly.

'I can't tell,' said Shawn, 'whether it would be so that other people could know you, or so that you could know yourself.'

'You're kind of full of yourself this mornin', kid,' declared Joe. 'You need work, I'd say. You've been stall-fed too long, and nobody's been ridin' you. Now leave that saddle alone.' For his guest was bending over the carving.

'What might this be, Joe?' asked Shawn, pointing.

'What would you take it for?'

'A fat woman out of a circus, running through fire,' was Terry's guess.

'You've got no eye,' said Joe scornfully. 'You fellows spend your time lookin' at cows and rocks until you don't see nothin' worthwhile. That's a Fiji belle doin' a dance.'

'Over here,' said Shawn, examining the

119

saddle further, 'is an ostrich, eating a rattlesnake.'

'Terry, you're a blockhead,' said Joe irritably. 'That's a lark that's found a worm.'

'I never knew that larks went in so heavy for legs, Joe.' Shawn shook his head sadly as he regarded the picture.

'You never knew nothing except guns and horses,' retorted Joe.

'It's got an enlarged hock, this here lark,' remarked the outlaw.

'Let me see,' said the anxious artist. 'Oh, I see what you mean. Nobody but a mean-hearted buzzard like you would ever take notice of a little thing like that. Well, a man's knife will slip once in a while.'

'Over here on this side,' said Shawn, 'I see that you've got a . . .'

'Never mind what I've got,' interrupted Joe hotly. 'I never met the mate of you, Terry, for spoilin' things with fool talk. Get out now. I'm busy.'

Instead, the outlaw sat down in a corner. 'Turn up some chuck, Joe,' he said. 'I'm hungry. And let's hear the news.'

Joe, grumbling but obedient, fell to work rousing a fire and preparing food. 'There ain't much news,' he said, 'except about one man.'

'Who is that?'

'The orneriest, lowest-down snake that ever bothered folks in this part of the world,' answered the other.

120

'I don't know who you mean,' said the outlaw.

'He came into town the other night and made eyes at pretty Kitty Bowen,' said Joe. 'The sheriff took pity on him and let him dance around with Kitty, but he expected that this here Shawn would stand and fight like a man after the dance was ended. Instead, what do you think this Shawn done? He jumped out a window and sneaked away like a low hound.'

'Maybe he didn't want to spoil the dance floor,' suggested Terry with a yawn.

'And now Lister is risin',' continued Joe.

'Lister is always rising,' remarked Shawn, 'and then sitting down again. How d'you know it's rising?'

'The Patrick boys came riding by . . . they'd had a telephone message from town. It seems this here Shawn had ridden Bowen pretty rough, and Bowen's just out and offered twenty-five hundred spot cash on top of the reward.'

Shawn sat up, his eyes bright and narrowed with attention. 'And why's that?' he asked.

'I don't know. But it seems that Shawn has been gallivantin' around the Bowen house . . . still after Kitty. And folks are tired of Shawn. They say,' explained Joe, 'that they don't mind him lifting the cash out of a bank safe or holding up a train once in a while. They don't mind him killing greasers or dropping a thug once in a while, because it gives the boys

121

something to talk about when the winter nights get long and the magazines give out in the bunkhouse. But what they do mind terrible much, kid, is having you fool around with the prettiest girl in the county.'

'They want her?' asked Shawn scornfully. 'Then why don't they take her?'

'D'you want her?' asked Joe suddenly.

'What if I do? Whose business is it?' asked Shawn.

'Your business. It's your business if you want her. It's her pa's business, too,' Joe told him.

'I don't know that I follow that.'

'Her old man would be askin' what would you do with her?'

'Suppose that I was to shake the old game and turn straight for her, Joe?' said Shawn suddenly.

'When did you start on your own?' parried Joe.

'I was thirteen.'

'That's ten years ago?'

'It is,' said Terry.

'How many days' work have you done in them ten years?'

'I suppose . . . oh, I don't know, if you come down to that,' said Terry, turning sullen.

'It's what it does come down to,' replied Joe. 'You've floated along for ten years and now you say that you want to turn and swim back upstream. Kid, you never could even get back to where you started from.'

'I hear you croaking,' said Shawn in a rising

122

temper, 'but it don't mean nothing to me.'

'You couldn't live without a gun in your hand,' said Joe thoughtfully.

'Me? I couldn't?' asked Shawn belligerently. 'Joe, you don't know nothing about me. I could settle down and work twenty hours a day for twenty years. Guns? I could leave 'em off forever. I'm tired of the weight of packing them around.'

'You couldn't even sleep without a gun beside you,' said Joe, laughing.

'Joe, there ain't a man in the world that's got the makings of a peaceable gent more than I. Fighting? I could quit it. I will quit it. I tell you right now, I'll never pull another gun. You wait and see if I ever do.'

'Never pull another gun?' asked Joe.

'Never,' was Terry's firm reply.

'Not even on a rabbit?'

'Don't be foolish . . . I mean on a man, of course. No, I'm through with all that.'

'Kid, will you let me tell you something?'

'I hear you,' said Shawn.

'You'll never change,' Joe told him gravely. 'It's in the blood of you. It's in your bones. Hitch wings to a bird and it'll fly, won't it? Same way with you. You've got to have a little hellfire around you once in a while or you'd curl up and die.'

'Hellfire? Hellfire?' repeated Shawn with a growing irritation. 'I don't know that I like the way you put that, Joe.'

123

'I put it again . . . you've got a taste for meanness and fighting.'

'Joe,' said the other sternly, 'you've said about enough.'

'Work? The kind of work that you'd do would be reaching into the pockets of other folks.'

'Joe, you're stepping over the line!' cried Shawn. He turned white with rage. 'You low rat,' he added, 'you wear a gun! Go for it before you try to talk to me like that!'

Instead of reaching for his gun, Joe relaxed, with a broad smile. 'You see for yourself,' he said. 'You were just promising that you would never pull a gun again. In half a minute I got you right up to the murder stage. Trust you? Why, kid, you can see that you can't trust yourself.'

Shawn listened and bit his lip. He turned toward the door, then turned back again. 'Joe,' he said in a broken voice.

'Leave out the rest of it,' said Joe cheerfully. 'Sit down and rest your feet, and eat something. We'll tie to some sort of an idea out of all of this.'

But Terry Shawn sat disconsolate, his elbows on his knees, staring with great eyes into space. The future had been to him like a land of gold and glory but a few minutes ago, and now it had shrunk to a flat plain of gray despair.

'We'll talk about this girl,' said Joe. 'We'll see what right you've got to her.'

Chapter Eighteen

For all of an hour they talked, therefore, about young Terry Shawn's right to Kitty Bowen, and by the time Joe had finished his careful analysis of the situation, it was plain to them both that Terry had no right at all. For that very day he had given proof that he could not control his temper in a pinch, and so long as he could not depend upon himself, how could a woman hope to depend upon him? Gloomily Shawn stood up and went to his horse. He saddled and bridled it with savage gestures, while Joe watched from the doorway, deeming it wise to come no nearer. He saw that his speeches had cut deep, and he wanted to assuage the outlaw's despair, but he found few words to use on this occasion.

'Where you going, Terry?' he asked.

'I don't know,' said Shawn dully.

'Wait a minute. I'll toss a saddle onto the pinto and come along,' said Joe.

'You've got some artist work waiting for you,' said Shawn. 'Maybe you can put another curb on the hock of that ostrich . . . lark, I mean. You stay here . . . I'll go alone.'

This last was uttered in a peremptory tone, and Joe shrank under it. But when his friend was out of sight across the hill, he nevertheless saddled the pinto and flew in pursuit, taking a short cut. He had barely rounded the side of the second hill when a rider moved out from the edge of the towering boulders and confronted him. It was Terry Shawn.

'Will you go back and stay at home?' he demanded.

'I'm worried about you,' explained Joe. 'You've got a bad look in your eye, like a gent who's about to chuck his last penny on the table and shoot the dice for it. Now, old-timer, no matter what you've got in mind, I'll ride with you and stick with you to the finish.'

'I've ridden alone all of my life,' said Terry Shawn. 'I've fought alone, robbed alone, played alone, and I'm not going to start working double now. Joe, go back home and don't come after me again. I ask you special.'

He whirled his horse around when he had said this, and jogged it straight on across the hills. After that encounter Joe dared not pursue, but he sat his saddle for a long time, marking the outlaw's course in the distance as he dipped up and down from sight on his hilly path.

That course led to Lister, as Joe well knew, and nothing but some desperate scheme should be carrying famous Terry Shawn toward the town in broad daylight. What scheme it could be Joe could not guess, but he felt that it must have been suggested by their last gloomy talk together. Bitterly did Joe repent his admonitions now. Kitty Bowen was a very pretty girl, a very kind girl, but, after all, what was her welfare compared with the welfare of such a man as Terence Shawn? However, he turned back sadly toward his shack, for he dreaded the wrath of Shawn as he dreaded fire.

*   *   *

He had not been wrong. Straight across the hills rode Terence Shawn, toward the little town of Lister. The afternoon sun was in its fullest power, and the vegetation of the earth seemed to bake and wither under the blast of that oven heat. No wind stirred. The perspiration rolled down his face, there was a salt taste upon his lips, and his eyes were stinging. The very cattle, which could defy the terrible cold and the biting winds of winter, could scarcely endure this fiery heat, and they had gathered in motionless, dejected groups under the trees here and there, or in the shadows of the taller rocks, or wherever they could find temporary relief from the sun. Now and again, however, some old veteran of many seasons was seen standing fully exposed, as though age had thinned and chilled its blood so that it dared to absorb this white radiance.

Yet Shawn paid no heed to this fiery blast, although it made the ground wave before his eyes and seemed to breathe forth a thin mist that steamed constantly upward. Yet he knew that no mist could be there, for during months and months there had been no more moisture than that which the fog of the morning brought to the range. That fog was gone now; only on the southern horizon was there visible a dull, gray bank that might spread north again during the hours of darkness. But weather was of no importance to young Shawn now.

Sometimes he was filled with such wrath against Joe that he wanted to turn about and ride to the shack and shoot his friend in the doorway. But he never could bring himself to such a mad act, for he knew that Joe loved him, and that all the counsel that the lanky, wise cowpuncher had spoken had been given, purely and simply, for his own good.

Nevertheless, he was ill at ease. Of all the treasures of his mind, the picture of Kitty as she had appeared to him that morning was the most vivid and the most recurrent. He saw her so plainly that it almost seemed her ghost was still beside him, cool and damp of cheek, with smiling lips and gentle eyes. He had been through a hundred flirtations, but never before had he loved, and the anguish and the joy of it overpowered him. For there was no mental stability in Terry Shawn. He could ride ten days without food and with little water. He could fight far beyond the limit of most men's endurance, but he could not build a fence against the torments of the mind.

Sometimes he felt, during this ride, that he

would soon break through the restraint that Joe had placed upon him, and again he felt that he rather would throw away his life than place Kitty Bowen in the slightest danger of future unhappiness at his own hands. The good and evil spirits never tugged so hard at one poor mortal soul as they tugged at the outlaw during that hot ride.

His conclusion was merely that which had flashed across his brain back at the house of Joe. He must have diversion. He must have some means of pacifying his outraged nerves and revolting soul, and therefore he would go into Lister—ride into Lister by the open light of day.

It was no more dangerous, say, than a visit of Paris would have been to the tents of the Greeks, but the very danger was what intrigued Shawn. He turned to peril as another man turns to whiskey in a similar crisis. And is it not strange that man never commits such follies and crimes as when the peace of his mind has been disturbed by love of woman?

Now, from the top of the last hill, he looked down into the valley. The town looked half buried in cool greenery, but he knew the terrible and humid heat that reigned there in the shadows. Only in the distance the silver face of the river was alluring, with the broad and clumsy etching of trees against its surface.

A whirlwind suddenly began at the upper end of the valley and, covering Lister with a cloud of white dust, left it clean again, and circled aimlessly onward until it disappeared as suddenly as it had risen.

That's the way with me today, thought the outlaw. *I'll raise a dust when I come in, and I'll go out like nothing at all.* He chuckled with a savage enjoyment of that grim idea, and then cantered his horse down the slope. He had made up his mind where he would go in the town—he would go to Lowrie's, and there he would stretch his legs in the cool shade and order a drink, and watch the dice roll and the cards fall. He might even play a little himself.

When he came down from the hill, however, he did not turn to the little back alley that led by a secret way to Lowrie's. Instead, on a sudden whim, he cantered straight on down the main street of the town. A dust cloud was pitched into the air before him by a brisk wind, but that mist obscured him too well, and therefore, since what he wanted was excitement, Shawn brought his horse back to a walk. The dust settled; he now was visible to all men.

So he waited, his nerves tingling, while many and many a curious, half-anxious glance was cast toward him. He always managed to pass by before a definite alarm was given out. The slowness of his pace allowed him to drift easily into the view of the passers-by, and each time he passed out of their ken again, without intervention.

In this manner was the outlaw welcomed in the town of Lister—merely by a few casual turns of the head—until he came to the bridge that lay across the river. On the arch of the bridge sat two small boys, chattering. They looked up as the rider passed them.

'Hey, Billy! Don't that look like Terry Shawn, though?' asked one of them excitedly.

'Don't it look like Christmas,' responded the other disgustedly. 'Would Shawn ride into Lister in broad daylight? He ain't crazy, I guess.'

We see what we expect to see.

So the heart of young Terry Shawn lightened a little. He began to smile somewhat to himself, and very confidently he turned to the left on the far side of the bridge, and entered the alley where the gaming house of Lowrie stood. He tied his horse under a tree, then kicked the swinging door that commanded the entrance of the gaming house. He found, within, a tolerantly cool atmosphere, an odor of liquor, a lazy bartender, and half a dozen men, half asleep in a corner around a table.

Terence Shawn strode to the bar and struck upon it with the flat of his hand, so hard that it was like the report of a revolver.

'Stand up on your hind legs and come and get it,' he commanded. 'Stand up and raise your thirst because I'm going to quench it, boys. Who'll have a drink with Terry Shawn?'

Chapter Nineteen

They rose and they came swiftly in answer to that call—the drunken yegg, the pair of darkly handsome professional gamesters, the jockey, retired from the turf because of certain unsavory practices, the treasure seeker from south of the Rio Grande, filled with wonderful stories but carrying no gold, the hired gunman who wandered across the West, selling his services and dividing his time between jobs with liquor and gun practice.

These men arose silently as shadows, and as silently they came about the bar, ranging before the slender, brown-faced lad with covert smiles of pleasure. They themselves were not without their reputations. They had done their share of deviltry, and they would labor again and again when the opportunity arose, but they had not achieved such a position in the eyes of the world as had Terry Shawn. He had made crime brilliant, beautiful; young boys and old men read or heard of his exploits with fast-beating hearts, and because of his gallant course, the whole profession of the lawbreaker was raised on high.

The gunman, in particular, rejoiced. He could say, someday: 'My partner, Terry Shawn . . . one day when we was drinking together down in Lowrie's, in Lister . . .'

So thinking, he glided silent as a falling leaf behind the outlaw, and the famous man stirred a little, as though touched with a spur-point of suspicion. Nevertheless, Shawn hardened himself against the danger and watched the glasses filled by a bartender as furtive, as shifty-eyed as any of the guests who stood before him.

Young Shawn beat again on the bar before him and shouted: 'Who else is here? Who's hanging around the corner, there? Come and drink, but don't stay and listen, or you'll be dead before you're five minutes older.'

And not one, but three men came slowly from an inner room and paused in the doorway while they fixed their bright, small eyes on the noisy Terry, then they stepped to the bar. They accepted their drinks with the left hand. Their manner of taking their potions was by waving the glass briskly to one side and then the other, and then tossing off the whiskey with a swift movement, so that the drink was tipped down the throat without making it necessary for them to turn back their heads. How often has a man been shot through the heart while his eyes examined the ceiling and whiskey poured down his throat?

'You with the black mustache,' said Terry Shawn, 'step up here and talk to me.' He repeated suddenly: 'You with the black mustache and the cat eyes, step up here and talk to me, I said!'

The desperate ring in his voice had its effect. For one thing, he was in the most terrible danger, for all that evil crew faced toward him, unafraid and calculating. The little bartender leaned against the bar, touching it softly with the tips of his delicate fingers. He, too, was thinking, and Shawn knew that one gesture of those delicate fingers would bring guns and knives at his throat.

Nevertheless, no signal was given, and the appointed man stepped slowly forward. He stood close to Terry, tall, unafraid, and out of his curious animal eyes he looked straight into the soul of Terry Shawn. He looked steadily and unflinchingly.

'I know you, don't I?' asked Shawn.

'Maybe you do, Shawn.'

'You're Slippery Joe of Boston, ain't you?'

'You have me wrong,' said the other, and his pearly white teeth showed as he spoke. Such are the teeth of a cat—translucent, white, and pointed.

'I don't think that I've got you wrong,' insisted Shawn. 'You're Boston Joe, the fellow that can ring up a pack three times and knock three crimps in it. Miss the first one and you'll hit the second, and Joe can read them wherever you cut. Is that right, Joe?'

The latter raised a dainty hand—his left hand—and just touched his mustaches. But the first touch against their waxed and polished surface made him remove his hand in haste, as though he feared to spoil that triumph of the toilet.

'You're Boston Joe, all right,' continued the garrulous outlaw. 'You're the fellow that got the tenderfoot from Manhattan and grabbed his wad, that night down in Phoenix. He shot himself the next morning. You remember?'

'I never was in Phoenix in my life,' said the other gently.

'It must have been you,' declared Terry Shawn. 'You're the fellow that rolled the tame pair of dice all night in El Paso . . . all night, on a blanket and bouncing 'em on one wall. That was the night that you took that San Antone kid . . . he cut his throat the next day. You remember, Blackie?'

Blackie shrank a little, as though the roughly found nickname offended his delicate soul to its very depths.

'I never saw you in El Paso,' he said.

'You must be mistaken,' said the outlaw.

'I'm never mistaken,' answered the other in the same delicate and chilled voice.

'Then why have you got this?' asked the outlaw.

Very swift was Blackie as he went for his gun with a gesture as fast, say, as the play of light from the face of a little hand mirror, but he was not fast enough for the speed with which Terry Shawn reached out and caught him by the wrist.

Under that iron pressure, Blackie's fingers

turned numb and he dropped on the floor a shining little automatic—small enough to be hidden in a coat pocket, in a sleeve, say—small and infinitely deadly, with a shower of seven bullets to be launched at a single touch of the finger. That weapon fell, and Terry Shawn clipped it out of mid-air, just as it was touching the boards. So an eagle stoops and catches the fish that he has made the hawk disgorge.

'I'm mistaken about you?' asked Terry Shawn cheerfully. 'But then explain what I see here?' He turned the slender hand of the other over on the bar and exposed the soft and folded palm and the long, long, slender fingers. 'Otherwise,' said Terry, 'how did you get a hand like that? There's no honest work in that. It could pick a watch out of a stranger's pocket . . . better still, it could pick the right card out of a pack. Am I right?'

Blackie returned no answer. Since he had lost his gun, he showed not the slightest perturbation, and his strange eyes never left the face of the outlaw.

'And so,' said Shawn, 'suppose that you and I and a couple of others sit down to a game of poker, where you can use your arts and I can use mine? What do you say, Blackie of Phoenix and El Paso?'

With this he offered back the automatic, but he offered it muzzle first, only slowly relaxing his grip on the handle. Blackie accepted the weapon in the same gingerly style in which it

136

was offered, and now the faintest of smiles appeared on his lips—one could hardly say whether it were a smile of purest pleasure or a smile of purest malice.

'We might sit in at a little friendly game,' he said.

'And who else?' asked Shawn, stepping back and looking over the crowd again.

At that moment he noticed another form, not a whit less sinister than any of the others— it was José, the Mexican, standing in the inner doorway.

'There's another man with a hand for cards,' he said. 'José, will you make one?'

'*Señor*, a poor man must do as he is bidden,' said José, but his glittering eye belied the humility of his speech.

The five were made up, then, of José, Blackie, Shawn, and those two silken-handed gentlemen who had appeared with Blackie from the interior of the house. To that interior room they now returned, all five, and, as they settled around the round table, the little bartender like a shadow drifted near them.

'What'll you drink, gents?' he asked.

'Something that you'll drink before us,' said Terry Shawn. 'Something honest, to go with an honest game of cards.'

He smiled as he said this last, and the bartender smiled in sympathetic understanding, and all were pleasant and at ease around that table except José, who sat stiffly in his chair and had grown a little pale. The lust of gold hunger showed in José, then; he was a famished man set at a board that was heaped with delicacies just to his taste, and, as the cards rattled in the first deal, a shudder ran through his body. He rubbed his hands slowly and violently together. He flexed the fingers one by one, and then he picked up his deal as though each card weighed a pound. Terry Shawn looked steadily across at him; the Mexican flashed back a single glance; they understood one another perfectly.

Indeed, there was singular harmony all around that table. Each man knew that the other four were quite capable of handling the pack with cunning crookedness, and each man trusted that his own skill would be greater than that of the others. The betting was very odd. Men laid down three of a kind without risking a penny. Again, two pair saw $500 on the table, and $500 won.

There was no conversation. Bets were laid in silence or with the quiet signal of a lifted finger, and there was no sound other than the light *click, rattle,* and whisper of the cards. What dealing it was. Sometimes all four cards in the air at once, spinning low to the table, hovering, descending like birds, very accurately. The three gamblers were three pillars of ice. Terry Shawn was one keenly amused, and the Mexican fierce and tense.

So hours began to drop away. Piles of

money appeared, and shifted this way and that.

Then Blackie pushed back his chair. 'I'll step out and take a breath of air.'

'But you won't come back to this game,' said José gently.

And suddenly the dealer stopped in the midst of his deal. A little waiting silence dropped upon the group.

Chapter Twenty

Now when Blackie had waited his moment he smiled again and nodded. Then he stood up and left the room. His two fellow gamblers stared after him.

'But he can't pull out like that,' said one of them.

'I'm two hundred down to him,' said the other. 'Let's get him back!'

They sprang up from the table. 'Friends,' said Shawn, 'that ends the game, you know.'

'Don't you believe it,' said one in hasty answer as he parted, and the two disappeared through an opposite room.

The bartender laid five drinks noiselessly on the edge of the table and withdrew, but, as he was going, the long arm of José darted out and caught him. The Mexican made an eloquent motion of drinking.

'Have a glass,' insisted Terry Shawn. 'Drink

139

it up, bartender. That's what José means.'

The little bartender fawned upon them, smiling, with eyes that wrinkled out of sight, but he shook his head and strove to slip away.

'D'you hear me?' cried Shawn. 'Drink it up, man. You're not a temperance lecturer, I suppose? Take a glass . . . here.'

'Thank you,' said the bartender, suddenly changing his mind, and he picked up a drink with a little bow.

'It won't do,' replied Shawn. 'Not that one, but this very same glass that you set down before me. I'm going to give you the honor of having my own drink, d'you hear? So down with it.' He rose and stood above the bartender with a sinister laugh, and now the little man shrank away before him. 'I'll give you one more second before I pour it down your throat,' said Shawn.

Like a cornered rat, silent but savage, the bartender shook a knife from his sleeve and drove it straight at the breast of Shawn, but his aim was spoiled by a glassful of burning liquor that was cast into his eyes. Then knuckles of steel rapped him on the jaw and he toppled headlong to the floor and lay still.

'Poison, José,' said Shawn. 'What a fine gang they are. Poison to turn the trick . . . if they couldn't handle the cards well enough.'

José was long since on his feet, a heavy, old-fashioned Colt in his hand. 'It is time to leave,' he said.

'And how, José?'

'By the door, *señor,* of course.'

'Well, try that way.'

José stepped to the first door; the heavy *click* of the lock against the bolt answered the pressure of his hand. He tried each of the other two doors in turn, and each was similarly secured.

There was no time for comment; the voice of a man beyond the last of the doors now came to them like a purr.

'Terry Shawn.'

'There's my good friend Blackie on the far side of that door,' said Shawn. 'We'd better have a little conversation with him. Hello, Blackie. Do you want to get back inside?'

Blackie laughed sweetly. 'I'm worried about you, Shawn,' he said.

'Thanks,' said Shawn. 'That's real friendly.'

'A gunman,' continued Blackie, 'and the crookedest dealer that ever took a poker deck in the palm of his hand . . . and yet you walk into a trap like this, Shawn. I'm really cut up about it. I see that even the cleverest fellows have their weak sides.'

'They have,' answered Shawn. 'There's no doubt about it. The cleverest man in the world may be killed with poison or a shot in the back. That's the way that you'll go, for instance, Blackie. Poison . . . or a knife in your throat.'

Blackie swore with a sudden fury and malice. 'Say what you want, Shawn, I've got you in my pocket, now, and you'll pay to get out of that place.'

'Pay what, Blackie?'

'You and the greaser lifted fifteen hundred from the three of us this evening. We want that money passed under the door,' said Blackie.

'And then we're free to go?'

'Maybe you are, then.'

'What will be our surety, Blackie?'

'My word of honor,' said Blackie.

'Your word?' echoed Shawn.

'Yes.'

'Your honor?' said Shawn tauntingly.

'Then stay there and rot!' shouted the gambler. 'I'll do no more for you. Let Lank Heney take charge of you. Unless you're lynched on your way to jail, you'll spend the rest of your life wearing stripes, and I'm glad of it.'

He departed.

The bartender, at the same moment, recovered a little and crawled to his knees.

Shawn, jerking a thumb at him, said quietly: 'Look at that worm, José. Go through him and see if he has any other weapons.'

José obeyed, but his procedure with the little man was strange. He stood him against the wall and sat in a chair behind him, with the point of a great Bowie knife resting against the small of the bartender's spine. Then José went leisurely over the clothes of his captive and began to produce a most interesting collection

142

of weapons. He took out a second knife, the twin brother of the first weapon with which the little fellow had attacked Shawn. Then he took a short-nosed, two-barreled pistol, very small, but throwing a large bullet—one of those guns that kill effectively enough at ten paces and yet make hardly enough noise to be heard above the sound of conversation and laughter in a room. There was, also, a very small automatic of minute bore; it would make a wound hardly larger than the thrust of a needle, but would penetrate flesh and bone to the very center of life.

'Murder,' said José gravely. 'This is a murderer, *señor.* Do you know what we used to do with such men in Mexico?'

'Tell me, José.'

'We stripped them and threw them into an *ocotillo* . . . the thorns killed them in one way and the sun killed them in another. They were spitted and roasted. And this devil would die well like that.'

'A good idea,' said the outlaw, 'but we can't spare him now. We're inside the can, José, and we have to use him as the can opener. Blackie and the rest probably have sent for the sheriff by this time.'

José grew a pale yellow.

'Listen to me, Shorty,' said Shawn to the bartender. 'There's a way out of this room, I suspect. Suppose that you show me how, and we'll call it square between you and me.'

143

Shorty sat down in a corner and folded his arms and closed his eyes.

'Stubborn,' said Shawn briefly, and began to clean his guns, although already they were polished brightly.

José strode swiftly and restlessly about the room. 'We could smash the lock of one of those doors and rush it,' he suggested.

'It works in books but never in fact,' answered Shawn. 'All they want is a chance to turn loose on us if we try to break away. No, no, José, they've got all these doors watched.'

José shuddered, and his fingers worked in and out. 'Do we do nothing, *señor?*'

'We only wait for Shorty, here. He'll change his mind pretty soon. You understand, Shorty? The minute that the sheriff arrives, you die.'

At this the eyes of Shorty opened as far as they were able and stared at the outlaw.

'Otherwise,' said Shawn, 'you show us the way out and go safe yourself.'

Shorty smiled.

'You don't doubt my word, Shorty?' asked the outlaw. 'It's better, my son, than gold in the wallet.'

At the same moment there was a sound of many feet in the outer hall, and then the well-known nasal voice of the sheriff: 'Where are they? Back here? Loftus, this is a good day's work for you. You'll have half the reward, if I land him. Have you got the doors watched?'

Apparently the answer was satisfactory;

there was the sound of scattering footsteps.

Shawn produced a Colt and leveled it.

'How will you take it, Shorty?' he asked. 'Sitting down or standing? The sheriff has come . . . understand?'

'It's murder,' said Shorty, leaning forward and gripping the edge of his chair.

'Better than poison,' said Shawn. 'A good deal better than that, old-timer.'

'Nothin' but a knock-out drop,' declared Shorty, beginning to tremble.

'Sure,' said Shawn, 'and a cut-throat would finish the work after the dope started working on me. No malice, Shorty. But I've told you what to expect.'

Shorty threw up a hand. 'Will you give me one chance?'

'Of course.'

'Then wait a minute.' The bartender stepped to a corner of the room and there dropped to his knees. He fumbled for a moment, and presently lifted up a board three feet long and six inches wide. Another and another came away in his active hand, and, leaning beside him, Shawn looked down into a deep, dark pit.

A hand beat on the door.

'You inside!' said the voice of Lank Heney. 'We've blocked every way out. Will you be sensible and surrender, Shawn, or will we have to smoke you out?'

Chapter Twenty-One

Kneeling beside the gaping hole in the floor, Shawn turned his head to the side and listened. 'Do you hear, José? The old sheriff is drawling away like he was talking about the weather. Mind you, if ever we have trouble with any man, it's apt to be old man Heney, though he goes about a manhunt the way most folks would go about making a cup of tea.'

'Merciful heaven!' exclaimed the Mexican. 'They will break through the door in another moment.'

Shawn shrugged his shoulders.

'I'll go first,' said the bartender. 'I'll show you the way.'

The hard hand of the outlaw caught Shorty by the shoulder and spun him halfway across the room, and then Shawn dropped a lighted match into the cavity beneath him. It showed a short drop to a platform, and beneath this a flight of steps. To the platform, therefore, he dropped, and, scratching a match, he lighted the way for José to follow him.

Above, there was a sudden screeching voice: 'Lou! Pete! He's got into the underground! He's working out! Lou, get 'im!'

'Are you ready, José?' asked Shawn.

'I go mad waiting, *señor!*'

They sprang down the narrow little rounded

146

tunnel, the Mexican close to the shoulder of Terry Shawn. In a few leaps they reached the end of the passage. There, by thrusting up at the ceiling, they jerked open a section of it and issued into the cool and quiet evening.

From the house of the gamblers, just behind them, issued the sound of battering and splintering, as though doors were being broken down, and above all was the screeching of Shorty, who seemed to have turned mad with fury. The fugitives stood in a patch of shrubbery that shielded them, shoulder high, and, looking over or through the brush, they could see people hurrying to the saloon to discover the cause of the disturbance. Around the place were the sheriff's men, naked guns in their hands, and the determination to use them in their faces.

'This way, this way!' said José eagerly. 'We can get into the backyard of that house.'

'Teddy Morgan has joined the manhunt,' said the outlaw, interrupting his companion. 'Teddy Morgan wants the blood money, too. And there's his pride and joy . . . his bay mare, José. I've a mind to ride out of Lister on Teddy's bay.'

'*Señor* Shawn, I tell you . . . ,' José started to protest.

'Go the back way, if you wish. I'm going down the main street of Lister. If they get me, they're welcome to me, but I've got to have a touch of fun, José. I'll meet you at your shack, if you can break through. Go ahead . . . I'll pick my time.'

José cast one earnest look at his companion, then he turned without further question and vanished silently through the brush.

Shawn, watching him, thought to himself: *He that steps like a cat may act like a cat. The greaser has claws.* Then he turned his attention again to the saloon.

The crowd about it was growing every moment, for Lister had finished its day's work, and now it thronged to take in this show. It was as if a magic circle were drawn fifty yards from the house, but outside of that line the crowd gathered and packed together, men, women, and children. They swarmed even to the verge of the shrubbery, and, as they began to pour about his hiding place, Terry Shawn simply stepped out and mingled with them.

Their eyes were all forward. He slipped among them without drawing so much as a glance in his direction, and so he came to the inner edge of the throng, just in front of the saloon, at the same time that there was an outbreak of loud voices behind the place, and there came the nasal, ringing cry of the sheriff: 'This way, boys! They've come out of the ground here!'

So at last they had worked their way down the tunnel and come out in the patch of shrubbery.

Shawn could hear the voice of Shorty as he

yelled hysterically: 'Didn't I tell you? Didn't I tell you what they was doing? They're gone! They're gone clean!'

His voice was abruptly subdued to a strange spluttering, as though a hard fist had landed on his mouth. In the meantime, there stood Teddy Morgan's fine bay mare, the reins thrown, near the hitching rack. Teddy was an upcountry lad who farmed in a small way and ran a few cattle and hired himself out from time to time. He was a thrifty fellow, and he had taken the money of the outlaw more than once in return for a night's lodging. To have loaned his hand to the state in a manhunt for the sake of blood money was, in the eyes of Shawn, rank treason—it was against the code and the unwritten laws of honor.

Straight out of the throng stepped Shawn, therefore, and, tossing the reins over the neck of the mare once more, he leaped into the saddle.

On foot he had managed to pass unnoticed, but the instant his feet were in the stirrups and the keen mare was prancing beneath him, some woman in the crowd screamed: 'There's Terry Shawn! There!'

The crowd fell into confusion. Shake iron filings on a sheet of white paper and you will see them scatter wildly here, pile into tiny heaps there, run toward the edges in another place. So that heap of humanity ran wild, some driving toward the outlaw, but most of them rushing away. Some were pitched to the ground in their haste; others tumbled over the prostrate, but what chiefly concerned Terry was a narrow little lane that opened up through the thick of the press, and through that lane he galloped the mare.

She was a trained cutting horse; he could guide her with the grip of his knees and the sway of his body, which left his hands free to manage two heavy Colts, and, as the good bay picked her way daintily through the crowd, swerving lightly to avoid the press, he turned in the saddle and watched for the pursuit.

Behind the house he saw Lank Heney leaping into his saddle, and he brought down a gun to cover him. But at the last minute he could not fire. For the second time that day he had the man at his mercy, and for the second time he hesitated and turned away. Behind him he heard the wild cry of Morgan as the latter came for his favorite cow pony and found it gone, and Shawn laughed in savage glee as he turned the mare into the open and let her race away down the street at last.

Bullets began to sing. He looked back and saw that three or four men on the verge of the crowd were opening fire on him. He pitched forward in the saddle and jerked the bay sharply around the next corner of the street.

He was safe, and, if the mare were fresh, he would laugh at Lank Heney again on this day. Whether fresh or no, she lengthened her stride beautifully and rushed down the street, and, with his guns, Terry Shawn made game on either side. As he rode he shouted like a wild Indian, and his guns exploded rapidly—at an upper windowpane, at the sign of Lucas, the blacksmith, at a weather-vane over the little bakery. Then he shot at the wooden Indian that for so many years had stood defiant in front of Bowen's General Merchandise Store. Looking back at it as he flew along, he saw that the big nose had disappeared, and Terry Shawn laughed joyously.

The last house of the village was left behind him. The hoofs of the mare rang hollow on the bridge that arched a tributary creek of the river, and now he had open country, with only a scattering of little houses before him.

He was well away, and the mare running like quicksilver, when, looking back, he saw the head of the sheriff's procession just beginning to turn out from Lister, rocking from side to side like the front of a speeding locomotive, and with a steam of white dust spouting high above the riders.

He saw the beating arms that urged on the horses. He saw, also, that they gained not at all. He would have preferred to turn straight to the left and into the mouth of the first little ravine, but he had promised the Mexican to meet him at his house, and therefore he hugged the bank of the river where the ground was high and the footing was of soft, deep turf.

So he made good time until he saw the shack of José before him. Surely the Mexican never could have got there so soon—but there, beyond all expectation, was certainly José, riding out on a roan mustang and leading, at the end of a long rope, Sky Pilot.

He waved to the oncoming outlaw, and at that gesture the stallion pitched sharply back, jerking the rope through the hand of his master and flinging the end of the lariat high into the air.

But as it came snakily down, and as the chestnut pitched forward, ready to run, Shawn came under like a bolt from the blue and caught the dropping rope in mid-air. He handed it to José.

'Well done, my brother!' cried José as they straightened down the trail together, the led horse galloping lightly at the end of the rope. 'I should have killed him before I left him behind for the others to take. Well done, *Don* Terry. We have our wings with us, and who knows? We may learn how they may be used before the end of our ride!'

'Let the roan run,' commanded Shawn tersely. 'That's the important thing.'

The roan could run. Freshly stolen by wise José as he slipped behind the houses to make his escape, he had not picked the worst horse in Lister, and now, matching strides with the bay mare, they saw the smoking train of riders behind them slow, and then at last turn back.

'It only takes a small crowd to kill off the best horse in the world,' observed José, looking back in turn. 'They are in our hands, *señor.* Which way shall we ride?'

'Straight up the valley.'

'That goes to the place of Bowen . . . he is not a friend to you,' José warned.

'It goes to the place of Bowen, and that's where I want to go. Keep on!' ordered Terry Shawn.

Chapter Twenty-Two

Soon they left the open. The trees began to rise about them, and the trail wound in and out among the trunks, while the noise of the hoof beats behind came to them in pulses—loudly in the open, veiled and muffled as they entered the woods again.

'The roan?' asked Terry Shawn. 'Is he equal to the race?'

The Mexican threw his hands out in a wide gesture. 'The roan says that I am nothing on his back, *señor.* I am a feather and he is a bird. He laughs at such a burden. He is happy, and his back muscles are bunching as though he thought of bucking with every jump. He will run to the end of the world and there is no barrier that he will not jump. Never fear for him, *señor.'* He added: 'And the mare?'

'She feels as strong as a rock,' answered the outlaw. 'But,' he added, looking down at her dripping flanks, 'she is a little soft. Confound men who won't grain their best horses. They're not worth stealing, José. However, I think we have that lot beaten.'

A long gap opened before them. They were well across it and entering the woodland on the farther side before Lank Heney appeared at the head of his posse, riding like a jockey, with his long frame doubled to the work.

José marked him specially. 'Shall I persuade him to turn back?' he asked, touching the rifle that was holstered beneath his knee.

'Let him be,' said the outlaw briefly. 'This isn't his day to die. Keep straight on, José. Here's the lead rope. Don't turn, even if I turn. Keep straight up the valley.'

They had issued from the trees again, and before them, to the left, was the wide front of the Bowen house, with the brightly colored pattern of its garden spread out in front. But what the keen eye of the outlaw marked was a woman in sunbonnet and apron, on her knees, trowel in hand.

It might be Mrs. Bowen; it might be a servant of the house. But no. Now she started to her feet, and he told himself that only one creature in the whole world could move like that. It was Kitty Bowen, he could swear.

He cast one glance behind as he galloped for the Bowen house.

154

José rode on hard and fast up the valley, but, as one man, the entire posse had swept to the left and followed Terry Shawn. He was the prize in their eyes; there was no blood money on the head of the Mexican. And still Lank Heney rode in the front, jockeying his tough little horse along, and never slackening his pace. However, there was a broad gap between him and his goal, and that gap might enable Shawn to do what he wished to do.

Shawn saw Kitty Bowen—plainly it was she, now—turn and run toward the house. But she hesitated and turned back as he shouted. He saw Bowen himself run for the house onto the front porch, with a rifle in his hand. The screen door slammed loudly behind him, and the merchant raised the weapon to his shoulder. He had left his store on this one day, it seemed, breaking the habit of long years to guard his girl from such another encounter as Heney warned him she had had that same morning.

'Keep off! Keep off!' Shawn heard the man cry.

He merely set his teeth, and, steadying the mare, he put her at the front fence and cleared it. At the very peak of that leap the rifle *clanged*. It was as though a hand had snatched the hat from the head of Terry Shawn; his hair blew freely backward as the mare came down inside the yard.

And there was Terry, leaning from the

saddle, above Kitty Bowen. Bowen himself on the verandah, twice raised his rifle to his shoulder, and twice he lowered it again.

'Do you hear, Kitty?' said the outlaw. 'I've thought the thing over. I'm not fit for you. I've tested myself, and I couldn't stand the test. I've showed that my word's no good. And I'm going to leave you free. There's ten thousand men all worth more to you than I am. God bless you, dear. Forgive me, and forget me!'

He leaned lower, kissed the pale face that was turned up to him, and started the mare away with a deep thrust of the spurs. He could not swing immediately to the right and out of the yard, for the sheriff was rushing close behind him. Instead, he bolted along the side of the house, leaped the rear fence, and swerved among the sheds behind the place.

Then, bearing to the right, he headed up the valley again and thanked the kind fortune that made the sheriff follow blindly, like a bulldog, in his tracks. The whole front portion of the parade had gone with Lank Heney. And a year of time and trouble would be needed to repair the damage that plunging hoofs had done to the garden of Mr. Bowen.

The last of the stream of riders had not had time to get up to the house before Shawn was away, and these swung to the side and made straight on after the flying mare and her rider.

Behind him, too, came Lank Heney and the rest of his best mounted riders. A few had come to grief at the fences, but four or five remained in the race, and these joined with the dozen or more laggards who unexpectedly found themselves in the fore of the chase.

They were in easy pistol range now, and, as the least speedy horses in the posse began to fall back once more while the mare straightened up the ravine, the riders pulled their Colts and opened with a shower of bullets. There was no defense for Shawn except to lie on the neck of the good mare and trust to luck.

Certainly her strong heart could be trusted. Unfalteringly she strode. Her neck and shoulders had been whipped to a lather by the chafing of the reins, and her sides were wet, but still she kept in her stride and held her head straight before her, as a good horse should. And the heart of Terry Shawn swelled with gratitude for the noble creature's effort.

In the olden days, men hard pressed for their lives were apt to pledge themselves to some sort of good work—to a candle to be lighted, say, at the shrine of some patron saint, or a large donation to the poor, or perhaps they would take on some vow of penance.

Terry Shawn, riding for his life in this Twentieth Century, looked upward to the blue of the sky and pledged in his heart of hearts: *If ever I settle down in a place, I'm going to put one field apart for broken-down ponies. I'll take 'em deaf and blind and lame, and I'll turn 'em out on grass all summer, and I'll take 'em in and feed 'em all winter. I'll groom 'em myself and doctor 'em myself. And if ever I have a son, I'll teach him to be a man by letting him watch a proper horse work.*

He had crossed the wide open stretch above the Bowen house now, and the woods were just before him, but, jockey the mare as he would, he was unable to draw her ahead of the pursuit. Only her brave spirit enabled her to keep to a gallop, and, although it was true that she had beaten off the great majority of the riders who followed, still, Lank Heney on his strong-limbed mustang and five other men, close behind, stuck in the traces of the mare and now—bitterly the outlaw admitted it— they were gaining. It was not a swift or sudden gain, but very steady and sure, and Shawn felt that his last day had surely come—indeed his last hour, unless a miracle happened.

Out of the dense copse before him, Shawn saw the twinkle of the sun on a long rifle barrel before the weapon *clanged*. His Colt was in his hand at first sight of that glinting peril, but the instant the rifle *cracked* he knew that it had not been aimed at him, for, far behind, he heard a loud yell of pain.

He glanced back and saw one of the posse trying to pull up his mustang with one hand while the other arm dangled helplessly beside him. Still Lank Heney and the rest poured on, and a *crash* of guns answered that single bullet.

158

A twitch of Shawn's shoulder and another at the side of his coat told him that he had been shaved twice by death. Then the rifle rang before him again, and, once more glancing back, he saw a horse and man go down in a heap. The rider spun head over heels, came blindly staggering to his feet again, only to pitch on his face and lie still—badly stunned, beyond a doubt, and very lucky not to have broken his neck in such a fall.

Even the resolution of Lank Heney was not strong enough to give him courage to ride on into the face of such deadly marksmanship as this. There were four fighting men left, but against them they had that hidden rifleman and Terry Shawn, whose value as a gunman was attested by the price upon his head.

Lank Heney, maintaining a steady fire with his revolver, swerved to the side, and his three fol lowers turned in the other direction, heading for cover.

So Shawn's staggering mare came in under the shelter of the trees, and José, laughing with delight, joined his companion.

The bay mare dropped at once to a dog-trot, and her rider pulled her back to a walk, and, leaning down, loosened the cinches. Five minutes' quiet breathing while the sheriff and his men rode through the woods, hunting them, might give the bay new life.

In the meantime he turned to José. 'You, José!' he said roughly. 'Why did you do that?'

The Mexican grinned broadly.

'In my country, *señor*, we are very kind to wild children.'

Chapter Twenty-Three

Checked by the deadly fire of the Mexican, nevertheless the sheriff did not hesitate long, but forged ahead through the trees in order to come again on the traces of the fugitives. Well and keenly did he hunt for sign of the two, but, although he ranged well up the ravine, he did not find what he wanted. There were trails, to be sure, but they looked a day old—some might be even older.

The reason was simply that José and his companion remained in the woodland covert, and only when their horses were well rested did they drift to the side of the ravine and take shelter in a little blind corner of the cañon wall. So, when the patient sheriff came back down the ravine and combed the forest, he found nothing whatever and was forced to turn his face toward Lister again.

In their hiding, the two remained that night, for, although José was eager to go on toward the higher mountains, Shawn insisted that they wait. Fresh horses, he declared, would be better than a long start. So they rubbed down their mounts, and saw to it that they had

160

excellent grass for grazing.

Before it was dark, Shawn tried his hand once more with Sky Pilot.

On the lead, or grazing in the little pasture that they had found, the chestnut was quiet as a favorite child, and, even when the cinches were drawn up, he merely grunted and stamped in a mild ill-humor. But when the outlaw leaped into the saddle, Sky Pilot tried to climb the sky. He was checked, somewhat, by the long rope with which José held him, but inside that limited radius he fought like a lion. For ten mortal minutes Shawn stuck to the saddle. Then, battered, broken, dizzy, he was hurled from his stirrups and lay in a heap. Had he not fallen in limp unconsciousness, he must certainly have broken his neck. Even as it was, José had to work over him until night was dark about them before he wakened and sat up with a feeble groan.

Later they sat, side-by-side, and smoked— Shawn with his head leaning back against a tree trunk, a very battered man, indeed.

'So it was with me,' explained José. 'I was a rider, *señor*. I laughed at the wild horses that were brought in from the range . . . horses that had run free for eight or ten years. They could not buck me off any more than they could buck their skins off. The chestnut was different. I used to tie him to a tree and try to ride him. But he bucked in a circle around it, and finally I would go down. I had only one

161

care . . . to fall on the outside of the circle and roll out of his reach. Otherwise, he would have killed me as I lay on the ground. A hundred times I have tried that.

'You see this left leg is crooked. It was broken below the knee by the colt. I made splints with my own hands and tied up the colt. For a month, for six weeks, I crawled about and lived like an animal. I ate roots. I trapped little birds and ate them raw. But finally I could walk again. You see this scar across my forehead . . . that is where he flung me on a rock. I have had five ribs broken. Three times a collar bone has snapped. I have lain in pain and misery, on account of him, for a whole year, nursing myself, crawling out in wind and snow to forage like a beast. Tell me, *señor,* why I have not killed him long ago?'

Shawn was silent; he was almost too sick for speech. José turned toward the place where the chestnut was grazing contentedly and began to curse his horse with a soft and solemn eloquence.

They slept afterward, and in the gray morning they prepared to ride again.

They left the cañon and journeyed straight across the hills toward the house of Joe, where they could find food and get the latest news, and where they would not be apt to be hunted. On the way, José spoke of the subject nearest his heart.

'You have told me, my friend, of the old

162

man of the mountain who made the chestnut as docile as a child?'

'I have. I saw it, José.'

'Let us go up to him, then. If he has made the horse obedient once, perhaps he can do so again . . . and we, *Don* Terry, will watch and learn what he does.'

There was no objection from Shawn. He hardly cared what trail he followed now, so long as it led away from Lister and Kitty Bowen.

So they rode in wretched silence across the hills. There was no fog this morning. Instead, the sky was coated with pale gray clouds, and a steady mist of rain fell—a cold rain blowing steadily out of the north and turning their hands numb upon the reins. The two saddle horses plodded on with downcast heads, submitting to misery, but the chestnut danced and pranced through the storm with a heart as light as a feather.

'Why should he be sad?' said the Mexican, gloomily watching the colt. 'Men are the masters of everything, and he is a master of men. Therefore he laughs. He is outside the law of horses, *señor,* which says that they must work and obey. We, too,' philosophized José, 'are outside the law, but still we are not free. Is not that true? If we escape from men and the jail, still the sky sends its rain on us, and the wind to cut us to the bone . . . and we are starved and beaten. We say that we are free,

163

but still we are slaves. Tell me, *señor*, if I have said the truth?'

Shawn did not answer, but there was a deadly verity in what his companion had said, and in his heart he admitted it fully.

However, they now saw the shack of Joe, half drowned in the rain mists before them, and they brought their horses to a gallop until they came to the door of the little house. Joe appeared at the same instant, dragging in a log for firewood, his mustang hitched to the timber with a line.

He greeted them with a silent wave of the hand.

'Don't talk to him,' said Shawn softly to the Mexican. 'He's looking black this morning. Every man who lives alone like this has his ups and downs, and Joe is down this morning.'

So, with hardly a word spoken, they took their places at a little table and let Joe serve them with food.

The meal was eaten in continued silence. Only, when they rose to depart, Shawn pressed a little sheaf of bills into the hand of his host.

'It's a rainy day,' he explained, 'and here is something to warm you up a little, Joe.'

'I don't want it,' answered Joe gruffly, passing back the money.

'You don't understand, old fellow,' said Shawn. 'I'm flush. I'm not broke, Joe. Take that and you're welcome to it. There are other places where I can drop in and get a meal from time to time, but I'm never sure of the people. You're the only one that I can count on.'

'You've counted on me for the last time,' returned Joe.

Shawn tried to smile, searching for the jest, but the face of Joe remained utterly grim.

'I'm through with you,' he explained slowly. 'I never minded when you raised all kinds of trouble, except this last kind, kid. Now I'm finished.'

'What kind?' asked Shawn eagerly. 'Lifting money from a set of crooked gamblers, Joe? Do you balk at that?'

Joe turned aside in disgust. 'You know what I mean,' he said shortly.

But Shawn followed him and turned him about. 'I've got no idea at all,' he said earnestly.

'The next time,' cried Joe in a burst of anger, 'when the boys take after you, I'm going to be riding with them, and I'll have my gun on tap. Is that clear to you?'

'What on earth has happened?' asked Shawn.

'Nothing,' said Joe. 'To you it ain't a thing. To take a fine girl away from her home without a by your leave . . . that ain't worth thinking about, to you!'

'Take a girl from her home . . . what are you talking about, man?'

Joe pointed a grimy forefinger accusingly at Shawn. 'What did you do with her?' he asked savagely.

'With whom?'

'Where did you take her?' insisted Joe.

'Will you tell me who you mean?'

'It makes me utterly despise you to have you dodge me like this,' said Joe. 'Who would I mean but Kitty Bowen. Where is she?'

'At her home, where I last left her, I suppose. Of course she's there.'

'Is she?' snarled Joe. 'And that's why old Bowen is ridin' over the hills, half crazy with grief? And that's why the boys are promising you a rope this time? And that's why I'm going to help them get you, Shawn. Just because you left her at her home, where you found her? You don't think you can bamboozle me like that, do you?'

'Kitty Bowen. Kitty Bowen . . . ,' breathed Terry. 'Do you mean it, Joe?'

Here José put in honestly: 'It is not true, *señor.* I myself have been with *Don* Terry all this day. She has not been with us.'

'Greaser,' said Joe more savagely than ever, 'do you think that your lying makes any difference to me? The pair of you are cut out of one kind of cloth, and it's a kind that I've got no use for. Do you understand? Shawn, I never want to see you again, except in jail!' And turning on his heel, he stalked out of the house, mounted his horse, and rode off into the mist of rain.

Shawn followed to the doorway and looked

166

after him until he was out of sight. Then he mutely signaled to his companion and led the way back to their horses.

'But it is wrong!' cried José. 'You have not told them, my friend! You have not explained that they're wrong! She is not with us!'

There was no answer from Shawn until they had covered the first long mile toward Mount Shannon. Then he said sadly: 'What good is talking, José? What good is the word of a crook? Only . . . where could she be?'

Chapter Twenty-Four

They took the first straight trail toward the distant heights of Mount Shannon, and that way took them at once into the mouth of a cañon. It was ordinarily as quiet and commonplace as any of the half hundred ravines that split and wrinkled the face of the big mountain, but now it was transformed. That misty rain, which wrapped the plains and the lower hills, apparently had fallen in thick and solid torrents on the breast of the upper mountain, so that now a great stream was bounding and thundering down the valley. Stones the size of a man's fist were whirled along close to the surface, and, deeper down, heavy boulders staggered and turned before the blast of the current.

José blinked and shook his head at this uproar, but the confusion and the crashing fitted oddly with the humor of Terence Shawn, for heart and brain were consumed in the contemplation of his own woes. To his superstitious mind it appeared that all his troubles came from his first meeting with the chestnut colt. Or was it, indeed, that the strange deaf-mute who lived in the wilderness on Mount Shannon had put some sort of curse upon him because he took the chestnut away? There was enough superstition in Shawn to make him cringe at this idea.

So beset was his mind with these ideas that he took no heed of anything around him except the crash of the water down the ravine, and the occasional fall of a distant rock down the cañon walls. It was José who struck his shoulder sharply in warning and then turned his horse aside from the trail, leaping it into a thicket.

When Shawn had followed and cast an inquiring eye at his companion, José pointed, and through the foliage, far down the trail, Shawn could see two riders hurrying up the valley.

'Head hunters!' said Shawn savagely. 'José, we'll talk to those fellows. Head hunters they are indeed, José! Why else would they be riding horses like that?'

For as the pair drew nearer it could be seen that they rode magnificent long-limbed horses,

168

plainly of good breeding, and certainly not the type that usually is used for knocking about through the thickets and the rocks of the mountains.

'Do you know them?' murmured Shawn a moment later.

'I never have seen them, my friend.'

'I'll tell you. It's Hack Thomas and Jim Berry. They've worked with me in the old days. They've been pals of mine. I saw Hack out of Tucson one day when a hundred wild men were trying to take his scalp. I backed him up and covered him until he could get started. There's Berry, too. I've staked him twice . . . I've worked beside him, too. What difference do the old times make when there's a price on a man's head? No difference at all. Joe, too. He pretends it's because of the girl, but it ain't. He wants his chance to get in on the easy money. The price of a lucky bullet brings in five thousand for him. Do you see, José? But I'm going to make that pair wish that they'd never ridden on my trail. We'll lie low till they get past. Look at 'em. They're reading my trail.'

So spoke the outlaw, his fury growing fast, for, as the two came up the trail, it was plain to see that they leaned from the saddle time after time to read the sign before them. They came closer—two tall, thin-faced, dark men, enough alike to have passed for twin brothers, each riding with a matchless grace, each armed to the teeth with Bowie knife, revolvers, and the inevitable long Winchester that usually was carried in the holster under the right leg, but which these hunters now kept exposed, balancing the weight across the pommels of their saddles.

They had jogged their horses past the thicket, when Shawn, having dismounted, stepped from the shrubbery onto the trail behind them, a revolver balanced in either hand. José remained in cover, his rifle at his shoulder, prepared for emergencies. But the last stern word from Shawn was: 'This is my game. Hands off!'

Then the outlaw shouted: 'Hack!'

Hack Thomas and his companion whirled their horses about with exclamations of astonishment; they found themselves under the cover of Shawn's two steady guns.

'Hey, Terry!' cried Thomas. 'We've been looking for you!'

'Sure you have,' said Shawn. 'I could see that. Maybe you wanted to give me a cup of tea, or something. Or you just rode up here behind me to pass the time of day. Is that it?'

'He thinks that we've been after him,' said Hack grimly. 'How're you going to persuade him, Jim?'

Mr. Berry bit his lip. 'Why, Shawn,' he said, 'you know me, old-timer.'

'I ain't drunk,' declared Shawn. 'Neither are you. If you were, it'd make it easier for you to take what's coming.'

'And what's coming?' asked Berry with more curiosity than fear.

'I'll give you both an even break, one after the other,' answered Shawn. 'But I'm going to have this out with you here and now. You hear me talk?'

'I hear you talk right foolish,' broke in Hack Thomas. 'Do you think that we're after the reward?'

'You'd be above it, I guess?' sneered Terry Shawn. 'What's five thousand to a pair of high-minded gents like the two of you?'

'What's five thousand compared to fifty thousand?' returned Jim Berry, still calm of eye.

'You can't make a fool out of me,' declared Shawn.

'We can't,' said Berry. 'You've done that before for yourself. What's eating you? If we did drop you, how could we collect? Do you think that they don't know us? Do you think that we're not wanted, kid, near as bad as you?'

'Only,' admitted Thomas, 'we didn't ever make a play like yours, kid. We never sneaked girls away from their homes. What's come over you lately? That ain't your old style.'

Shawn, in doubt as he listened, drew back a little, watching them with a hawk-like sharpness, and neither of them stirred hand or muscle under that scrutiny. To have moved so much as a finger would have meant death, and they seemed to know it perfectly well.

'I want to believe you,' said Shawn gloomily. 'I want to believe that you boys didn't come up here to get me.'

'Go ahead and believe it, then.' Thomas grinned. 'We won't hold you back. And just shove those Colts away, kid. They make me feel terrible sick to look at 'em.'

'José,' said Shawn, 'keep a sharp watch.' And suddenly he put away his guns.

'The greaser is in the brush, is he?' asked Jim Berry, nodding in the correct direction.

'He is,' said Shawn, 'and he's covering you. I want to trust you fellows, but I can't, just yet. They've been riding me from wall to wall, boys, and they've got me a little nervous.'

'We've heard about it,' admitted Thomas. 'That was how we guessed where we'd find you.'

'This ravine, you mean?'

'Yes, because it's the shortest cut to the tall timber. Terry, we need you bad. We've got a little proposition to put up to you. That's why we're here.'

'Business?'

'Yes.'

'What kind?'

'You want us to talk with José listening?'

'Aye, fire away.'

'It's bank stuff, Terry.'

'I've quit teaming,' said Shawn. 'I do my

172

stuff alone. You ought to know that.'

'Sure, you work alone. But this deal is different. How about fifty thousand, kid?'

'As much as that?'

'That's the least it can be. It ought to pan out to a hundred and fifty. Now, kid, does that sound big enough for you to have a share in it?'

'Oh, never mind the money,' answered Shawn gloomily. 'But if there's any excitement to be had out of it . . . I dunno, Hack. It might tempt me a little.'

'Excitement?' murmured Hack Thomas. 'Well, all you've got to do is to ride into a certain town with us in broad daylight and help us stick up the bank. How does that sound to you?'

'Where?' asked Terry Shawn.

'Kline River.'

'You mean the new bank?'

'That's it.'

Terry sighed. 'They're loaded with cash,' he said, 'if you can only make the cashier toss out what's in the safe.'

'That shouldn't bother you, Shawn. Haven't lost the old knack, have you? Besides, what's one cashier against three old hands like us? Kid, throw your leg over your horse and come along with us now.'

Temptation made the eyes of Terry Shawn glitter, but suddenly he answered: 'It sounds good to me, boys. But I've got another job on now. Come up the mountain with me, spend a couple of days there, and then maybe I'll ride down with you.'

Chapter Twenty-Five

So they became a party of four. They established a point ahead, with one man riding at it; they established a point behind, for a rear guard, and in the center journeyed two. Now let Sheriff Lank Heney and his men beware. For in the first place they would hardly be able to surprise a party riding in this circumspect fashion, and in the second place they had numbers sufficient to hold off the challenge of a large body of armed men. José was given the rear guard, the post of honor; Hack Thomas journeyed ahead, and in the center were Jim Berry and Shawn. They could afford to be off their guard, and to center their attention on talk.

There was much useful information to be had from Berry. His first advice to Shawn was to clear out of that section of the country as quickly as possible.

'Why?' asked Shawn. 'I've done my work around here. I've made my friends around here. Why should I clear out?'

'Up to yesterday,' said Berry, who was a crisp-spoken fellow, 'you had as many friends as any long rider in the world, but today there aren't three men outside of the profession that would stand up for you.'

'Go on,' murmured Shawn, frowning.

'It's the girl,' said Jim Berry. 'People won't stand for that. Rob ten banks, if you please, and shoot up a couple of dozen "punchers of all kinds. But you ought to leave the women alone, kid. How come that you didn't know that, anyway?'

Terry Shawn turned a dark crimson, and his temples throbbed with rage, but there was something about the cold, steady eye of Jim Berry that discouraged a tirade. Besides, he was baffled and bewildered by these continual charges that he had removed Kitty Bowen from her home. He decided to use calm reason and try to get to the bottom of the matter.

'Kitty Bowen's left her home?' he began.

Berry nodded, with a quick side glance at his companion. It was very plain that, had it not been for the use which Thomas had for the expert assistance of this gunman and robber, he would have been hardly more kindly to Shawn than the others who ranged on his trail.

'She's gone,' said Berry. 'Well?'

'Look here, Jim. Was I ever a girl chaser?'

Berry shrugged his shoulders, like a man who makes no admissions.

'Matter of fact,' said Shawn eagerly, 'did you ever know me to have hardly anything to do with 'em?'

'Maybe not,' said the other grudgingly.

'Now, I ask you, would I be fool enough to bother a girl like Kitty Bowen, that has a thousand admirers . . . that's known everywhere?'

Berry grunted.

'Would I throw myself into danger like that?' said Shawn with increasing vehemence.

'She's gone,' said the other with significant emphasis.

'But what has that got to do with me?' cried Shawn. 'Have I got her with me? Is she in my pocket? Did I hide her in a hole in the ground?'

'Go on and jump me,' said Jim Berry. 'I'm not turning you down. I've come up here to get you in on a big job where I need you. The point is, you go to Lister and make a dead set at Kitty Bowen. Go out and see her at her house. Ride in under her old man's rifle to have ten words with her. And the next morning she's gone. Well, kid, what are folks going to think, unless they've got no brains in their heads? If you didn't steal her, who did?'

This evidence the outlaw considered with gloomy silence, for he saw that he could make no retort. It would be merely folly for him to bare his heart and show what woe and pain there was in it for the disappearance of pretty Kitty Bowen. He would be considered a mere hypocrite, and no more.

At that point there was a call from José in

176

the rear, and that keen horseman came flying up and announced that he had spotted a horseman following them in the distance.

Either they would have to turn aside and let the rider pass, or they must increase their pace, or else drive him away.

'Try a scare,' suggested Jim Berry. 'Throw a bullet between the front legs of his horse. Is there only one rider?'

'Only one.'

They went back to a point of vantage, all three, and they saw, presently, the rider of whom José had spoken. He seemed, in the distance, a small man, narrow shouldered like a cowpuncher who had spent his life in the saddle, and with a disproportionately huge gray sombrero of the cone-shaped Mexican fashion.

Shawn, being the most accurate shot in the group, was chosen to do the shooting. He dropped on one knee behind a rock and delivered his bullet exactly where Berry had suggested—at the very feet of the stranger's horse. The mustang pitched up high in the air, but, instead of bolting for cover or turning tail and retreating at full speed, the stranger took off his hat and waved it sweepingly about his head.

'Mocking us!' said Berry with heat. 'There's a cool one for you.'

Another bullet in the same place made the mustang pitch more violently and took him out of sight behind a great boulder, but to the last the rider's hat was violently waved in defiance.

The three fugitives looked gravely at one another, and then proceeded up the trail again. They discussed the event seriously. The stranger was a mere boy. So much José, whose eyes were like the eyes of a buzzard, was willing to swear. But a mere boy could be more dangerous than any grown man, as Billy the Kid had demonstrated for all time. A grown man possessed an element of reason that prevented him from taking certain risks, but a boy could be a mad creature who would hold headlong on his course, no matter what the obstacles that arose. You never could guess what a boy would do next.

Therefore, in view of the fact that the young daredevil had defied them so boldly, they determined that they would put a quick stop to his career if he showed near them again.

They had not gone another two miles up the cañon when José brought swift word that the same pursuer was dodging them in the rear.

Terry Shawn flushed a little. 'It's only one man, boys,' he said. 'I'll just drop back and argue with him a minute. You wait for me up here.'

Jim Berry chuckled with mirth. 'You'll go back and kill that gent or get yourself shot up,' he said. 'You're only a kid yourself, Shawn . . . no real sense. No, sir, we'll stop the kid, and we'll do it without blowing his head off José, can you put a slug through his horse?'

José grinned in appreciation, and the three drew back to the edge of a little covert of lodgepole pine to watch the performance of this ceremony.

Once more they saw the indomitable small rider come twisting into view near the flashing river, his mustang black and glistening with perspiration as it climbed up the difficult trail.

José took careful aim.

'Shoot when I whistle,' said Berry. 'We've got to warn the kid before we shoot.' So he put his two forefingers in his mouth and emitted a blast that shrieked loudly down the cañon, sounding even above the roar of the torrent.

The pursuer stopped his horse and jerked up his head so that the broad brim of the sombrero flared up around his face. That instant the rifle of José *clanged*, and the mustang dropped, lifeless, with sprawling legs.

The youth was out of the saddle instantly. His hat fell from his head. Long, blond, womanish hair streamed down over his shoulders. Even under this rifle fire he did not turn to shelter, but, snatching up a rifle from the holster of his fallen horse, he dropped to one knee and poured a rapid stream of bullets straight up among the pines, the very first of his shots cutting a twig beside the head of no less a hero than Terry Shawn himself, and sending the whole trio scampering back through the woods to a safer distance.

179

'You see?' Jim Berry grinned. 'Young enough to be crazy. Oh, I know the type. Jump off a thousand-foot cliff for a bet. Eat fire. Fight a hundred men. I don't know but it would have been wiser to send a bullet through him, instead of through the horse.'

Shawn answered with some dryness: 'That may be your idea of a game, Berry, but I make it a practice never to shoot at a man out of cover, and I guess that's the rule that we'll all follow so long as I'm with this party.'

Jim Berry turned a grimly challenging eye upon Shawn at this remark, and his look was met by a glance as cold as ice. Sudden silence fell upon the three, but Berry said no more, and José, as he fell back to the rear once more, was smiling faintly and unpleasantly.

Chapter Twenty-Six

The question of superiority between Berry and Shawn had been tacitly settled by this little exchange of views. A difference between the two had been inevitable from the beginning, and now it had occurred. For that reason José smiled wisely and a little cruelly as he fell back to his post of rear guard. Silence dropped down between the two riders in the center. It could be taken for granted that all good feelings in Berry toward Shawn had been killed by the silence to which he had been forced, and young Mr. Shawn could have testified of old experience that no good could come of this attitude between them.

However, he could hardly go back upon the position that he had taken, namely, that there was to be no firing from ambush upon men in the open. It was true that hardly another long rider in the cattle country would have insisted upon so stern an edict, but that was the very difference between Shawn and the rest. Men in the West were not apt to question what was done in a man's life so much as how it was accomplished, and if the way was decent, the thing itself could pass muster with all except the overcurious. There was this matter of the girl, of course, to harm him. But the truth must come out, his innocence be known when Kitty Bowen showed up somewhere to explain her disappearance, and then once more he would he spoken of and looked upon rather as a gentleman adventurer than as a murdering bandit. For, from the beginning, every man who rode on his trail knew that no secret danger would come from their quarry, but that he would fight with fair warning and man to man, with equal weapons.

So the repute of young Shawn had been established in the beginning, and now he would not tarnish his fame himself nor give his companions a chance to blacken his name. As for the anger of Jim Berry, he shrugged his shoulders and told himself that he had endured the wrath of much greater men.

Hack Thomas at last came back from the front, and Berry went out to the lead. However, Shawn refrained purposely from mentioning the difference that had occurred between him and Berry; he would let the story come out with all the prejudice that Jim Berry would lend it. He did, of course, tell the story of the long-haired boy who followed them and had been unhorsed. Thomas grinned and then grew sober.

'I know,' he said. 'I've heard about 'em, and I've seen 'em . . . these girlie kids. All they want to do is to get famous. They don't much care how. Just a chance to find danger somewhere and eat it. Think of that young fool dropping on one knee and opening fire on a whole forest. Well, you'll hear from that kid again, and take it from me you'll hear hard. He ain't going to be shuffled off the trail by the loss of one horse. Shawn, I tell you that this trip into the hills is a silly trick. Let's turn right around and slant straight for the town where we have our job staked out.'

For answer young Shawn turned in the saddle and glanced back. The Mexican was just coming into view, Sky Pilot beside him.

'You see that horse?' he said.

'Yes.'

'What would you give for it?'

Hack Thomas turned and looked at the

flashing beauty. Although, of course, the distance was too great for the distinguishing of points, far off as he was, the greatness of Sky Pilot was clearly revealed to him.

'I'd give two thousand cold, and I've got the cash with me,' he announced.

'Would you? That's a tall price.'

'I know the value of a horse . . . to me.'

'Well, Hack, suppose that you couldn't get it with money?'

'In that case . . . well, I ain't particular about my methods, kid.'

'Now,' said the other, 'when we get to the end of our march, I may have a chance to own that horse. So you see why it's no good to talk to me about anybody else or anything else.'

Hack Thomas took this answer as final and discreetly turned the talk into other channels. 'Where are we going?' he inquired.

'To the end of the trail,' answered Shawn curtly, and he fell deeply into his own profound thoughts.

For his own part, he would have been very glad to know whether the man on the mountainside was a saint, a criminal, or a devil. He would have suspected him of all three inspirations. For one thing was manifest—his power—and power is often attributed to some extra-human source.

They had no further sight or sound of the precocious young fighting boy who had been driving up behind them. That same evening they came to the foot of the rugged pass that led up to the brow of Mount Shannon, and pushed up a gorge dripping with water that trickled from the sides, welled from every crack, and seemed to creep up from the very rock underfoot.

They came out, finally, upon the little valley that the outlaw remembered so well. The time was just after sunset. They could look down from the eminence and see the lower mountains lost in the night, and all the broad, dark plain stretching away to the south, tinged with purple. But up here, reflected from the near sky all around, there was a strong and rosy twilight. From the horizon, north, east, south, and west, the radiance sprang upward, faded in the center of the sky, and covered the whole face of Mount Shannon with a rosy glory.

So the four, drawing together in a compact group, came up the little valley, and they saw before them the homestead that the hermit had made here on the very edge of the world. The hour was late, but he was employing the light in a strange fashion. He had put together a wooden plow, tying the tough timbers together with sun-dried and toughened withes, and, by dint of pressing down with all his weight on the handle, he managed to sink this Egyptian-style plow point into the rain-softened earth. Before him walked a saddled horse, and from the point of the saddle ran back a lariat that was hitched to the plow beam. Patiently the horse worked ahead and, scratching some sort of a feeble furrow behind it, answered the twitching of the reins, and, turning again at the end of the field, came back along the other side.

Young Shawn stopped his companions on the edge of the woods. 'Look, look!' he exclaimed. 'Do you see the old boy there? Do you see that horse? Tame, ain't it? But let me tell you, I never got a day's ride out of that devil without a full dose of bucking to warm up on. Bucking in the morning was bacon and eggs to him, and bucking at night was like coffee to a tired man. And now look at him . . . tame as a baby, and begging for more work! Look at his ears . . . pitched straight forward like he was eatin' apples. If that man ain't a witch, I'm a sucker.'

This speech was not greeted with a smile. José, even, took off his hat in a sort of odd reverence.

'Señores,' he said, 'that is a holy man . . . a saint.'

'No, not a saint,' said Hack Thomas. 'It's just some wise old shake. Why, kid, this is old Shannon, ain't it?'

'It is.'

'I've heard about him. Let's go have a look at him.'

They went up the valley from the woods, accordingly, and, when he saw them coming,

Shannon paused in his work and leaned upon his plow. Then, taking note of the lateness of the twilight, he abandoned the plowing and began to unknot the draw rope. The four greeted him in silence, knowing him to be deaf, but they waved most cheerfully, while Shawn explained to his companions.

'That was a soft brute. Soft and foolish, but now look at him. Shannon has made him hard and wise. Look at his eye. As understanding as a man's. That's Shannon's work.'

'Look!' said Hack Thomas.

Shannon, in the midst of his work, had paused with the loosened lariat in his hand to wave a courteous greeting to his guests. But at that very moment he was turned to stone, it appeared, by the sight of the young chestnut horse. They saw him stiffen, then he dropped the rope and went slowly forward.

'Keep back!' yelled José. 'Keep back! That horse is a man-eater, *señor!* Keep back beyond the length of his line!'

The deaf-mute did not falter, and Shawn called sharply, 'Be still, José! Are you going to teach the finest horse wrangler that ever walked how to handle a horse in his own home yard?'

José, anxious but silenced, fidgeted in the saddle, and even drew out a gun, so that he would be able to stop the murderous charge of the stallion, if it were necessary to resort to severe measures in the end.

Without the slightest hesitation, Shannon went straight up to Sky Pilot, who flattened his ears when he saw the man coming straight at him, and then made a little rear and plunge, as though about to hurl himself upon him. Yet he did not advance, but suddenly halted, with his legs widely braced, and his head stretched out, and his nostrils expanding and snorting.

On went Shannon, until he laid a hand on the starred brow of the beautiful animal. Sky Pilot at the same instant pointed forward his ears, and a whinny of joy rose from the very depths of his heart. He sniffed at the feet of Shannon. He sniffed at his ground-stained knees, at his hands, at his chest, and at his face, and at last he nipped slyly at the hair of Shannon's head.

The hermit smiled. He turned his back to Sky Pilot, and to Shawn he made a singularly graceful gesture.

'He's thanking me,' said Shawn, 'for bringing back his horse. Now, how can I explain? José, let go the rope and see what happens.'

'Let go a thunderbolt? *Señor,* we will never see the colt again!'

'We will, though. Let go and see,' commanded Shawn.

It was done, and Sky Pilot, after a lofty spring and a plunge or two, began to gallop swiftly around Shannon, shaking his head and pretending a vast fury, but finally bringing up behind the man of the mountain and trotting like a dog at his heels.

Chapter Twenty-Seven

At the open fire of Shannon, they cooked their supper, and Shannon, coming and going with perfect patience, never showed the slightest irritation when he saw his larder so heavily drawn upon to meet the needs of the strangers. It was a very dark night. There were enough high-flying clouds to shut out the stars, and now and again some downward blast of wind came rushing and roaring through the forest in the valley like a warning of danger to come.

They finished their meal and sat about; the fire was built larger, whole logs and small trees being cast upon the blaze out of Shannon's stock of well-dried and seasoned timber, but still he made no protest.

'We'll have to pay high for this,' suggested Thomas.

'He won't take money,' declared Shawn. 'I know him . . . he'd throw your money back at you. He's a queer one, this Shannon is. He won't take money. He trades in skins for everything that he wants. Never uses coin at all.'

Thomas fell into thought. 'We could send

him up some stuff like guns, and ammunition and such. He'd need that up here.'

'You try it,' said Shawn. 'He'll take nothing. I know him, I tell you.'

'But,' exclaimed Thomas, 'then we're just calmly sitting at our ease, here, and usin' up things that he's worked hard for and that we can't repay?'

'It looks like it,' said Shawn. 'Except that I've been figuring on the thing, and I'll find a way sometime.'

'What way? What way is there that ain't got money in it?' asked Thomas with vigor. 'Tell me that, Shawn?'

'Money ain't the only thing in the world, I suppose?' suggested Shawn with warmth.

Thomas then grew irritatingly logical. 'Look here. What have you ever had in your life that you didn't steal?'

Shawn was silent, growing hot with anger.

'I ain't insulting you,' the other assured him. 'I just mean to tell you that all a man can steal is money, or things that you exchange for money. And so that's all you've got to make a payment to Shannon. Well, money is nothing to him. So that makes us unable to pay our debt. We can't have anything to do with him. We can't be square with him. If we take anything, we never can pay it back.'

He had warmed to his words, and now he finished with such emphasis that Berry stared upon him, mouth agape. He turned toward

189

young Shawn, forgetting his recent enmity, merely curious to hear what the answer could be.

Shawn had no answer. He reached deeply into his mind and almost felt that he had words to reply with, but in every instance his heart failed him. He said at last: 'I don't know, Thomas. I can't sling words the way that you can. Only, I feel that there's something that could be said by a clever talker.' He stared gloomily at Thomas as he spoke. 'You can give a fellow a helping hand, Thomas. I'd call that something that ain't money.'

'Sure,' agreed Thomas instantly. 'You're going to take this old goat's horse that he cottons to so close, and afterward you're going to wait till he's in trouble so's you can pay him back. Likely that he'll be in trouble up here, ain't it? He's got so many neighbors that'll bother him, eh?'

Shawn's only reply was to fall into a passion. He leaped violently to his feet and started to burst into a tirade. Then, thinking better of it, but unable to control his anger, he turned and hurried away into the darkness.

It left the Mexican, Thomas, and Jim Berry alone by the fire. This had died down a little, but still it stained the hands and the faces of the men with streaks of blood-red. They remained subdued and quiet for a moment after the departure of their companion.

Then José took up a handful of pine

needles and tossed them into the coals. There was a brief *crackling,* and then an arm of fire wagged high in the air.

'So,' said José. 'My friend, he is that.' He assisted his meaning by throwing up both hands in an aspiring gesture. Then he relapsed into a chuckle.

'Nice fellow,' said Jim Berry with sarcasm. 'Nice, even temper. A lamb . . . he is. I say,' he added with greater warmth, 'that he's been spoiled. He's been runnin' with people that he could walk over and sink his spurs into, but the time's come when . . .'

He was distracted by the heel of Thomas, which descended with force upon his toes, and, as he turned a furious face on his companion, he was directed toward José with a nod. It could be seen that José was looking gloomily downward, his brow contracted into a deep frown.

'The kid is all right,' said Thomas heartily.

'Oh, maybe he is,' agreed Berry, massaging his injured foot. 'Only he gets on my nerves a little. It ain't anything I have against him, only look how close he was to a fight just then.'

'That is true,' murmured José, reassured by this change of tone in the conversation. 'But look, friends, it needs a hot fire before iron can be melted. What good is a little yellow flame?'

They broke up their fireside group to clean the kitchen utensils and knives that they had used in their cookery, and, when they had finished that duty, they found Shannon waiting for them on the edge of the dim circle of firelight. Behind him was a splendid and shimmering form of black and crimson—Sky Pilot, still at the heels of the hermit.

Shannon beckoned to them, and, leading the way to his shack, he kindled a lantern there and pointed out four beds that he had made with pine boughs and hay, with warm skins for blankets. The three thanked him with gestures and turned in for the night. But when Shannon had gone they conversed softly, as though for fear of being overheard.

Was it fear of them that had made their host treat them with such hospitality? Or was it a sense of hospitable duty that had ruled his actions? In the meantime, where was Shawn? Gone to walk off his evil temper and try to devise a way of getting the chestnut colt, undoubtedly.

This made Berry put the question: 'But how will Shawn settle with you, José, if he wants the horse? Sky Pilot belongs to you, I suppose?'

José laughed softly. 'That is nothing to worry about,' he said. 'Who is there that can handle the devil . . . except a saint, my friends?'

They fell asleep, at last, and were not disturbed when Shawn, in turn, entered softly, found his bunk prepared, and turned in. He slept a short and broken sleep, however, and, when the early mountain dawn had come, he was up and about once more. Early as he had risen, however, he was behindhand with the trapper. He saw Shannon already in the meadow, carrying a saddle and bridle, and Sky Pilot cantering eagerly toward him.

With rather a cruel smile of expectation, Shawn crouched behind the pile of newly cut wood that stood beside the shack and watched what was to follow. It was all very well for Sky Pilot to welcome the man on foot, but what would it be when there was a saddle on his back and feet in the stirrups? A little shudder went through Shawn, and many recently bruised places ached violently, in sympathy.

In fact, when the chestnut spied the saddle, he paused with a snort, and swept in a rapid circle around Shannon. Then, coming up from the rear, he sniffed at the saddle and flattened his ears. Shawn grinned again with dark foreknowledge of what was about to take place. He had little sympathy for Shannon. That elderly hermit was so far removed from the ways and the speeches of ordinary mortals that the outlaw could not help feeling that a fall on the turf of the soft meadow could do him no harm, and might give his conceit a tumble. He felt this the more so as he noted the unhesitant manner in which the lone dweller went about the work of saddling.

There was one miracle, to begin with, and that was that Sky Pilot stood unroped for the burden to be strapped upon his back. Once he side-stepped and shook himself like a wet dog. But after that he was calm enough while saddle and bridle were fitted on and made secure. Now for the mounting!

To the amazement of Shawn the hermit approached the fire-eating colt from the wrong side, and still Sky Pilot endured. He stood still while a clumsy foot was raised and thrust into the stirrup, only twisting his head around and biting softly at the arm of Shannon. A heave and a sway, and there was Shannon in the saddle at last.

The chestnut crouched suddenly low, ears flattened so that his head had a snaky appearance, and every muscle of his splendid body stood out as though carved in stone, so tense were his muscles with fear.

Now for the bolt forward or the lunge into the air. Shannon clucked; the chestnut crouched lower, and now he was urged forward by a heavy *thump* of a heel against his ribs. Shawn caught his breath, for who shall urge on the lightning?

Yet there was no explosion. Instead, the colt straightened, shook his head as though to resolve his doubts, and then obediently and softly trotted off with his master, who was such an inexpert horseman that even at that silken gait he bounced violently in the saddle.

The dark of the morning woods received them, and Shawn stood up with a still greater darkness upon his face, for this was such a miracle as even seeing could hardly make him believe.

Chapter Twenty-Eight

The situation in the valley on Mount Shannon grew rapidly tense. Berry and Thomas pressed for a departure; they had assented to this trip up into the wilderness only in order to please a foolish whim of young Shawn, because they wanted his promised assistance in the matter of the bank robbery, but now they had arrived in the valley and the business of Shawn appeared hopeless and ridiculous. They urged instant departure.

As Thomas put it briefly and vigorously: 'You ought to get out of this section of the country where the law is looking for you. We offer to take you through the dangerous ground and get you away to a safe region and fill your pockets with coin, besides. You prefer to stay here and look at a wild horse. Why?'

And Shawn could only answer: 'The longer I look at that horse the more I want it. If the old man can use the horse, then maybe I can learn how, too.'

'The old man has that pony hypnotized,' declared Hack Thomas. 'He's got something about him. *All* the horses like him.'

This was obvious truth, and the implied challenge was: unless you, also, have a touch of that natural magic, how can you hope to exercise any power over a bad one like Sky Pilot?

'Besides,' added Thomas, 'even if you could handle the chestnut, he ain't yours . . . he belongs to José.'

Shawn could be reduced to a point when he could argue no longer, but he could not be made to leave the valley. So Jim Berry took his companion aside and declared firmly in favor of chucking the more famous outlaw and going about their work without him. He pointed out that all of their plans were perfect. If they needed a third man, they could pick him up somewhere—*any* hireling gun-fighter.

Thomas listened. He was the sort of man who hears everything to the end, and then makes his answer.

'Three is all we want,' he replied. 'Four makes a crowd of it. Four men attract too much attention . . . but three is just right. One man for each end of the big bank room. Number three is the steely devil who shoves his gun under the cashier's nose and paralyzes him and takes the cash away. Neither of us, kid, is good enough to play the part of number three, and Shawn is the only man we know that is good enough. That's why we'll wait here for Shawn.'

Against this argument Jim Berry fought, but

he fought unsuccessfully, for in his heart of hearts he recognized the truth of what Thomas had said.

In the meantime, José was dreaming his hours away in the sun, smoking cigarettes, or fishing in the stream with great success. And Shawn spent all his hours on the study of Shannon and the stallion. He followed on foot when Shannon rode out along his trap line. He raced and scrambled and tore through trees, up rocky slopes, down sheer pitches, in order to keep his eye on the old fellow and try to penetrate his secret. But always it remained hidden. Sometimes he felt that he had got a line on something—in the touch of the hand of Shannon, in his manner of sitting on the wild horse. But in the end he realized that these thoughts were the worst sort of folly. Plainly Shannon rarely wasted caresses on the chestnut, and, as for his sitting the saddle, the miracle was simply that he was permitted to stay in it at all. No, it was a control of spirit over spirit, rather than of flesh over flesh, and the more irritated and perplexed he grew, the keener became the interest of Shawn.

Whenever the stallion was away from Shannon, Shawn improved by striving with all his might to cultivate its friendship, offering choice bunches of seed grass or succulent dainties that would appeal to the tooth of Sky Pilot. Yet he never could draw near without having Sky Pilot shrink away from him. He

197

never came really close without having the
stallion toss his head with an upper lip thrust
out stiffly and a foolish look in his eyes—the
folly of blank terror and dislike.

'What have I done to you?' Shawn was apt
to say through his teeth. And he confided to
Jim Berry and Thomas: 'That horse is two-
thirds fool. What've I ever done to him? But
he's scared to death.'

'How many times you tried to ride him?'
asked Thomas.

'Oh, half a dozen.'

'You weren't wearing spurs, I suppose?'

'Well, maybe.'

'You didn't have a quirt?'

'Sure I did.'

'And you ask why he's scared of you.'

Certainly those wild interviews with Sky
Pilot had not been of the sort to fill his soul
with trust and peace, but, on the second
evening, Shannon saw fit to interest himself in
the hopeless attachment of Shawn to the
chestnut.

The outlaw had followed the stallion down
the meadows to a spot where the stream
entered a pleasant grove. There it widened
and spread to a still-faced pool, all covered
with shadow, with a long branch thrusting up
out of the water like a black, skeleton arm.
The grass grew long and rank around the
edges of this pool, and, as every good horse
loves changes of diet, so Sky Pilot had come

here to vary his food. Shawn, carefully following with a handful of grain and a bit of sugar, strove to slip up to the red beauty.

The maneuvers of Sky Pilot were those of a naturally wicked and cool-headed horse, for he would allow the man to come almost up to him before he whipped his tail into the face of his pursuer and moved on. Or he would stand patiently and let Shawn reach his shoulder, before he swerved just a little, and kept on swerving to mock and baffle Shawn as completely as a wide gallop across the fields could have done.

Shawn paused, at last, gritting his teeth to keep back the curses, and, half lost in the pattern of the shadows, he was suddenly aware that eyes were watching him. He started erect, ready for trouble, and then he made out that it was old Shannon, smiling faintly through the beard that now grew long and gray, and descended far down his breast, matching the almost equally long hair that fell over his shoulders.

He nodded when he saw that he was observed, and came forward at once. Sky Pilot, as though to show his unmistakable preference, flirted his heels toward Shawn, and cantered eagerly to meet his master. Shannon waved the colt aside as though it were a human being, and, going on to Shawn, he took the lean hand of the outlaw in his and led him to the chestnut. It was exactly, thought Terry

Shawn, like a child being presented, but at the touch of that hand awe overcame him, and he went gravely forward.

Sky Pilot, as one who would have none of this, whirled off in a crimson streak, but he came back in a wide circle, looped swiftly around them, and halted suddenly before them again, snorting and stamping. As clearly as with words he said to Shannon: 'That man is dangerous. I know all about him, and he's full of harm.' Yet the raised hand of Shannon subdued the stallion, and, although he trembled violently, Sky Pilot allowed the two to come up, allowed the hand of the master to carry the hand of the outlaw to his muzzle, his forehead, allowed the hand of Shawn, alone, to pass down his silky neck, although at this Sky Pilot shook his head and whinnied softly to Shannon for help. For half an hour in that darkening place the introduction continued, and then they walked out from the trees side-by-side—Terry Shawn leading the stallion by the mane.

He could feel that he was under bare endurance; it was the presence of old Shannon that made the thing possible, and yet even that hardly diminished the delight of Terry Shawn in his first victory. Through that tangle of mane he felt a tremor vibrate under his hand, and it was very like holding a smoking thunderbolt, ready to be launched. Nevertheless, by the delicate thread of the will of Shannon, the stallion was held. Some day, perhaps, with his own unaided hand he might do as much.

The spell was snapped by the sudden exclamation of José, who came out of the woods with half a dozen fish dangling from his hand and cried out at this sight.

Sky Pilot veered away with a neigh, and Shannon went on to catch him for the night and put him away in the shed.

José came up to Terry Shawn with blazing, dark eyes. 'What is the trick, *amigo?*' he asked. 'How did you manage to do that?'

'There's no trick,' said Shawn, gazing earnestly after Sky Pilot. 'It's all in the head of Shannon. Heaven knows how he does it, but he seems to have a rope on the colt all the time.'

'Bah!' snapped José, growing angry. 'I saw you lead him with your own hand. Is that no trick?'

'I'll tell you what,' said Shawn, rolling a cigarette, but keeping his glance fully on the face of the Mexican, 'I'm feeling near enough to winning to want to buy your claim in that horse. What do you say, José?'

'What price?' asked the other sullenly, but curious.

'I can give you a thousand, spot cash. I'll pay you that much, José.'

'Why should I sell?' asked José. 'I take him down to a town and charge five dollars a ride. I make two or three hundred dollars a month that way. Why should I sell him, *señor?*'

'Because it's a dangerous game. You have ten men pitched on their heads. One day somebody breaks his neck. And that man's brother or father or son will come gunning for you.'

'I wear a gun, also,' said José scornfully.

'Aye, and you can use it,' admitted the other. 'You're a straight shooter, both ways from the start. But still you know what I mean. It's dangerous. Now, José, I'm offering you a fat little stake for that pony. What do you say?'

The thoughts of José were on another matter.

'How much did you pay *Señor* Shannon to learn the trick? I, José, have no money to pay to him.' He said it bitterly, a glimmer of anger in his eyes.

'I didn't pay a penny,' said Shawn with perfect truthfulness.

The Mexican shrugged with impatience. 'I am a child,' he suggested. 'I must believe everything you tell me.'

'Believe a thousand dollars,' said the outlaw. 'Will that sound right to you, old son?'

'Bother a thousand dollars.'

The patience of Terry Shawn came to an abrupt end. 'Look here, José, what's your real claim to Sky Pilot? You've told me the yarn with your own mouth. What right have you got to him?' he demanded.

'I have paid,' said José slowly, 'nearly three years of hell. Who else has paid so much for him?'

'What would a judge say to that?' asked Shawn with a sneer. 'What new kind of a bill of sale is that, José?'

'Villain!' shouted José, growing wild. 'You would take him?'

'Steady,' urged Terry Shawn. 'I'll never take him against your will. I'm just asking you to be reasonable. There's a horse that'll bring you in ten dollars' worth of trouble for every penny of cash that you can get out of him. I offer you a thousand bucks. Look here, man, right in my hand.'

He extended the bills, but José, with a furious oath, struck the money from that extended hand and turned on his heel. The bills fluttered slowly down to the ground and Shawn stood transfixed, staring at his hand, at the falling money, and at the departing form of the Mexican. Never before had he endured so much from any man, and by that blow he felt all the amenities and ties that existed between them were wiped away and made as nothing.

Chapter Twenty-Nine

Let a wolf smell bear near his home, and he will sleep lightly, for a month at least. So it was with Terry Shawn that night in the shack, dozing for a moment, then opening his eyes suddenly and lying with all senses alert, listening to the breathing of the other four in the little room. When he heard a little rustling sound, late in the night, he raised his head silently, and waited.

A shadow was moving through the dark—something to be guessed at rather than seen—something to be felt rather than heard. He could have sworn that a form leaned above him through the darkness, and, with a ready revolver, Terry Shawn waited. After an instant, the sense of imminent danger became so great that he was about to sweep a hand before him and fire if that hand struck any obstacle, but at that moment he saw a form, indistinct but real, step into the doorway, and out again into the starlit night.

He followed at once, picking his way in soft silence, with fastidious care. Outside the door, he flattened himself against the wall of the house, while he enjoyed a few deep breaths of the cold, pure, outer air. Wine-like, it made his blood leap, blew the weariness out of his brain, and made him perfectly alert and collected.

A thin night mist covered the woods, so that it was hard to tell which was forest and which was fog, save that close by the black trunks that seemed stepping toward the shack. Overhead, through wide pockets in the mist, he saw the stars, hanging as if from wires, out of the thick black velvet of the sky. There was not a ghost of wind; there was not a murmur of sound, except an occasional stamp and rumble from the horse shed. Very late for the horses still to be standing.

So thinking, he looked to his revolver again, spun the cylinder, weighed the weapon with affectionate familiarity, and then stole around the edge of the shack and the horse shed.

He was barely in time. José had not many moments the start, but José worked fast, indeed. There he sat on a saddled horse—Shawn's own mount he had selected for this occasion—and behind him he was drawing Sky Pilot out of the shed door at the end of a long lariat. Unwillingly the stallion came out into the cold of the night, with flattened ears and expanded nostrils.

'Hello, José,' said the outlaw.

José groaned, and, dropping the lead rope, he fired from the hip.

Good reason had Terry Shawn for commending the accuracy of the Mexican with firearms, and if hitherto he had seen no proof of that skill, now he could bear personal testimony hereafter. At the first stir of José's hand he had dropped toward the ground, but even so the skill of José, shooting by starlight, sent a bullet that clipped open the shoulder of Shawn's coat, cut through the bottom of the coat, and blew away half the heel of his boot. Also, before he struck the ground in falling, Shawn sent in his own fire.

That bullet ended the battle, for it apparently struck the right arm or shoulder of José. Out of his hand, the gun slipped to the ground, and, leaning well over the saddle bow, flattening himself like an Indian, José drove away through the night. The mist opened its arms to receive him.

'José! José!' shouted Terry Shawn. 'Come back! I'll do you no harm. You're hurt! Come back!'

But José was gone in the mists, and the dull, hollow echo of his own voice came back to Shawn in empty answer.

Other noises, of course, soon joined in. The three roused sleepers rushed from the house, Jim Berry in the lead, a Colt in either hand. He found Terry Shawn closing the door of the horse shed, and in a most uncommunicative humor.

'What's happened, Terry?'

'José wanted a little exercise by night,' said Shawn slowly. 'I just gave him a little send-off.'

Berry wasted no further time in questions. He gave one glance at the downcast head of Terry, and then stepped past him and opened the shed. By match light he made his examination and came out to report to the other two. Terry Shawn had gone quietly back to his blankets.

'Sky Pilot is loose with a lariat around his neck, and Terry's own nag is gone,' he informed them. 'José must have tried to get away with both of them. Think of it. To steal Shawn's own horse!' He whistled softly.

'There you are,' announced the philosophical Thomas. 'He was a good greaser, too. Enough grit to supply a couple of bears and a painter . . . hard as nails . . . straight as they come . . . but too dog-gone' changeable. Lovin' the kid one day . . . tryin' to murder him the same night.'

Old Shannon went into the shed to examine things for himself.

'Nothing better could have happened,' declared Jim Berry. 'The kid has been hangin' on here, wasting his time. Now he'll have to move, because it's a cinch that the Mexican will never stop till he's brought trouble back to us.'

'He'll have to move,' agreed Thomas. 'Listen to that.'

Out from the stable came a soft, deep-throated whinny, such a sound as a horse makes to a dear friend.

'Poor Shannon,' whispered Thomas. 'And he can't speak a word back to that colt. It's enough to break your heart.'

Now that a double death scene had been averted, all went calmly back to sleep, and not five minutes after his gun had sent a bullet into poor José, Terry Shawn had closed his eyes in profound slumber. Thomas and Berry paused in the doorway to listen in astonishment to the soft snoring of the youth.

'That's nerve,' said Thomas in quiet reverence. 'Most likely he had a bullet fanning his ear . . . most likely he about finished that greaser . . . and now he's sound asleep again. He's a lamb, Jim, ain't he?'

Jim agreed with a gloomy murmur; nothing could make him admit much good in the character of Shawn.

Neither did Shawn speak a word about the fight in the morning. The damage that his clothes and boots had suffered spoke for themselves, but since nothing was volunteered, nothing was asked by his two companions. As for old Shannon, he seemed above an interest in such things, and made an early departure to ride the round of his traps.

That day the upper crests of Mount Shannon were hidden under a gray shawl of clouds, and far to the north the fringes of that garment flickered across the sky. Snow undoubtedly was falling, yonder on the heights, and, although the wind was from the south, it seemed a cold wind. By noon the creek had lost half of its volume, and Thomas pointed out the cause.

Up there on the heights the snow was coming down in thick layers; the melting that supplied that stream had stopped. Before the next morning, no doubt, a heavy freeze would lock the whole upper reaches of Mount Shannon in the first embrace of winter. And, indeed, at any time a heavy fall of snow might wrap the great mountain in white far down its sides, and make the rocky trails perilous, and fill the bottoms of the ravines with great wind drifts of crusted white, impassable for man or horse.

'It's time to start, kid.'

'It won't snow. It's just a touch of cold,' said Shawn morosely.

'Then look there!'

As if by special intent, the wind, shifting a little, opened the gray mantle that hid the shoulders of Mount Shannon, and exposed a dazzling patch of white that instantly was veiled again.

'Now what do you say to that?' exclaimed Jim Berry. 'Good grief, man, are you going to wait to be snowed in here?'

For answer Shawn walked sullenly away, his head hanging a little as if in thought.

'It's too much,' said Thomas, touched at last. 'Let him go . . . we'll try for a third man somewhere else . . . the kid's gone crazy.'

Chapter Thirty

The cold increased every moment. It thickened the mist that kept pouring up from the south through the trees; it set the horses trembling in the meadow, and it herded them into the lee of the trees; it filled the solidly built shack with a damp, disheartening chill.

When Shannon came back from his traps in the mid-afternoon, his first greeting was an eloquent gesture toward the mountaintop, and then, by signs, he indicated that the snow that was falling there might soon be heaped thick along the floor of the valley. Thomas and Berry, ready to be impressed, tried a last appeal with young Shawn, but Terry refused to answer.

'We've waited a long time,' said Thomas, biting his lip with angry impatience. 'Tomorrow morning we start, old son. Think it over tonight, will you?'

Terry Shawn nodded, but plainly his heart was still too strongly bent upon the stallion. The horse was no sooner back from the round of the traps that day than he went out to work over it.

Slow work for Terry Shawn. He could not stalk the horse, but when he found the section of grass on which it chose to graze—for the cold weather seemed to make no difference

210

whatever to this hardy creature—Terry sat down on a half-crumbled, fallen tree trunk, and gradually the stallion drew nearer. He was troubled by the presence of this man, but nevertheless, in that particular place, Sky Pilot chose to graze, and, since the man sat quietly and merely talked in a gentle voice, there seemed no particular harm.

And so Terry Shawn sat in the damp cold and picked seed grass, and patiently offered it. It was scorned for a long time; at length, as he held forth a large and choice bunch, Sky Pilot turned away and stared up the mountain. The clouds had parted and blown clean away from the mountain head, streaming toward the west with a shifting of the wind, and all the summit of Mount Shannon was revealed, heavily coated with white except where the shadowy ravines made streaks of black. That expanse of dazzling brightness made Terry Shawn shudder more deeply than before, and then Sky Pilot turned deliberately and, without a sign of fear, took the seed grass from the hand of Shawn!

It was done so suddenly that Terry Shawn hardly could believe that the thing had happened. Amazed and delighted, he stretched out the empty hand. Sky Pilot, eyes blazing with fear and curiosity and hatred, stretched his head in answer, sniffed at the naked hand, and then flung away in a wildly frightened gallop.

Much, much to do! Indeed, the outlaw felt that he hardly had his foot on the bottom rung of the ladder, but this much at least had been accomplished—by the will of the mysterious Shannon, he had led the horse by the mane, and by his own patience and calm he had induced Sky Pilot to take food from that same hand. Well, much could be done after that. A step at a time, little by little.

Somewhere he had heard the Chinese fable of the old woman who sat at the roadside, grinding an iron pestle in an empty mortar. 'What are you doing, mother?' she was asked. 'I am grinding the pestle down to make a needle,' was her answer.

Patience would be its own reward, in that case, but here there was something profoundly more important—there was Sky Pilot.

Ah, let other men live as they would with wealth and comfort around them, while he flashed through the wide Western ranges with such speed under him that cities and mountains and rivers would be spurned under foot. With such a horse beneath him what could he not do? So he soared in his imagination, as any wild-hearted boy, looking up from a fairy tale, flies through the sky from Harun-al-Rashid's Baghdad to Valhalla.

He rose and followed the stallion then, but this time the chestnut made as if to charge him, and fled away across the meadow, squealing with rage. Enough had been done for that day, so he turned his back reluctantly on the horse and wandered to the creek.

By now its waters were fallen still farther, and, instead of the loud and solemn thunder with which it had gone down through the trees before, it had dropped to a quiet and melancholy singing. Now, as the sound grew more gentle and mournful, Terry Shawn listened with a swelling heart and a gloomy soul. It was as though this song had been made especially for him—he whose spirit had soared in the sky a moment before, simply because he saw a distant hope of riding a wild and stolen horse; he whose ladylove had been swept away mysteriously; he whose existence was a shadowy thing of but small, elusive pleasures, and an abundance of sorrow.

Berry and Hack Thomas strolled down the bank toward him. He turned resolutely upon them.

'Jim and Hack,' he said.

'He's talkin' like a soldier,' said Hack, nodding. 'Got his little hands right by his sides, and got his little chin tucked in, and his little stomach, too. What do you want, honey?'

'Oh, cut it out.' The outlaw sighed.

'He's pickin' up a little,' Hack Thomas said, nodding. 'What's ridin' you, kid?'

'I never should have dragged you two up here with me. I thought I'd take a little fling at the horse, and then call it quits. Well, boys, I find that the horse means a lot more to me than I had thought.' He waited.

Jim Berry exclaimed: 'Well, dog-gone if I ever heard of a . . .'

'Oh, never mind,' said Hack Thomas gently. 'You do what you want to do, kid. It's your right. Stay right here till you get snowed in. If it's too deep for you to move, it's goin' to be sort of hard for the sheriff to get at you, too. You'll have a snug winter, and you'll get to know the horse fine by the time the spring thaws come around. Maybe you'll work up a sort of sign language with old Shannon, too.'

The irony of these remarks did not escape Terry Shawn, but he let the arrows fly without heeding them.

Before another remark could be made, Jim Berry exclaimed: 'There he is! There he goes through the trees! On foot!' And he snatched out a revolver and tried a pot shot. They heard the bullet go crackling through the branches, and a thin fall of leaves followed its course.

'There's who?' asked Shawn.

'The kid . . . the one that chased us up the ravine. I saw him there just now. He's tracked us on foot all this way. That kid wants blood!' He pointed into the trees in the direction in which he had seen the stranger.

They were excited enough. Guns in hand, they scanned the trees and made their plans.

Big Hack Thomas and Berry decided to go down the creek and cut into the woods in the course of a hundred or so yards, trying to pick up the trail. Terry Shawn should move up the creek and enter softly, trying to cut off the advance of the enemy if he went in that direction.

He saw his two confederates slip down the creek while he crossed to the farther bank and turned up in the opposite direction. He entered the trees where there was a narrow opening through a dense thicket. Behind this he came to a more open bit, through which he could look to a considerable distance. And here he took his place to watch and wait, for he felt reasonably sure that the youngster would skirmish up through the woods, avoiding the thicket because of the noise that must be made in pressing through it. This was the place to wait.

Now, lying prone between a pine and a birch, where he was sheltered by a tall, spare growth of grass, he scanned the trees before him steadily, and all his senses grew gradually more and more alert.

He heard the whisper of the wind in the branches, a flutter of wings as a bird made off from a lofty perch, and then the singing of the creek in the near distance. Finally there was the indubitable sound of a gun exploding, farther down the valley; it brought him to his knees, but he sank back again after a moment.

One shot could hardly have begun and ended the battle. There would be a fusillade before the two men brought down that elusive and dangerous youngster with his accurate rifle, and certainly with one shot the latter could not have dropped the pair of them.

So he settled himself to his vigil again and had barely made himself alert and comfortable when a low voice said behind him: 'Hands up, Shawn!'

He jerked his head around, and there stood the youth. There was a bright gleam of hair beneath the brim of the ridiculously large hat, but the brim descended so low that all the face was in shadow, only the rounded lines of an absurdly youthful chin could be seen.

'Lie quiet,' said the same low voice, 'and take your hands away from that Colt.'

He removed his hands from his gun, but turned and rose to his knees in spite of the leveled rifle, stood up, made a hesitant step forward, and then drew a great breath of astonishment.

'Kitty!' cried Terry Shawn. 'Kitty! What are you doing here?'

Chapter Thirty-One

'I don't know whether it's me or my ghost,' said Kitty with a twisted smile.

Meanwhile, Shawn took the rifle from her hand and the hat from her head, so that her hair slipped out of the loose knot in which it

216

was done and cascaded down across her shoulders. It was so bright and rich that it seemed to cast a light upon the face of Kitty, and, with her glowing eyes and the crimson of her lips, she seemed to the outlaw a radiant and precious vision. He touched her reverently, hardly daring to kiss her.

'You've been riding along after me,' said Terry Shawn in awed and wondering tones. 'So you were that crazy kid we tried to turn back.'

'Me? Crazy?' cried Kitty Bowen. 'If I were a man,' she added, 'I'd never turn loose a gun on a man who'd had no warning.'

'Those were placed shots, Kitty, to turn you back. Do you see?'

'And then to shoot me when I wouldn't turn back?' asked Kitty with a bitter smile.

'No. They were aimed for the horse, just to stop you.'

'Look!' She pointed to a rent across the right knee of her trousers. 'That's where the bullet went on the way to the heart of poor old Mopsy. Oh, Terry, how could you kill her?'

'Was she a pet, Kitty?'

'I loved her! She used to come when I whistled,' said Kitty. 'She loved me, too.'

'I'm going to hunt the whole world over and find a mare that you will like as well,' vowed Terry Shawn.

'That's just like a man,' said Kitty.

'What more can I do?'

'You could never have touched her.'

Shawn began to be irritated. Also, he was a little afraid of those shining eyes. 'I didn't. It was another!' he protested.

'Who?' asked Kitty.

'I can't tell you that, of course.'

'I don't see why.'

'It wouldn't be honorable,' said Shawn firmly.

'Honor! Honor!' cried Kitty, and stamped her foot furiously.

Shawn never had seen her in such a rage. He was amazed and mute.

'I tell you, you have to tell me!' she stormed. 'I want to know who killed her!'

'We wanted to stop you . . . wasn't it better to shoot at the horse than at the rider?' asked Terry gently.

'I wonder you didn't, Terry Shawn. I just wonder that you didn't shoot at a poor helpless girl that was riding after you with a heart full of love.'

'How could I know it was you, dear?' asked Terry.

'You didn't much care.'

'Care? Kitty, you aren't very reasonable.'

'You could have guessed. You'd heard that I'd left home,' Kitty charged.

'I had,' admitted Shawn, 'but I couldn't have dreamed that you'd come after me.'

'Do you think I'd go after some other man?' demanded Kitty.

'Kitty, you're just talking like a child.'

'Is that so?' said Kitty. She swept up her

218

shining hair and knotted it swiftly again. She snatched the hat from his hand and jerked it on her head. 'I won't stand to be insulted,' said Kitty.

'Kitty!' cried Terry Shawn in despair.

She turned her back on him and hurried away, so that he had to run to place himself in front of her.

'Listen to me!' he begged.

'Don't you dare to touch me!'

'I'm not going to, dear. But where are you going to go?'

'Home!'

'Will you only let me get you a horse and ride along with you?'

'I wish I'd never met you,' she said.

'Most likely you do,' he said sadly. 'I never had a right to so much as look at you. I'll take you home.'

'I'll go alone,' said Kitty coldly.

'I can't let you. Look how the snows are beginning. It'll be a lucky chance to get through the passes before they're blocked.'

'I don't care.'

'Kitty, don't you care anything about me, any more?' he asked piteously.

'No!' Kitty snapped, and she struck the butt of her rifle on the ground to emphasize the point.

He stared silently at her, lost in woe, tight-lipped with grief. Then: 'I don't believe you,' he declared.

'I don't care what you believe,' she answered.

Suddenly he stepped closer.

'Don't you dare touch me, Terry Shawn. I won't let you touch me!'

'You can't help yourself,' he said.

'I . . . I have a gun in my hand.'

He brushed hand and rifle aside. It fell unregarded to the ground while he picked her up lightly in his arms, and carried her, struggling, to a seat on the crumbling top of a fallen log. Then he sat down beside her.

'You coward!' cried Kitty Bowen in tears.

'I'm mortal scared of you,' said Terry Shawn, 'but I know that you've got to care for me. You aren't the kind of a girl that changes so quick . . . you're only mad at me. But do try to look at things reasonably, dear.'

'Let me go,' said Kitty.

'I will, when you stop crying,' he declared.

'I'm not crying. I just hate you,' she sobbed.

'Sure you do. I'm not going to bother you. You just go ahead and cry,' soothed Terry. He began to cradle her softly in his arms.

'D-don't you dare to treat me like a b-baby,' she said between sobs.

'I'm not. I'm just loving you and caring for you,' said Shawn gently.

'You killed poor Mopsy!' she accused.

He waited, saying nothing, and, because the tears and the sobs came faster and faster, she fell forward against his shoulder, trembling with grief and excitement.

'You didn't want me!' cried Kitty through her tears. 'You just tried to head me away from you.'

'Steady up. Steady up,' he said. 'There's nothing to shy at . . . it's all straight road. There's no trouble ahead . . . and we're pointed home.'

'You needn't talk to me as if I were a horse, Terry Shawn.'

He was silent. The sobbing grew fainter; the body was less shaken by grief.

Then: 'Oh, Terry!'

He waited, still cradling her, his heart aching with grief at her unhappiness, yet glad at the same time, too, because of her presence. He would take her back to her home, he decided, and say to her father and mother: *Forgive me. I thought she was grown up . . . I didn't know she was only a baby, like this.*

'I'm mortal tired,' she sighed, as the weeping ended.

'You're going to rest, now.'

An arm passed around his neck, and she drew herself closer.

'I thought you were trying to drive me away, with your guns,' she whispered. 'It was a terrible time.'

'You made us run, honey,' he assured her. 'You scared us, worse than we scared you.'

'I wasn't afraid. But my heart was broken. I just came on because there was no other place for me to go. I couldn't really go home, to face them and all their questions.'

'They love you, honey. There'd be no questions . . . just love for you an' gladness to have you back.'

She stiffened suddenly and sat up. 'Terry,' she said. 'You wouldn't send me back to them?'

'Me?' he echoed vaguely.

She caught the lapels of his coat, and her eyes were wild. 'I'd go and kill myself, first!' she cried. 'I couldn't stand it. Terry, you're going to keep me always with you. You must promise me that!'

'I want to do what's best,' he said. He took one of her hands and kissed it, then he spread it across his own brown palm, and, brooding over its wonderful delicacy and slenderness, he felt again that sick rush of shame and grief and tenderness. He had taken a child.

Somehow the man's clothes accented her youth, and reminded him of her wild-hearted folly, and the more mightily he loved her, the more certainly he saw that he must protect her.

'Terry,' she whispered.

'Yes, honey?'

'Do you love me, really?'

He made no answer, nor even glanced down at her, merely drawing her a little closer, and, as he did so, she stared up at him and fell quiet, as a child falls quiet when it sees the far-off trouble in a parent's eyes.

Chapter Thirty-Two

When Jim Berry and Hack Thomas slipped cautiously out from the woods, having found no trail, they were amazed to observe their quarry walking boldly ahead of them, rifle in hand, with Terry Shawn. They approached with speed and silence. Nevertheless, that sensitive ear of Terry Shawn detected them, and, turning, he called: 'I've got him, boys!'

The slender form turned, also. 'Yes, he got me, boys!'

Hack Thomas stopped as one suddenly struck in the face, but Jim Berry hurried forward. 'It's Kitty!' he cried.

And she, equally excited, ran to meet him, took both his hands, and laughed joyously up into his face. 'Jim! Where have you been?' she asked.

Their answers crossed each other. They walked aimlessly up the meadow, side-by-side, stopping now and again with bursts of cheerful laughter. And Terry Shawn remained behind, stroking his chin.

Hack Thomas came up to him. 'There you are,' said Hack. 'That's the weak side of Jim. Now, you take a young gent like him, with a punch like a mule and a sure shot, ready to fight ten wildcats and eat 'em up . . . but still he's got to have a weak side. I say it's too bad.'

'Weak?' echoed Shawn. 'Why, it kind of appears to me like he's acting strong, here.'

'The girls can't help lovin' Jim,' admitted Hack. 'It's his handsome face and the bigness of him, you see.'

Shawn glanced down at himself, not even by standing on tiptoe could he give himself the size of Jim Berry.

'I recollect down in Tucson,' went on Hack, 'where we were teaming with Doc Gray. We ran a faro layout on the quiet, and the boys patronized us, because they knew that our deal was square. We were all making good money . . . getting rich . . . no trouble with anybody until Jim busted it up. Doc had a girl, you see, and she was a corker. There were other girls in that town, and, when Jim walked down the street in a long-tailed coat and a pale hat, he could have had any of them. But you take a high-flyer like him, nothing but the best will do for him. He began to pay attention to Benita, and Benita paid attention back. Doc noticed and began to lose weight.'

'Why do you have to tell me all about this?' cut in Shawn coldly.

'Aren't you interested?' asked the guileless Hack.

'Well, go on,' said Shawn grudgingly.

'I got Jim to one side,' went on Hack.

' "Jim," says I, "you ornery rhinoceros, you bow-legged, blink-eyed buckstang, you're goin' to spoil the whole layout. Doc Gray is dyin' of jealousy."

' "It ain't possible," says Jim, real flippant.

' "Aren't there any other girls in the town?" I asks him.

' "Yes. But I've picked out the best," says he.

' "Gray'll kill you," says I.

' "I'd rather be right than be President," says Jim.

'What could I do? Nothin' but sit back and feel sick. Three days later the bust came. It was Doc that started the shooting, and Jim that finished it . . . and then he had to hoof it out of town for murder, as they called it for a while. The faro and I went bust. Everything was spoiled. And that's what women always do to a man and his business. You keep shut of them, and you keep shut of trouble.'

To this speech, Shawn made no reply, but he looked earnestly at the retreating forms of Berry and the girl. And Hack Thomas began to observe aloud, although he might have known that what is left unsaid is at least left without a poisoned point.

'Look at 'em now,' said Hack. 'Look at the way he's holding her by the arm. Why, you'd think that she could hardly walk . . . she that has rode a wild mustang up the valleys, and scared us all to death, and trailed us right to here. You'd think that Jim thought that she needed help. But he doesn't really think that . . . it's only his way. To see him around a girl, you'd think that she was faintin', or about to faint, and he's got to take care of her. It's always too hot, or too cold, or too drafty for a girl, according to Jim Berry, and he's got to make things right for her.

'And that's one way that he makes his hit with them. You and me, and ordinary 'punchers like us, we've got an idea that the women are about as strong as the men, and we act according. If you take a girl to a dance where she's goin' to spin and whirl and run and chatter and act up from nine p.m. to five-thirty the next morning, what's the use of half carryin' her up the stairs to the dance hall? When there's a hundred chairs along the wall, each like every other one, what's the use in askin' her if that chair will do? When she knows everybody in the county, what's the use of askin' her what folks she wants to dance with and can he bring anybody around? When it gets warm, will she have a glass of punch? When it gets chilly, will she have a wrap? No, of course she won't . . . but she's tickled to hear him talk that way. You take some ornery freckle-faced girl that's milked twenty cows twice a day since she was ten, and taken a hand in the haying, and ridden a horse farther than an automobile can run in a lifetime . . . a long-legged, spindle-shanked, square-jawed girl that can tie a buckin' mustang into a figure eight . . . and when she hears talk like old Jim slings, she begins to blink. It's like fine champagne to her. It goes to her head . . . and pretty soon

226

she's rollin' calf's eyes at Jim.'

'*Aw*, forget it, Hack,' said the outlaw in disgust. 'He wouldn't play the fool like that over any girl!'

'Wouldn't he? You don't know him,' said Hack earnestly. 'Makin' the girls cock-eyed is a sort of a profession with Jim, and he's always practicing. What chance, I ask you, would a gent like me or you have against a fellow like Berry? None whatever. He can relieve a man of his wife or his best girl so easy that the gent don't know what's happened until he's left alone.'

This was a long speech, even for Hack, but it was a subject on which, apparently, he felt deeply.

'He's kept you out of double harness, maybe?' suggested Shawn curiously.

'Oh, well,' said Hack Thomas, rather red of face, 'let him go. What difference does it make what he's done? Only, kid, you look after him, now. He's making a dead set at her. I've given you a fair warning.'

He said it in such a pointblank manner that Terry Shawn set his teeth and lengthened his stride as he hurried up the valley. Hack Thomas made no effort to follow, but, contenting himself with falling to the rear, he smiled and chuckled softly to himself. He even rubbed his hands and laughed until his shoulders shook.

'Now, Jimmy,' he said aloud, but to himself.

227

'Now, Jimmy, you watch yourself pretty careful, old feller.'

Jimmy had no apparent thought of watching over himself, however. When they reached the shack, he set about making himself busy, preparing for the girl a basin of hot water for washing, to brace her after her long journey. And he piled the pine boughs of two beds one on top of the other and heaped it deep with soft skins so that she could lie down and rest.

It made no difference that she declined the invitation, but sat on the edge of the bed, her hands locked around her knees, perfectly cheerful and gay and chatty, for it seemed to be fixed in the mind of Jim Berry that she was a languishing and exhausted creature who must be handled as wilting flowers are handled.

'I'm not going to fade, Jim,' she said, 'until time does it to me. Get away and take care of yourself . . . but I don't mind a bit of coffee, if you've got some handy.'

He looked on her and sadly shook his head, then he turned with a sigh.

'You look kind of weak yourself, Jim,' she said.

'Letting you come here . . . I ought not to say anything,' said Berry, 'but I can't help coming out with it. What was Shawn thinking of?'

'Nothing. He didn't know that I was coming.'

228

'He didn't?' Mr. Berry laughed gently and wisely.

'Did he think that I'd really trail along after him?' cried the girl, flushed with instant pride and anger. 'Did he expect me to come trailing after him?'

'I'm not saying anything,' said Berry, with a most eloquent shrug of the shoulders. 'Only . . .' He bit his lips, as though to keep something back.

'I've got to know!' cried Kitty.

'How can I talk?' he asked in obvious distress.

'He did think that I'd come then! Oh!' she cried, and covered her crimsoned face.

He answered obliquely, speaking as a strong man should to a woman in distress, with a tenderly deepened voice. 'Don't you worry none. I'm goin' to see you through this, Kitty. I'm goin' to take charge of things. Don't you worry. You just lay back and rest a while.'

Chapter Thirty-Three

Plainly the weather was changing. The strong wind had fallen away, and the last remnant of cloud mantle had been snatched from the head and shoulders of old Mount Shannon. When sunset came, the colors streamed up all across the sky, tinting it deeply at the horizon, and blending with a mysterious delicacy in the zenith. For the moment, there was no atmospheric depth, and the sky looked like a vast Chinese bowl of porcelain, polished, and with the stark blackness of the mountains and their fringings of magnificent trees stamped against a softer background.

It was below freezing point. There was no fireplace or hearth inside the shack, for Shannon used fire for cookery alone. Even in midwinter, he sat in his house wrapped heavily with skins, but with no heat in the placeindeed, he was rarely inside, except to clean and stretch skins, and to sleep.

However, this manner of living did not please Jim Berry, because, he said, one could not expose a delicately nurtured girl like Kitty Bowen to the evil damp and cold of that cabin. He would not have it.

'Stuff!' said Kitty. 'I'm big and strong, and cold doesn't bother me.'

However, he insisted, and, by his direction and chiefly by his work, a great bonfire was built close to the door of the house, so that a flood of heat and brightness entered every part of the shack. Kitty had protested once; afterward, she luxuriated in the warmth and in the comfort.

Shannon came home in the midst of the preparations for dinner. Hack Thomas, that same morning, had shot a fat buck and brought in the carcass on his mighty shoulders.

That venison had been roasted in the Dutch oven, and, when the iron lids were removed, through the still air stole a pervading fragrance, richer, to their eager nostrils, than the fragrance of roses, more delightful than the pure odor of the pines.

Into that happy scene, at that lucky moment, came Shannon. He greeted them solemnly, with raised hand and a charming smile. Then he saw the girl, and his smile went out. He scanned the group hastily, and suddenly pointed to Jim Berry with a frown. It was perfectly clear that he objected to the girl's presence. Berry merely shrugged his shoulders and pointed in turn to Terry Shawn. Under the sparkling, angry eyes of this hermit, Shawn was subdued and troubled.

'Look here, Shannon,' he said. 'I want to tell you how it is. You see, Miss Bowen, yonder . . .' He broke off then. 'What's the use?' he said. 'He can't understand.'

Shannon, however, seemed to master his first emotion of annoyance. He approached the girl and raised his hat as he bowed before her, so that it seemed, for a moment, that words must come from the speaking courtesy of his expression. Then he went on into the horse shed, the beautiful chestnut following at his heels, and dancing and shying away from the proximity of the others.

Kitty, tears in her eyes, faced the others. 'Isn't there some way of telling him who I am?'

she asked.

'He doesn't blame you for coming,' said Terry Shawn. 'He heaps it all on me, thanks to Jim.'

He turned to Jim Berry with a cold glance that bored into the eyes of Berry and left his brain icy and numb with a sudden fear. However, he shook off that unpleasant feeling and bent his attention upon the girl. He had given her a comfortable place to sit near the oven. He had insisted in wrapping a goatskin around her feet for warmth, and by that means had rendered her helpless, so that she was forced to accept his other ministrations. Restlessly and eagerly he fetched and carried for her—coffee, roasted meat, a tin plate, a knife, a bit of clean-whittled birch bark for a fork or spoon as occasion should demand, and, while he tended on her, he kept up a cheerful and gentle current of talk.

Terry Shawn, on the obscure verge of the circle, spoke not a word, but the keen eye of Hack Thomas found him out, and there was malice in that eye. He went to him and touched his shoulder.

'Cheer up, kid,' he whispered. 'You'd better buck up and take a hand. Girls hate a dummy, you know.'

'Oh, don't bother me,' answered Terry Shawn, and sank into his black silence once more. He was growing more and more ugly, and his lower jaw was thrust out menacingly.

When Shannon came for dinner, way was made for him instantly, but the portion he took was small. He ate rapidly, and the minute he had finished he was gone again, toward the horse shed.

'He doesn't like it,' said the girl unhappily. 'He doesn't like having me here. I don't know what to do.'

She looked at Shawn, whose eyes were on the ground, then she turned to Berry. 'What shall I do, Jim?' she asked.

'I'll write out a note for him,' said Jim. 'Don't you worry none.'

He was as good as his word, and, retiring away from the others, he scratched on the back of an envelope:

DON'T MAKE A MISTAKE. KITTY BOWEN IS A FINE GIRL. IT'S SHAWN'S FAULT. HE GOT HER TO COME UP HERE.

Then he went to find the master of the house and discovered him only by chance, concealed in a little clump of shrubbery near the rear corner of the house. The man of the mountain was on his knees, his face raised, absorbed in prayer, and, for a moment, even the keen mind of Jim Berry was impressed— almost as forcefully as it had been by the dangerous glance of Terry Shawn, a little before. For it seemed as though there were some strong connection between this silent hermit and the bright, cold faces of the stars above him.

At length, he touched the shoulder of old Shannon, and, when the latter rose stiffly, he scratched a match so that the old man could read what was written.

Shannon read, and then slowly raised his eyes and looked fully into the face, into the very soul of the other. There was neither accusation nor doubt in that look, but rather a profound inquiry, and for some reason Jim Berry was unable to endure the question.

With the last flame of the match, he touched the envelope, and saw it burst into fire, curl in the heat, blacken, and fall to the ground a wisp of carbon, instantly dissolved by the first touch of wind.

He went back to the fire, then, and straightway set to work preparing the sleeping place of the girl for the night. He set up, with skin stretchers and cured pelts, a little screen in a corner of the shack, and inside this compartment he built up a comfortable pile of the softest pine boughs, overlaid with more pelts.

'You're played out,' he said to the girl. 'You'd better turn in and have a long sleep. Come along, and I'll fix up a light for you.'

He led the way into the shack and left Hack Thomas with the outlaw, alone.

'You been watching?' asked Hack Thomas

with the same quiet malice. 'See how he's taken her in hand? Oh, he's smooth and he's deep.'

Terence Shawn made no reply; he was sunk in a deep and black reflection, and in his turn he went into the shack and rolled into his bed, while Jim Berry came out to sit by the fire and his friend, Hack.

They smoked in quiet, for a time.

'When'd you get to know her so well?' asked Thomas at last.

'I used to work on their place,' answered Jim Berry. 'Used to ride Bowen's range, and I taught the girl how to handle a horse. She had the nerve of a regular bronc' peeler, and a natural seat, and a firm pair of hands . . . so we got on. She was only a little kid, then, with a whip of pigtail hangin' down her back.'

'She's come on, since then,' suggested Hack Thomas.

'She's come on,' agreed the ladies' man.

'Tell me something,' said Hack Thomas, pretending to yawn. 'You ever hear from Lulu any more?'

'Who?' asked Berry, puzzled.

'Lu Perkins.'

'Oh, your old girl?'

'Maybe you could call her that,' admitted Hack with carefully studied indifference.

'I haven't heard from her for a year,' said Jim Berry. 'Got tired of writing all the time. That girl, she'd write you a book . . . took an

235

hour to read one of her letters. I chucked it . . . I got tired.'

Hack Thomas was silent for a moment, then he murmured: 'You always get tired, kid. You always chuck them, pretty quick.'

'A man's got to have variety,' remarked Jim Berry. 'Can't live on venison for a year . . . can't live on ice cream, either. I'm goin' to turn in.'

'Wait a minute,' said Hack. 'I just wanted to ask you . . . you been watching the kid?'

'Kitty?'

'Shawn, I mean.'

'What about him?'

'He's looking pretty black. If I were you, I'd keep my gun loose in the holster,' advised Hack.

Jim spoke savagely: 'I've let him come over me once, and I don't aim to let him try anything again. If he's wanting that girl, let him keep her. That's all I've got to say. Let him keep her, if he can. But if he wants another kind of trouble, I'm ready for him, night or day, with a knife or a gun or any way that he says.'

'That's the way,' said Hack Thomas dryly. 'Talk right up, Jimmy. Don't you back up a step till you back right into your grave.'

Jim Berry shrugged his shoulders, grunted, and retreated toward his sleeping quarters.

Chapter Thirty-Four

Hack Thomas had somewhat the nature of a politician. A politician, we take it, is one who controls, without seeming to have the upper hand. A politician works from the inside—by means of a smile he does more than by means of a blow. So it was with Hack Thomas.

He never had forgotten pretty Lu and the days when he had hoped to make her his wife. She was all that he had hoped for and wanted, and Jim Berry had taken her away. For a month, Hack had alternated between grief and rage, wondering whether or not he should go to Berry, gun in hand, and demand satisfaction, but he and Berry had been partners in crime for many years, and a little delay merely blunted the edge of his purpose, but never removed his malice.

That anger that is unexpressed enters the blood. At least, so it did with Hack Thomas, and he had waited through many a long month for the chance to break even with his companion. Now fortune had placed the chance in his hands. If he had been asked directly whether or not he wished the death of Terry Shawn or of Jim Berry, beyond a doubt he would have answered with horror that he desired neither. He was merely giving a certain shape and direction to events that would take care of themselves.

Bitterness poisoned the heart of Hack Thomas; he wanted the whip to be laid upon the back of Jim Berry, wanted to see him sick and broken, after which he dimly envisioned himself healing the wounds and caring for the stricken man. Suppose that the blow was one which could not be healed? Of that, he refused to think, but permitted himself to look only as far as the prospect proved agreeable.

The next morning saw the indefatigable Jim Berry again at work to please and care for Kitty Bowen, while Shannon went off hunting, and Hack lingered around the cabin with no care on his hands except to watch young Terry Shawn earnestly at work with the chestnut. It seemed to Hack Thomas that the youth was making little enough progress, but the patience of Shawn seemed limitless.

Many small steps at last make a mile, and Shawn worked over Sky Pilot with endless endurance. He had reached a point, now, where Sky Pilot accepted him as a necessary part of the landscape, even if not a pleasant one. He would graze to the very feet of Terry Shawn; he would take grain, after some snorting and precautionary starts and stampings, from the very hand of the gunfighter. It seemed almost as if Sky Pilot realized there was some sort of game that he and this man were playing together. At least, he saw no harm in taking delicious tidbits from this fellow, nor even in allowing his smooth back to be stroked, while he reached for a tuft of seed grass.

Many a wise old mustang, a hardened veteran of the range, might have told him that familiarity with man is apt to bring loss of independence, and that, by cunning kindness, man breaks the spirit, as well as by the use of whip, and spur, and jaw-breaking curb, but there was no such warning for Sky Pilot.

He had in mind only one sort of man-fashioned danger, and that was the danger of spur and quirt and gripping cinches. So now he allowed this former enemy, this smooth-voiced youngster, to while away the time with him, wandering idly about with him over the rich grass of the meadow, silently and patiently.

Jim Berry and the girl disappeared up the stream, finally, on a fishing excursion. They returned just before noon, their voices ringing out in gay laughter, and, as Berry went off to cut fresh evergreen boughs and resinous wood for the fire, Shawn came into the shack and met the girl.

She was cleaning the fish and preparing them for cooking, and Shawn stood over her and looked down with a melancholy interest on the flying, supple hands. Hack Thomas arose and wandered away toward the trees, perhaps to help Jim Berry, perhaps to mask his contented grin.

'Be useful, Terry,' said the girl. 'Bring me a

bucket of water.'

'Kitty,' he said.

'Hurry,' she said impatiently.

'Kitty,' he repeated pleadingly, and she looked up at him.

'Now what's up? Have you got a toothache, Terry? You've been glooming around long enough.'

He hooked his thumb over his shoulder in the direction of Berry. 'I want to talk to you about Berry,' he said.

'Go on, then.'

'How long have you known him?'

'About twenty times as long as I've known you,' she said promptly. 'Why?'

'I only wanted to say that Berry has got a name, do you understand?'

She stood up. 'A name for what?'

'For being a lady-killer. He's caused a lot of unhappiness.'

She paused, stared, and then spoke sharply: 'Terry Shawn, I'm surprised!'

'Ask anybody,' said Shawn. 'Everybody knows.'

'To come here like this,' she said, 'and talk behind the back of a man.'

His teeth came together with a sharp *click*.

'If you wanted to say something about him, why not talk right out in front of him?' she demanded.

'I'm talking to you,' said Terry Shawn, 'because I have a right to talk. I don't want to see you losing your head over that man.'

'Losing my head!' she cried. 'How dare you talk to me like that?'

'You've made up your mind to get mad,' said Shawn sullenly. 'There's no use in my saying anything more.'

'There's a lot of use,' she cried, growing more and more angry. 'You've accused poor Jim Berry when his back was turned, just because he was polite. You might learn something from him, Terence Shawn!'

He regarded her sadly, without anger, and then turned slowly away.

'I'm not through. I have something more to say!' exclaimed Kitty Bowen.

He went back to her, grim of face.

'He's a quick worker,' said Shawn bitterly. 'It took him one evening and a morning to show you that I'm not worth bothering over. I've got to hand it to him. He's slick.'

'Oh!' said Kitty, trembling with wrath. 'Terence Shawn, there's not a speck of shame in you.'

'He'd be glad to hear us talk like this,' said Terry Shawn. 'Well, I'll tell you, Kitty. When he comes back from the woods, don't you let him go around here with any wrong ideas about me. You tell him out and out what I think about him, will you?'

'Jim Berry is a gentleman!' defended the girl hotly. 'I never met a kinder, better, straighter, gentler . . .'

'Rat,' said Terry Shawn. 'You might tell him that's what I said he was. A rat. A low-down, sneaking yellow rat. When you're telling him the other things, you just speak up and tell him that I called him that. And when I come back here, I aim to expect that he'll know what I said.'

This last speech Shawn delivered very slowly, haltingly, as though he were hunting for the proper words and was satisfied with those that he found. It reduced Kitty Bowen to a frozen silence that held her while Shawn turned on his heel and sauntered down the meadow to the place where the shining chestnut was standing.

She seemed about to start after him, but at this point Jim Berry came out of the woods, heavily laden with pine boughs. He came up to the shack with his burden. Dropping the boughs, Berry looked keenly at the girl, her white face turned toward the distant and retreating form of Terry Shawn. The faintest of smiles appeared upon the lips of Jim Berry, but he banished it at once, and said quietly: 'Is there anything wrong, Kitty? You look sort of upset.'

'Anything wrong?' cried the girl, clasping her hands excitedly. 'Everything's wrong, and something terrible is going to happen!'

'I hope not,' murmured Jim Berry solicitously.

'He's going to fight,' said Kitty Bowen. 'I

could see it in his face. He'll . . . Jim, saddle
your horse and ride away as fast as you can,
because if he comes back here and finds you,
he'll make trouble.'

Jim Berry lost a great deal of color on the
instant. He stared at the girl, and he stared at
the far-off form of the gunfighter. Instinctively
he reached for a gun and froze his grip on the
handle of it in readiness for instant action.
'What's happened?' he asked hoarsely.

'It's me,' said Kitty ungrammatically. 'He
thinks that you've been paying too much
attention to me, and he's furious . . . he won't
listen to reason. Go quickly, Jim, or something
terrible will happen. I know!'

Berry moistened his white lips. He was
rather glad that the girl, instead of glancing at
him, kept her frightened eyes still fixed on
Terence Shawn, down in the lower meadow.

'I run away from no man,' he said bravely.

At that, she turned sharply and suddenly on
him. 'You don't mean that you'd stand up to
Terry Shawn?' she asked incredulously.

'I mean that I won't be bullied,' said Jim
Berry. 'Who's Shawn? I've met harder men
than him. He can bully cowards, and he can
bully women,' added Jim Berry, laying his
hand on her arm gently, 'but he can't bully
me.'

'Good heavens,' moaned Kitty Bowen. 'If
you stay . . .' She did not finish her sentence; it
needed no finishing, as a matter of fact, and

243

she turned back to stare apprehensively toward Shawn in the distance.

Jim Berry, having made his proud boast, slipped around the corner of the house and into the horse shed.

Chapter Thirty-Five

The courage of Jim Berry was, of course, undoubted, but it was of a peculiarly quiet type. It appeared only when he wanted to use it, and it might safely be said that his discretion was at least as great as his valor. He had been known to stand up to three armed men, but he knew the three men against whom he stood. On this occasion, he knew the man against whom he had to stand, and, although he was certain that few men in all the world were more accurate than Jim Berry with a revolver or a rifle, he was sure that the young outlaw was among those few. Not for an instant did he intend to make his boast good, but when he reached the horse shed, he jerked his saddle from its hook and tossed it on the back of his horse.

Even as he saddled and bridled the mare, he was listening with alert ears to all sounds outside of the shed, and, when a step approached the door, he whirled about and waited with a drawn revolver and set jaw.

There might be some difference between his marksmanship and that of young Terence Shawn, but if Shawn came through a door at him, Berry would certainly wipe that difference out.

It was not Shawn. Instead, the broad-shouldered Hack Thomas came through the door. With desperate haste, Jim Berry strove to put his revolver out of sight, but he was much too late. Hack had seen; he leaned one hand against the wall and smiled benevolently upon his old friend.

'Cuttin' and runnin', Jimmy?' he wanted to know.

'Why should I cut and run?' asked Jimmy.

The answer came with disheartening certainty: 'Shawn.'

'And why should I have any trouble with that Shawn, will you tell me?'

'Sure I'll tell you. You've been spending too much time with Terry's girl,' Hack told him.

'Confound Terry, an' his girl, too!' replied the other savagely. 'I wish that I'd never laid eyes on the pair of them!'

'Maybe so,' answered Hack Thomas. 'Only, kid, I'd like you to take notice of this . . . chuck Shawn and we chuck the biggest and the surest job that we ever tackled. There's enough coin in it to retire on, I'd say.'

'Is he the only fightin' man in the world?' asked Berry with heat and scorn.

'No, he ain't the best,' said Hack Thomas.

'He's only the best that I ever met up with, or ever had anything to do with. He's twice as straight a shot and twice as quick, as anybody I ever saw pull a gun. And we need him, kid.'

'You've got him,' answered Berry. 'Well, take him along. If you can't replace him, you can replace me. Stand aside, Hack. I'm on my way.'

'Sonny, you're actin' rash,' replied the older of the two. 'Throw your reins, and climb down, and talk common sense. How long have we been workin' together, old son?'

'I dunno. What's that got to do with it?' growled Jim.

'We've teamed for near six years, ain't we?'

'About that. Hack, clear out of the doorway and let me through.'

'Oh, back up!' exclaimed the other. 'Kid, in those six years have we ever been in jail?'

'I don't suppose we have,' admitted Jim Berry.

'Can we ride through nearly any part of the range and pass as good, ordinary, honest cowpunchers?' continued Hack.

'I suppose that we can.'

'Now, do you think that I'm going to chuck six years of luck, even for the sake of a gent like young Shawn?'

'I like what you say fine,' answered Jim Berry. 'Only there's this to say . . . am I to stay around here and get my head blown off by Shawn?'

246

'That's straight and that's frank,' replied the other. 'The fact is, he would kill you, Jimmy . . . you know it, and I know it. But here's another fact . . . he's not going to get the chance.'

'What'll stop him?' asked Berry. 'He's hot as fire, already. He wants my scalp, and, if he has a chance at me, he'll fill me full of lead.'

'You could back up a little, Jim, knowing the stake that we're playing for.'

'Back up?' asked Berry, flushing dark. 'I back up and let the girl see me do it? No matter how I may feel, I've never backed up yet, and I'll never start taking it for any gunfighter that ever stepped on two legs. You write that down in red, Hack. What sort of a man do you think I am?'

'I understand,' said Hack Thomas. He paused and considered.

'I'll be on my way, then,' repeated Berry.

'Hold still!' commanded his older companion. 'I'm going to see my way through this, and I'm going to keep you and keep the kid, too. I want him, and I've got to have you. Now, old son, you know that I can manage things pretty well. Only tell me, first, if you really want to cut and go?'

'No! I never hated anything worse. Aside from leaving you, I've thrown a bluff with the girl, and, if I go off now, she'll write me down as a yellow dog. Only it's better for me to quit now, than it is for me to back up under the gun of the kid.'

'I tell you what,' said Hack suddenly. 'I'm going to handle the kid, and you'll have no trouble out of him.'

'And if you fail, then I'm simply a dead man. Is that right?' asked Jim.

'Not so certain. No gunfight ever is certain. You'd have one chance in four, even on an even break,' Hack assured him.

'Thanks,' said Berry. 'That's not the kind of odds that I play.'

'Well,' answered Thomas, 'tell me this, then . . . could he beat the pair of us?'

'The pair of us?' repeated Jim.

'Kid,' cried Hack Thomas, 'don't you understand? The minute that the pinch comes and he starts an actual gunfight with you, I'll be at him. He won't be expecting me. I'll shoot Terry Shawn down before he has a chance to get his guns out. Will you trust me?'

Jim Berry listened with unbelieving eyes. 'Do you mean that?' he asked huskily.

'I mean that, son.'

'It'd save my face before the girl,' commented Berry. 'Give me your hand, Hack. You always had a head for everything.'

'Leave it all to me,' said Hack with the air of a commander addressing his officers before action. 'All you've got to do is to pipe down small and not kill yourself bein' nice to the girl. I guess you've had a little lesson out of this, Jim?'

Jim Berry mopped his forehead; no other rejoinder was needed.

'You'll be keeping out of the way of the other fellows' girls, after this,' went on Hack Thomas with more sternness than before, 'and, if you do that, you'll be keeping out of trouble. Now, kid, listen to me. Shawn ain't a bully. He won't press too far, and, if he just sees that you aren't bothering the girl any more, he'll be contented. I can have a few words with him, and smooth things over fine. But if anything should go wrong, I'll fill him full of lead before he can aim at you.'

'Good old man.' Barry sighed, and moisture appeared in his eyes as though he were overwhelmed by the goodness of his companion.

So they arranged the thing, and Jim Berry, left alone in the shed, slowly stripped saddle and bridle from his horse. He made many pauses, for he was still far from sure that he was following the wisest course.

At last, however, his mind was fully made up, and he stepped from the shed into the open. He walked slowly; gravity was in his face; gravity was in his heart, and he felt that the entire world had changed. Certainly the atmosphere in the valley had altered, for now the bright sunlight was gone, and in its place there was again the creeping, chilling mist of gray, growing momentarily thicker. It seemed to breathe forth from the very trees that were hidden by it. The lower meadow, too, was clouding over, so that Terence Shawn and the chestnut were well-nigh lost to Berry's view, although big Hack Thomas, as he strode toward them, could be made out plainly. At the edge of the shack, Jim Berry glanced earnestly after his partner.

Kitty Bowen, on her knees stirring up the fire in the oven, said to him: 'You've sent Hack out to make peace, Jim?'

'What makes you think that?' he asked sullenly.

'You don't need to be ashamed,' said the girl gravely. 'To turn an ordinary fellow against Terry is like turning a wolf against a tiger. Well, I hope that Hack has luck, but I'll tell you what . . .' She hesitated.

'Go on,' urged Berry.

'If I were you, I'd back up . . . I'd saddle my horse . . . and I'd slide out of the valley.'

He looked calmly on her. His courage was returning; he could even smile. 'I never back up, Kitty,' he said. 'You ought to know that. And I'm too old to start learning.'

'Ah,' cried Kitty, coming to her feet, 'maybe it'll turn out all right, after all!'

'What makes you think that?'

'Look. Now that he's done that, he won't care for anything, he'll be so happy.' She pointed, and, out of the mist, Berry saw Shawn coming toward them, leading Sky Pilot easily along, his hand on the chestnut's neck.

Chapter Thirty-Six

In fact, all thought of danger was forgotten by Jim Berry in the bewilderment he felt as he stared toward the outlaw and the horse that walked beside him. Just as an eagle, formerly restrained by clipped wings, is altered when its strong wing feathers have grown, so it seemed, to those who watched, that Shawn, as he walked by the side of the half-tamed horse, had been given wings that made him mightier and somewhat more than human.

Hack Thomas, striding at the side of the youngster, had more on his mind than the subduing of a wild horse. Nevertheless, he was filled with admiration. He knew the appalling record of Sky Pilot, yet here was that same horse, literally in the hand of a human enemy.

The chestnut walked jauntily at the side of the outlaw, not in the fashion of one who has to obey, but rather as of his own free will, content in the knowledge that he could go whenever he chose. Now and again he paused a little, and sometimes he would turn his lordly head and stare into the distance toward the white crags of the upper mountain, and sometimes he would turn and nose the man who walked beside him. It was as though he were torn between a love of the wilderness on the one hand, and love of man on the other.

'How'd you do it, kid?' asked big Hack Thomas, coming up to him.

'Keep still and leave him alone, will you?' said Shawn nervously. 'Don't you see him tremble when you speak? I haven't got him, yet . . . I've only got a fingertip on him. He only endures me while it pleases him.'

Yet, unquestionably, the divide between enmity and friendship had been passed, and the chestnut trusted Shawn, or had at least begun to trust him. Shawn paused, and Sky Pilot walked on, but he walked in a circle and soon came back to this new human acquaintance. Terry Shawn, much moved, rubbed the horse's nose and stroked his neck.

'It's as if I'd opened a door and stepped inside the house,' said Shawn, half to the horse and half to Thomas. 'I've hung my saddle and bridle on the peg, and I'm getting hospitality. Hack, what's the good of whips and spurs, when a little time and conversation will give you a horse like this? You hear me talk? I'll never again break a horse with floggings and the spurs. I'll break 'em with an open hand.'

'It'll cost you valuable time,' said Hack Thomas.

'It's worth every extra hour it takes,' answered the youth.

'Well, tell me how you figure that,' said Hack.

'What's the difference between a friend and a hired man?' asked Shawn, by way of reply.

Thomas was silent. At last he said: 'They're not all like the stallion there, though.'

'A poor friend is better than the best of hired men,' said Terry Shawn with an infinite conviction. 'Run along with you, Sky Pilot,' he added, turning upon the horse. He clapped his hands and waved them, and the horse whirled away, tossing his heels in the air and snorting.

'You've lost him, you idiot!' cried Hack Thomas.

'You watch and see,' admonished Shawn. 'Do you think that he doesn't know the difference between that and the crack of a whip? He knows, well enough. Watch that.'

The chestnut had circled the meadow like a flash of red lightning, and now he drew up well ahead of Shawn, head high, feet planted wide, eyes flashing, for all the world like a playful child ready for a game.

'Get out, you scoundrel!' yelled Shawn, and leaped forward with menacing fist.

Sky Pilot reared, smashed at the turf with his descending hoofs, and backed away. Shawn made another lunge; the horse squealed in answer, and, flinging himself into the air, bucked and cavorted in such a way that not the most cunning of jockeys could have kept a seat on him for ten seconds.

'He's gone amuck again!' shouted Hack Thomas. 'Look at him! Oh, Terry, you blockhead, you've broken the charm!'

Terence Shawn merely laughed and,

stepping forward with outstretched hand, in another moment his arm was around the neck of the horse, leading him along passively enough. 'I've got him by more than a fingerhold,' said Terence Shawn, exulting. 'I've got him by a lot more than that, and, heaven willing, Hack, I'll make him mine forever.'

'What'll José say to that?'

'He had him,' said Shawn grimly, 'and he chucked him away. He had him and couldn't manage him. He's lost his chance.'

'And what about old man Shannon, then? He didn't chuck his opportunity?' For answer, Terry Shawn scowled savagely and spoke not a word. Thomas shrugged his shoulders and smiled a little. It was plain that he had touched on Shawn's weakness. Nor did Thomas wonder at it; he himself would have paid much good coin of the realm to gain the love of the chestnut as Shawn had. Thomas spoke after a moment: 'You can take the horse, I suppose, and get away with it. All the same, there may be trouble.'

'What kind of trouble?' asked Shawn sourly.

'I mean,' answered Thomas, 'that the best man most usually wins, in any sort of a game.'

'And Shannon is the strongest man in this here valley?' challenged Terry Shawn.

'He's the strongest man here . . . we're in the hollow of his old hands . . . I've felt it ever since I first laid eyes on him,' said Hack. 'Hey, what's going on up yonder?' He pointed.

The lofty head of Mount Shannon had lain naked and crystal white but a moment before, yet now it was abruptly changed, for, with a wind rushing out of the north, the familiar mantle of clouds was being flung around the shoulders of the giant. It looked as though a vast explosion had occurred, as though the center of the mountain were being rent, and the smoke and fury of the convulsion were escaping through the cleft ribs of the monster and ascending toward the sky. Wideflung on either side, the mantling clouds streamed upward, and, in another moment, the summit of Shannon was in the midst of a gigantic confusion. Long arms of shadow were seen reaching down into the ravines, and then the clouds began to fling out faster and faster from the summit, breaking off from the main cloud masses, sailing in frantic haste across the southern sky.

'What has broken loose up there?' asked Thomas again.

'It's winter,' answered Shawn. 'That's the first storm. We may have a white valley here before many hours.'

'I hope things don't break loose in any other place,' remarked Hack Thomas with sudden meaning.

'What other place do you mean?'

'Here in this valley.'

'I don't know that I follow you, Hack,' said Shawn.

'Kid,' said the older man, 'I know you, and I know when you mean trouble. If you haven't got trouble in your eye right now, I'll eat my hat. Who is it for? Berry?'

'I've said nothing about Berry,' returned Shawn darkly.

' "I've said nothing about Berry," ' mimicked the other. 'You don't have to say . . . you look the part. You're goin' to bust loose, roaring like the wind up yonder . . . listen.'

As they paused and raised their heads, they could hear it plainly enough. It seemed at first to come from the trees, then out of the very ground at their feet the noise appeared to rise. It was a deep note like thunder, but unbroken, and with a weird, high, complaining falsetto note running through it, as though something tender were being crushed under the hands of a roaring giant. Both of the men had heard that noise before, although never quite so clearly as in the sounding box of this ravine. It was the sound of the storm, which was shooting through the upper regions of the air, and sending the echo of its bellowing along the mountainside.

'Look yonder, kid,' said Thomas in awed tones. 'There are the ghosts, rising as the magician calls to them.' He pointed.

Toward the south, the white and low-lying mists that had been crawling thicker and thicker into the woods, now began to stream upward, rising like long, white draped arms

256

toward the upper sky. Presently they seemed to touch the invisible force that flew through the middle air, and were snatched away bodily. Other arms rose, more and more rapidly; in a trice the whole body of the clinging mist had been snatched away, and the woods lay sullenly revealed down the whole slope of the mountain.

'Something is goin' to happen,' said Hack Thomas grimly. 'I can feel it. These are signs. And it looks like he was the gent that sent them.'

He indicated old Shannon, who was striding from the edge of the woods with the carcass of a young deer slung across his shoulders. He came with great strides, and, whether it was the gray-bearded majesty of his presence, or the infernal commotion in the sky above them, reacting upon their awed minds, it did seem, for the moment, that the hermit was larger and more formidable than a human being. The two regarded him with awe.

'Now, kid,' said Hack Thomas, reverting to his former subject, 'I see that we're all fixed up. You've got your horse just about in hand . . . and there's the job waiting for us down yonder in the plains. Do we start tomorrow morning, or this evening? Or are you goin' to insist on raising a row with Jim Berry?'

The other looked curiously at him. 'What makes you think that I want to have trouble with Jim Berry?' he asked. 'You started in by warning me about him . . . now you talk small about him. What's the idea?'

'He's had his lesson,' said Thomas eagerly. 'He's scared to death, old son. He knows what he's headed for, now.'

'He's had his lesson?' repeated the other with a burst of white anger. 'His lesson ain't started, even.'

Chapter Thirty-Seven

This touch of temper made Hack Thomas, in turn, grow very grave. He came close to Terry Shawn and laid a heavy hand on his shoulder. 'Listen to me, kid,' he murmured. 'You feel kind of hard against Jim.'

'Never mind what I feel.'

'Let me tell you something,' went on Hack. 'Jim is scared to death. He sees what he's done, and he hopes that it's not too late. Matter of fact, kid, I've had a hard job to keep him from clearing out of the camp.'

'Why did he want to go?' asked Shawn.

'Because of you. Berry's game enough, but he doesn't want to commit suicide.'

'I don't get what you're driving at!' exclaimed Shawn with a burst of impatience. 'First you steer me at Berry, and point out that he's apt to turn the head of a girl. Afterward, you come around and tell me that Berry's sorry. Well, Thomas, I don't know that that's much good to me. Suppose that somebody picks your pocket and throws your purse away. Are you going to let him say that he's sorry, and call it quits? Or are you going to jail him?'

'Of course I see what you mean,' replied Hack Thomas. 'I see what you're driving at. You think that Jim Berry has made a great head with the girl. You think that they're pretty thick, eh? Let me tell you, kid, he means nothin' in her young life. Nothin' at all. He was handy and useful . . . he stood around smilin', and she just smiled back a little. That's all.'

'Did she send you over here to give me this line of chatter?' asked the gunman, lowering his head a little and looking grimly at the other.

'She sent me nowhere at all,' Hack assured him. 'It's just because I like you, Terry, that I'm tryin' to stave off any trouble. I like you, and I like Berry. So will you, when you get a better chance to know him.'

'Study your horse when he's tired, and your man when you're in a pinch,' said Shawn. 'I guess that I know him fairly well.'

'Not a mite. But whether you know him or not, whether you hate him or not, you need money, and you need big money, old son.'

'What makes you say that?'

'Can you settle down with a girl like that without a stake?' inquired the other.

Terry Shawn's face blackened. 'We're not

259

settling down,' he said savagely. 'Besides, I've talked enough.'

Hack Thomas saw the youth stride past him, and, furious at himself for touching on the wrong topic, he gritted his teeth and drove his sharp heel into the turf. Then he hurried after Shawn and laid a restraining hand on his arm.

'Kid,' he said, 'will you listen to this? Is it better to kill Jim Berry now, and lose about fifty thousand beans, or is it better to wait till you've got the money in your pocket? Answer me that, will you?'

Shawn hesitated, growing sullen. 'I don't know,' he muttered at last. Then he flung out, rather in agony than in rage: 'I don't know much about anything, Hack. All I know is that I'm in wrong all around. I've lost everything . . . I've got nothing left. I used to have a thousand friends, like old Joe. Well, I chucked them for the sake of a girl. And now I've lost the girl . . . had her taken out of my hands. I don't ask for sympathy . . . only I say that there isn't anything straight before me that's worth looking at except the chestnut. Look at him. He's all that I've got. And what's he good for? Simply to take me into one patch of trouble and out again, faster than the eye can follow. That's all he's good for.'

His manner, however, denied these words, for, as he spoke, he dropped his head against the muscular cheek of the stallion, and Sky Pilot pricked his ears and stood like a rock.

Hack Thomas, really moved, saw that it was a time to waste few words, and he merely said: 'I leave it with you to act like a sensible fellow, old-timer. I'll only say that you're wrong in what you think about the girl . . . she's for you as much as ever. But she's gay . . . she likes to have a jolly time . . . she wants to chatter a bit . . . and Jim Berry has been playin' up to her. I only ask you this . . . watch him tonight, and see how he acts. If he wastes much time around her, then call me a liar. Son, he's going to keep hands off.'

'Because he doesn't want her,' suggested the bitter Shawn. 'Because he's tired of her already.'

He writhed at the thought, while Hack Thomas, seeing that words of no sort would now avail him, walked slowly ahead. He passed Shannon, coming in with the deer, and, for lack of anything better to do, or perhaps to show his respect for that grave-faced hunter, he took the burden from the strong old shoulders and carried it on toward the fire.

Shannon turned off and went toward Shawn, and the chestnut whirled away from its new friend and raced joyously toward the old one. The hermit waved it aside, and, pausing in front of Terry Shawn, he nodded to the horse and then smiled with the utmost cheerfulness and kindness on the outlaw. After that, he did not stay, but this brief instant of meeting impressed Shawn more than the longest of speeches would have done, for it seemed to say: *Welcome, my friend, into the companionship of the chestnut. You and I are now of one world. Good luck be with you.* All this did the smile of Shannon seem to say, at the very moment when Shawn would have expected jealousy and hatred for the sharing of the affection and the trust of Sky Pilot.

So Terry Shawn, almost forgetting the girl and Jim Berry, lingered by himself and communed with a portion of his nature that had never before been revealed to him. Call it the higher self, or the inner mind, or the voice of conscience, whatever it was, that instant of meeting with Shannon had revealed it, and altered life for Terry Shawn.

He remained alone with the new idea— although it was hardly an idea, but rather a form as vague as the mist that lately had lifted from the trees. Thinking of that, he raised his face to the cloud masses that were streaming through the upper sky. Less high, they seemed now, and ever sweeping lower and lower, brushing down toward the earth while the booming echo of the storm rolled faintly and terribly through the cañon. The head of Mount Shannon was quite lost in the storm, now, except for an occasional glimpse, as the very fury of the wind lifted the cloud screen for an instant, and the solemn face of the peak looked forth again.

And it seemed to Shawn that so it was with

the man he had just met. Silence and gentleness ruled his life, but in his breast there were mighty emotions, cast on a greater scale than those of most men, just as the form and the features of Mount Shannon were vaster than those of all of the surrounding summits. Here in this cañon, living in this little shack, was a truly regal and extraordinary presence, and Terry Shawn was overwhelmed by it.

If the recognition of this presence brought more solemnly beautiful ideas of life to Shawn, also it brought a sense of fear and of loss. For one thing, his own strength that always had seemed so great, now seemed a petty matter, and he no longer felt that he could claim possession of the horse. Whatever the coin that Shannon had paid for Sky Pilot, the youth felt that he could never duplicate the price.

The present, however, was not the time for such reflections. Shawn went on toward the house, slowly, his head hanging a little. At least one thing had been gained by this awakening of his soul, for, whereas a moment before all his thoughts had been turning toward big Jim Berry and a crushing vengeance, now Berry and vengeance seemed paltry things—so even did Kitty Bowen—so certainly did Terry Shawn. Such had been the flash of divine light and kindness that had shone on the gunfighter from the hermit's eyes that he began to understand, although dimly, the possibilities of a greater life and a broader

263

comprehension. He breathed uneasily. So great became the commotion in his mind that all the turbulence of the upper sky was unnoticed by his downcast eyes.

In the lee of the house he sat down, crosslegged, and looked down the ravine with eyes that saw nothing of the coming of the storm; neither did he regard Kitty Bowen close by him, nor Jim Berry, quietly at work in the repair of his bridle, nor Hack Thomas, singing in the horse shed, nor old Shannon, cleaning a pelt.

But all work was suspended, from time to time, and all eyes turned up to the sky, for it was now plain that the storm would never stop until it had swept the cañon clean through. Just above their heads the clouds were pouring, rolling wildly, heaving and leaping like animate creatures, and now and again the smoky arm of the storm reached down to the shack and shook it, and made the very ground tremble.

In the same manner, those arms of fury reached down into the woods, and, whenever that happened, the listeners would hear crashings and batterings, and sometimes the loud screech of boughs, ground crushingly, against one another. All the leaves that had been hanging to the trees, in bright autumnal splashes of russet, and gold, and purple, and yellow, and red—all of these leaves were now stripped away wherever the storm wind reached. Whereas the ravine had been a flowing tide of color, now there were spots that had suddenly been harvested of all richness and left barren and brown.

Even Kitty Bowen paid some attention to this vast battle. In all the world there were few more literal-minded and serenely practical persons than Kitty, but now she left her household task, and, standing by the corner of the shack, she faced the downward torrent of the storm.

'That's the way that life is,' said Kitty, the philosopher. 'If you're the tallest tree, you're stripped first, and you're stripped the cleanest, and you're left the most naked for the winter.'

Chapter Thirty-Eight

The storm wind, which had been raging just above the top of the house, now rose, shunted higher, perhaps, by some twisting of the wind currents as they gushed through the mountain passes. As streams of water from two fire hoses meet and make a vast white flower of spray blossom in mid-air, so now, as the counter currents of the storm came rushing together around Mount Shannon, the sky began to boil. Clouds were born and dissolved momentarily, and a vast riot raged over Shannon's peak.

However, this was a thing to be seen rather than heard, for the small group of people in the shack, or around it, were aware only occasionally now, of far-away screamings and moanings, indescribably terrible and sad. But for these echoes of the storm, however, they were relieved from the main burden of noise and could speak again.

So Terence Shawn left his broodings about life and Nature and himself, and turned suddenly to the grim facts that had filled his mind before. There was Kitty Bowen who once had loved him—there was Jim Berry who, he felt, had stolen her away—and here sat Terence Shawn with idle hands.

He looked down at those bony, strong hands in amazement, as though they were capable of answering his question about their idleness, then he began to scrutinize the girl and Berry more carefully.

So darkly hooded was the sky that, even in the full day, there was as much light from the fire as from the heavens, and Kitty Bowen worked in a rosy glow. She seemed permanently stained, for, when she turned from the fire, there still was color on her face and hands. She appeared to be totally absorbed in her cooking, but now and again, cautiously, she cast a side glance toward Shawn, a clever, measuring look, he thought, as though she were coolly appraising him. It angered Shawn intensely; he felt like springing to his feet and crying: *You don't know me! You've never seen me in action, but you're going to, soon!* What was in her mind? Cold dislike, no doubt, because he would not raise his hand against Jim Berry.

As for Berry, he sedulously avoided the eye of young Terry Shawn. It was true that he did not pour his offers of assistance upon the girl now, and, in this respect, it might seem that he was striving to avoid giving further offense to Shawn. Still, there is no use insulting a loser, and it was plain in Shawn's mind that the tall and handsome Jim already had won, and was merely ignoring him, his former rival. And anger rose darkly in the mind of Terry Shawn.

In the meantime, Hack Thomas was making a little idle conversation. 'We're going to get it pretty quick,' he declared. 'The wind has done a little retreat, but pretty soon it'll come again and swamp the whole dog-gone' valley. It's goin' to be full of snow when it comes, too. You mark what I say, things are going to break loose around here pretty soon.'

And he looked anxiously up to the over-massed heavens above them.

Suddenly Shawn stood up, stretched himself with care as though to make sure that every muscle was in smoothest working order, and then turned to Jim Berry.

'Jim, I want to talk to you.'

Jim Berry nodded, without glancing back. 'All right. Go ahead,' he said.

'It's private talk,' said Shawn. 'Just come away from the shack with me, will you?'

He saw Berry stiffen a little; he saw Kitty Bowen catch her hands suddenly together, almost as though she had burned herself at the fire. And that maddened him, but he told himself that this was a plain token that she was wild with anxiety about the welfare of her new lover.

'I don't see any reason,' said Jim Berry, speaking slowly and thereby retaining control of his voice, 'why you can't talk right here, Shawn.'

'I'll tell you the reasons, later on,' Shawn assured him.

But Berry would not move. 'We'll have the wind smashing around the shack in another minute or two,' he said. 'Why not keep here, under cover?'

'Berry,' said the other solemnly, 'what I've got to say isn't the sort of thing that a woman should hear. You understand what I mean?'

Berry, before he answered, cast one eager glance at Hack Thomas, asking a volume of questions in that brief instant, and, in return, he had a sullen nod from Thomas, who was observing matters in the background.

Kitty Bowen sprang to her feet. 'Jim,' she said, 'don't you go a step away with him. I know what he wants.'

'You're a mind-reader, maybe,' said Shawn with bitterness. 'What do I want?'

'You want trouble,' she answered. 'You want to fight because you think . . . well, we all know what you think.'

He was badgered to the last limit of indiscretion. 'Since you all know,' he said, 'I'll say it out loud. Berry has cut the ground from under my feet . . . he's made his set at me, and he's won out. Well, that's all right. He can have you . . . I don't want a girl who changes quicker than the wind. But because he's played low with a partner and played the sneak with me when I trusted him, him and me have got to settle our little account. Berry, will you come out here with me?'

It was odd to see the change that came over Shawn as he spoke. Up to this time, he had appeared the least significant person in that camp, not to be matched, certainly, against the mysterious grandeur of old Shannon, or against the lofty stature and good looks of Hack Thomas and Berry, but now he had altered, and, just as some down-headed undersize pony that has passed unregarded in the pasture, steps on the track with sudden fire in its eye and the manner of an emperor, so Shawn stood before them, now, burning with anger, and terrible as flame.

Had he been totally unknown to them, still he would have commanded their attention and inspired fear in them, but he was known well to them all, and the record of his wild achievements stood sternly behind him. Both

Thomas and Berry were frozen in their places, but Kitty Bowen stepped straight before Shawn and caught him by the sleeves of his coat.

'Terry, dear,' she said, 'are you going to listen to reason for a minute?'

' "Terry . . . dear!" ' he mocked her furiously. ' "Terry . . . dear." I know that I'm nothing to you, girl, and I wish that you were nothing to me, but whatever you are, you can't make me blind and twist me around your finger. Will you stand back? Will you keep out of this?'

'I won't move,' said Kitty, trembling and breathing deeply. 'I'm going to make you see what a . . .'

She could get no further, for Shawn picked her up suddenly and lightly and placed her inside the shack. He slammed the door and thrust home the bolt on the outside. There was a cry, and then a scream from inside.

'Terry, Terry! Let me out! You've been all wrong. I love you, Terry! Don't hurt Jim Berry . . . he's done no wrong!' She could not have spoken more foolishly, for her words seemed a direct appeal to him to save Berry.

Shawn turned on his two companions, and a cold and terrible smile curved his lips. 'You, Berry,' he said. 'Are you ready?'

'I'm ready,' said Jim Berry grimly. 'Mind you, you're wrong. But I won't back down. You've gone a long ways, kid, and you've raised your share of trouble, but you've come to the end of your rope. Go for your gun.'

'Me go for my gun?' sneered Terence Shawn. 'I'm going to kill you, Berry, and I'd kill you if I started with my back turned to you. I give you a flying start. Begin it, Berry.'

The glance of Jim Berry flickered ever so slightly toward Hack Thomas, and there was an imperceptible nod from that grim-faced man. Matters were not going as Hack had wished to have them go, but he was not foolish enough to try protests at a time like this. The game had gone too far for retreat, and he knew it. There was only one choice, as it appeared to him, and that was between the two who were about to fight: should Berry or Shawn live? That question he had answered for himself long before.

'I'll never begin it,' said Jim Berry sullenly. A little, nervous convulsion twisted his mouth into a grimace, and he flushed hot with shame at this betrayal of his state of mind. 'I'll finish, but I won't start.'

'Stand over there, Hack,' commanded Terry Shawn. 'Stand over there and drop your handkerchief for us, will you? That'll do as a signal.'

A great noise of battering began inside the shack. Doubtless it was old Shannon trying to smash down the door, and the wild, sobbing voice of the girl went shrilling out to them. That voice was lost completely, a moment later, and the battering against the door was made to seem small and far off, by the final attack of the storm. It had piled its mountains of clouds all around Mount Shannon and had filled the northern skies with towers that now began to topple and pour down the southern face of the great peak. Roarings and shoutings filled the ravine; the last words of Shawn were lost as the tumult of sound washed over them.

The blast of the wind struck Terry Shawn so violently that he was sent staggering before it, and that stagger saved his life. For Jim Berry, persisting in his non-aggressive attitude, had not touched his weapons, but Hack Thomas had made a quick draw, seeing that the final moment had come. The bullet was well aimed, but, as he pulled the trigger, the storm had knocked Shawn before it—his foot caught in a root that arched above the surface of the grass—and he pitched forward on his face.

Chapter Thirty-Nine

There is a saying, not wholly authenticated, unfortunately, that when Wild Bill the Great was shot through the brain from behind, and fell forward on the card table dead, he made his draw while he was falling. Certainly he was dead the instant the bullet touched him, and his hands were empty, then, except for his cards, yet, when they picked him up, they found a heavy revolver clutched in either hand. The last contraction of muscles, the last instinctive message that quivered down the nerves, had made the dead man draw and prepare for battle.

It was less miraculous, then, that Terence Shawn was able to equip himself with two Colts in the very instant when he was dropping to the ground, but it was wonderful indeed that, before his body actually struck the ground, his guns had spoken. One bullet went wild past the ear of Jim Berry, but the shot from his left hand struck Hack Thomas in the thigh, and he collapsed suddenly upon the ground.

Jim Berry had made his draw. He stood like a duelist, his left hand behind the small of his back, his side turned to the foe, and a barking revolver in his right hand. His first shot kicked a shower of dirt into the face of Shawn, half blinding him; his second surely would have ended the days of Shawn, but the impetus of the outlaw's fall was not ended at once, and he tumbled twice over on his side, still pumping bullets from both guns as he rolled.

A man lying on the ground, as soldiers know, makes an ugly and difficult target. Poor Jim Berry had a prone and rolling figure and he did very well with it. He chipped the toe of Shawn's left boot, and he split the face of his coat, just over the heart, but luck was against

273

him.

Shawn, coming at last to rest on the ground, steadied himself to drive home his last bullets, only to find that both his enemies were now down. Both had lost their guns, and both were groaning and cursing savagely.

With cautious guns balanced in his hands, Shawn rose, just as the door of the cabin burst open and Kitty slipped out before old Shannon. She ran at Terry like a fury, and crying—'Give me those guns, you murderer!' —she wrenched the weapons out of his nerveless hands and ran to where Jim Berry lay.

That, said Shawn to himself, was certain proof that she loved the fellow. She was holding his head in her arms and calling out to him, although the mad surging of the storm cut away her voice at her lips.

Old Shannon was with them, however, and, with his aid, Terry carried both his victims into the shack. There, the howling of the wind was kept away behind the stout log walls, and it was at least possible to attempt conversation.

Thomas had been hit only once, but Jim Berry was fairly peppered. A bullet had clipped through the calf of his left leg; another had grooved his right arm from wrist to elbow, a deep and dangerous wound; the third was the most dangerous, for the slug had passed through both legs above the knees, and on the left leg there was a cut artery.

As for Thomas, the bullet, flying on an upward course, had entered the thigh just above the knee, struck the bone, and come out through the back of the hip. He lay stiff with pain, but making no complaint.

When Shannon went to him, he knocked the hand of the hermit aside and pointed imperiously toward Jim Berry. When Kitty Bowen hurried over to him, he shook his head. 'Save Jim,' he said. 'I've only got what's coming to me.'

Kitty merely fell to work on him, silently, her face white and tense, her hands sure as steel. She cut the leg of the trouser to the entrance wound, and she gripped the thick muscles above it to cut off the flow.

'Quick, Terry! We've got to have a tourniquet, here!'

'I can't leave Jim,' answered the outlaw. 'If only the old man could help with Hack...'

It was literally as though Shannon understood what was said. He turned back to Thomas again, and fell to making, with perfect calm and efficiency, two powerful tourniquets for the weakened Hack.

They worked fiercely, and, as they toiled, the storm freshened and rose from one crescendo to another, until the wild, bellowing voices roared back and forth across the echoing valley with a continual booming.

For two long hours, patiently and carefully they worked, and at the end of that time the wounded men lay in some comfort, still tight-lipped with pain but braced with some heavy drams from brandy flasks.

'Terry,' said Hack Thomas at last, 'heaven knows that I've got no right to speak to you or any other honest man, but the fact is that Jim and me are partners. I couldn't see him tackle you alone. And even with the two of us fighting, and me taking the jump on you, this is the way that it turned out.'

'I don't blame you much,' replied Shawn gently. 'I know that some men figure different from others . . . he was your partner and you had to stand by him. Well, you had your own way of doing that. And here's the end of this game for me, boys. I'm saying good bye. Jim, there's my hand . . . and I wish you better luck with her than I've had. So long.'

He shook hands with Berry, wrung the hand of old Shannon, and then stepped to the door. There was no word from him to the girl, not so much as a glance at her, and she stood with downcast head in the corner. The force of the wind was falling rapidly, but still it howled wildly enough to give much point to Berry's admonition: 'Man, you'll be frozen in one hour, if you go out into that storm.'

'I've seen as bad before,' said Shawn. 'It doesn't worry me, Jim. So long!'

He jerked the door open. A long sighing draft ran through the cabin, and before him lay a blinding mist of flying snow. It was cleft for

276

an instant, and those within could see, now, that the entire ravine was cloaked with shining white. Into that whiteness stepped Shawn, and closed the door heavily behind him. A long silence held the people in the cabin.

'I didn't speak, Kitty,' said Jim Berry, 'because it didn't seem any use. If I told him that I meant nothing to you, what difference would it have made? He would only have laughed at me. How I wish that you could forgive the harm I've done you with him.'

She merely shrugged her shoulders.

And then old Shannon went to her, took her by the arm, and led her to the door. He raised his head, and the lips that had not spoken a human word for those many long months now said in a strangely hollow voice:

'Child, you love him. Go after him and bring him back. Or go after him and follow him where he rides.'

Thomas and Berry, their hair fairly lifting on their heads, raised themselves on their elbows and stared in mortal wonder, and Kitty Bowen looked up at the hermit as if at a ghost.

'Do you understand?' repeated Shannon. 'Go after him . . . fall on your knees before him . . . beg him to take you back. Are you afraid? I'll take you to him.'

And he led her, stunned and unresisting, out of the house and into the open. A great whirl of wind, filled with snow particles, formed around them, and the cold gripped them with a numbing power. Still he strode straight forward, threw open the door of the horse shed, and entered, leading Kitty Bowen like a captive behind him.

There they saw Shawn in the act of drawing up the cinches on a horse.

'Go to him now,' said the hermit. 'Fall on your knees. Tell him that you have been a foolish girl, but that you love him!'

The outlaw, more agape at Shannon than at the girl, stood back from the mustang. Kitty, like one hypnotized, did exactly as Shannon had directed. She fell on her knees before Terry Shawn.

'Oh, Terry, Terry,' said the girl. 'I've been a silly child, but I didn't mean harm. Will you forgive me? Will you take me back?'

Terry Shawn caught her from the floor and held her close in his arms. He had no time to speak a word, for Shannon's voice broke in on them again.

'Go back to the house, child. Take your coat, because you'll need all the warmth you can get. Come back here quickly. You must start away at once.'

She went, never dreaming of disobeying, but, as she hurried through the door of the shed, Shawn protested: 'It's not right to drive a girl like that into this sort of weather.'

'This is her last chance to get away,' he replied. 'Otherwise she'll be frozen in with the rest. You wouldn't want that.'

'Then I'll stay here with them,' said Shawn.

'And be trapped? I know the sheriff of this county, and, if he rides slowly on a trail, he rides forever. Boy, I have broken a great vow for your sake today . . . don't let me break it in vain. Do as I tell you, and begin by saddling Sky Pilot.'

'Are you riding with us?' asked Terry Shawn.

'I am riding with you to show you some short cuts through the lower ravines, so that you can escape the danger of a snow blockade. But I don't ride Sky Pilot. Put your own saddle on him.'

'Hold on!' cried Shawn.

'He is your horse,' said the hermit. 'I give my part in him freely to you, and no man has a greater right to him than I have. He is yours.'

Chapter Forty

You who love diamonds, suppose that the crown jewel, Kohinoor, were put in your hands? Still it was nothing compared with the joy that filled the heart of Terence Shawn as he heard this speech. But he sobered instantly, and exclaimed: 'I never could ride him!'

'Get into the saddle while I hold his head,' said the hermit, 'and he will never trouble you . . . he will be a good servant to you the rest of your life.'

279

'He is like a child to you,' said Terry Shawn. 'How can you give him away?'

'Like should go to like,' said the old man, his face nevertheless touched with a momentary pain. 'What is he to me except a plaything? To you, he's the other half of a soul.'

'Partner,' said Terry Shawn slowly, 'you're a white man to do this, but, if I let you, I'm a snake. I thought that you knew me, but you don't. I thought that you figured me for what I am, but I see that you think I'm some honest "puncher or farmer, maybe. Let me tell you the truth. If you never heard of Terence Shawn before, I'll tell you what he is . . . he's a robber, a waster, a no-good gent. And I can't take more from you than I've taken already.'

The hermit smiled. 'Those two inside my house,' he said, pointing, 'are much worse than they think. They have not been outlawed, and therefore they still think that they are worthy of living like honest men. You, my friend, have been outlawed, and you despise yourself because a sentence has been passed on you. Yet you are better than you think.'

'Ten states would like to have the hanging of me,' admitted Shawn gravely.

'A wise man,' said the other, 'once said that there are only two great sins . . . cruelty and cowardice. You never have been cruel, my young friend, and you never have been cowardly. If you have fought, it has been the

280

fighting of tiger with tiger . . . you have not taken advantage of help-less men. You are better than you dream, Terence Shawn, and, for the sake of this girl, you will settle down to a useful, steady life.'

'Who are you?' asked the outlaw, filled with wonder and awe. 'Heaven knows I hope that what you say about me may be right. Whether right or not, I'm going to give it a chance. But who are you? What brought you here?'

'Sin,' said the hermit gravely. 'Terrible, mortal sin brought me here, sin for which no repentance is complete enough. Silence and misery and cold and pain are not enough.'

The outlaw listened, struck dumb. To attempt to persuade or comfort this man never occurred to him, more than it would have occurred to him to attempt to persuade Mount Shannon's granite cliffs and yawning cañons. His own affairs seemed suddenly to shrink; his own troubles were as nothing; such matters as wind and weather were not to be regarded.

Kitty Bowen came hurrying back, bundled with wraps to face the long ride. For himself, the hermit flung over his shoulders a ragged sheepskin cloak of home manufacture, and gave another to Shawn. So they emerged from the shed with the three horses, and the whole white world lay before them.

'Which way do you wish to ride?' asked the hermit.

'North,' said Terry Shawn eagerly. 'Out of

this range as fast as I can go. But first I'm taking Kitty home.'

'I'd never go,' said the girl. 'Terry, what are you asking of me?' And her eyes grew big with tears.

'Do you think that I'd ride you over the mountains in weather like this?' asked Terry Shawn. 'Back you go.'

'Young man,' said the hermit, 'opportunity comes only once. Heaven has given her to you . . . therefore take her and keep her. You will find a minister in the first small village, no doubt. Be married there, then ride on . . . your home is where you two are found together . . . and before long, you will find a way of settling peacefully. From the moment you have her, you will never be tempted to commit any crime.'

'Listen to him,' said the girl. 'Oh, Terry, I think that we can believe him.'

'He's the law and the gospel to me,' answered the boy solemnly. 'What he asks, I'll do. Sir, would you lead the way?'

'I'll hold Sky Pilot while you mount him. Are you ready?'

'I'm ready. He'll heave me at the sky, though.'

'Watch, then.'

Standing at the head of the chestnut, Shannon soothed it with a word and laid his hand on the reins when Shawn approached and put his foot in the stirrup, but Sky Pilot

282

showed not the slightest concern, and, when Shawn swung into the saddle, the horse merely shook himself a little and then pricked cheerful ears.

Terry Shawn stared at Shannon in amazement. 'I think you're right. He's not going to pitch. What in the world did you do to him?'

'You did it yourself yesterday,' said Shannon, smiling.

'I only got him so that he would let me walk beside him,' protested the outlaw.

'Yes,' said the hermit, nodding, 'but in this world, what no longer fears us already has begun to love us or despise us, and not even Sky Pilot could despise you, my friend.'

With this explanation Shawn had to rest content; indeed, he had little chance even to think, during the next few moments, for Sky Pilot, if not viciously determined to dismount his new rider, was nevertheless so filled with high spirits that he could not and would not keep still. Up on his hind legs he reared suddenly and beat at the air with his armed hoofs, then wheeled and plunged away, frolicking and lashing out with his heels. Twice he skidded on snow-covered rocks on which his shoes rang loudly. Back and forth across the ravine he raced and cavorted like a lamb in spring. Then, as suddenly as he had begun this nonsense, he dropped it, and went calmly along beside the others.

'It's like sitting on the back of a bird,' said Shawn, in a voice trembling with excitement.

'Or a thunderbolt,' suggested the girl. 'Didn't he nearly put you down a dozen times?'

'Never once. He looked wild, didn't he? But once I lost a stirrup, and he was dog-trotting in a minute. I tell you, he's human, he's better than human . . . I never knew a man that was worthy of brushing his coat.'

'It is true,' said Shannon. 'He has learned how to hate and he has learned how to love, while he is still young. My young friend, he should go on to great things with you to ride him.'

'I'll only keep him,' said Shawn sincerely, 'so long as I have to ride hard to break away from this section of the range where I'm known, but, when I settle down to a straight life with Kitty, I'll send him back to you.'

'Is he meant,' asked the hermit with a smile, 'to carry an old man through a solitary forest, or to give pleasure to the eyes of ten thousand people?' Shawn would have protested, but the hermit continued: 'If you have a beautiful daughter someday, will you want to send her away to the woods, or keep her in the world where everyone may enjoy her beauty? Ah, lad, the setting is as important as the jewel, even if it doesn't cost as much. Take Sky Pilot, and may heaven bring you luck with him. When I came back and saw that you'd

284

mastered him, I knew that he should belong to you. Now say no more about it. Here's where the road forks. We can take either of the two ravines. That on the left would be dangerous going, but there are not apt to be any observers along the way. This on the right is easier and quicker, but you may meet other riders there.'

'We'll chance it,' answered Shawn. 'You think that the sheriff rides in all weathers . . . well, he does, but he can't get posses to follow through such a storm.'

'The storm has fallen away,' said Shannon, 'and that sheriff will always do more than you expect. Ride on, however. We'll take the right-hand ravine. Keep a little behind me . . . I'll go on first.'

So he broke trail for them, and the two drew together behind him. They spoke very little, but looked often and wonderingly on one another. And once Shawn saw that Kitty was crying silently and asked her what troubled her.

'It's just that I can hardly stand it, Terry, to think that everything is going to turn out right for us, after all the bitterness and trouble.'

'Not yet. We're a long way from that, Kitty, though I'd like to promise you nothing but success.'

'He said so, and he can't be wrong . . . he *can't* be wrong,' said Kitty firmly, nodding toward Shannon.

Shawn himself secretly felt the same conviction that the hermit spoke as an inspired man, and contentment and surety filled him as they jogged ever onward down the trail.

And now, rapidly, they passed into a new climate. The storm, which had been dying down every moment during the past hour, had now fallen to the dimensions of an ordinary snowfall, and even this, as they dropped lower and lower down the ravine, began to thin out.

Still they could look back and observe Mount Shannon wrapped, as it were, in thunder, but the southern sky momentarily grew brighter. They had come down to a warmer level, and their heavy wraps were almost too hot. Careless joy was rising in the hearts of the lovers, for before them rode a guide and guard who was, they felt, invincible, while behind them lay not only Mount Shannon but all the dangers and the follies and the mistakes of Shawn's past life. Like a region of shadows it appeared to him now.

They saw Shannon stop, suddenly throw out an arm, and then whirl his horse about. He came rap-idly back to them.

'Here,' said Shannon. 'We'll ride straight down that cañon. They're coming straight up to us. I was right . . . the sheriff and twenty men, I think, are on the trail, and every one of them is mounted on a fresh horse. Ride fast. And pray for one more touch of snow to cover our tracks.'

That prayer was instantly answered by the passing of a whirlpool of wind, heavily laden with snow, and, as the whirlwind dispersed, the floor of the ravine was loaded with fresh inches of snow.

Chapter Forty-One

Swiftly the trio went down the little cañon that opened off the course of the main ravine, and, doubling to the right, they came upon a second valley, broader, and leading well on in the direction that they were following.

'It is all the better,' said Shannon, whose cheerfulness was growing with every moment; 'we have better going here and . . .'

'On the right!' snapped Shawn warningly. 'They're coming. Ride, Kitty! Shannon, ride for it!'

They swung their horses about and got them into a gallop, just before a mass of riders burst out of the low woods ahead of them. How it had happened so quickly, they could not imagine, unless it were that the sheriff, catching a glimpse of his enemy in the first ravine, and seeing them disappear, had guessed that they would try this second passage. At any rate, there was the familiar gawky figure of the sheriff, riding with all his customary skill and boldness, and behind him came the pick of the country and the range.

With the very first volley that they poured upon the fugitives from long range, the hat was knocked from the head of Shannon, and the girl's horse was slashed across the hip—not a serious wound but one that made the animal begin to pitch wildly, so that Kitty was almost thrown to the ground.

Shawn turned in the saddle and began to drop shots around the pursuers. His bullets sang close to the ears of the sheriff. They kicked up the snow in white puffs before the feet of the horses, but not a man faltered, and not a man fell out of the race. They were riding today to make a kill, and that was apparent.

Shawn took stock of the horses on which the three of them were mounted. Kitty was a featherweight, and her nag would hold up. Sky Pilot, of course, could laugh at the whole world. That left Shannon. There was the weak point. He was no light burden in the saddle, and his horse could not stretch out, carrying such a weight. Cutting down their speed to keep with him, they were letting the posse climb up on their tracks slowly and surely. A worried glance from Kitty showed that she understood perfectly, but still Shannon was smiling and calm.

He shouted to Shawn: 'Keep a strong heart, my lad! I have an assurance that all will be well!'

No sooner had he spoken than a violent blow in the side made Shawn sway in the saddle, and he felt a bitter pain over his ribs. There was no concealing the fact that he was badly wounded. Even the men in the rear had seen the swaying of the rider, for there was a yell of exultation from them. There was no concealing that wound from Kitty, least of all.

She pulled her horse over beside Shawn, and watched him with a white face. 'We'll have to surrender, Terry,' she said.

'Never,' he answered grimly.

'Terry, we're lost, we're lost. Only trust to the sheriff . . .'

Shawn made a gesture, as though to signify that he would not waste his strength in argument, and then, turning a little in the saddle, he looked back with a sort of leonine fierceness upon his pursuers.

'This way . . . to the right!' called Shannon suddenly.

They swerved into the mouth of a shallow valley, and, riding at full speed, they gained enough to place a full bend of the ravine between them and the pursuit. Here Shannon reined close to Shawn and looked into the narrowing eyes of the youth, and the gray, set face.

'Pull into those trees!' he commanded. 'Dress that wound . . . and stay there till I come back. I'm going to play a game with this posse.'

'We'll stay together . . . ,' began Shawn but the other cut him short with an imperious gesture.

'Do as I say,' Shannon commanded. 'Into that cover, both of you!'

Like children they obeyed, and swung aside into the thicket. Shannon went straight ahead, and even to the two behind him, so did the echo multiply the sound of his running horse, that it seemed surely as if several riders must be pressing up the valley.

They were not well in shelter before the posse came by them, the men leaning forward to the pace, their horses shining with sweat, their ears laid back to their work and their snaky heads stretched forth. First came the tall sheriff. Behind him was the main body, and, a few hundred yards to the rear, a little clump of stragglers.

They saw this, then Shawn tore off coat and shirt, and the girl saw a long raw furrow on his side, scraping across the ribs. There was no danger from it. It was merely painful but would not be fatal, except through the loss of blood. Between them they had skill enough to take care of a worse hurt than this. If only Shannon could keep the posse employed—if only he could draw them sufficiently away.

*   *   *

The hermit had gone straight on down the

valley until it began to dwindle and the floor rose sharply. Mercilessly he drove his horse, and yet, for all his driving, he could not gain ground on the head of the pursuit, for there rode the sheriff and the best of his fighting men on chosen horses. They felt that their quarry was before them at last, and they were sparing neither whip nor spur.

The ground rose, now, to a low divide—a narrow pass littered with boulders, and here Shannon dismounted. Before him there was the beginning of another ravine, rapidly deepening as it progressed—a little valley with a rocky floor where the tracks even of galloping horses hardly would appear. There he might have ridden and striven to hide himself in some nook of the broken walls. Instead, he chose to dismount, and, letting his horse gallop away, took his place behind a great rock. When the sheriff came in sight, with the utmost care Shannon placed a bullet mere inches from the cheek of Lank Heney. Another ball, placed nearer than he had expected, clipped a horse on the shoulder.

The whole posse split, then, like rain on a roof. Some went to one side and some to another. Many dismounted. Shannon heard a clamoring of voices, and presently he had glimpses of men struggling up through the boulders to take him on the flanks.

He was not fighting. He was only pretending to fight, but all the skill that he had learned in hunting on the broad sides of Mount Shannon was brought into play, now. Whenever an enemy fairly showed himself, a bullet was sure to sing past close to his head, and the posse began to advance more slowly, more cautiously, although the voice of the sheriff could clearly be heard urging them on.

Down the farther ravine, the *clattering* hoofs of the riderless horse roused the echoes, and the sheriff was crying: 'There's only one of them here holding us back! Press on, boys! We're losing miles and miles . . . we're losing the whole game, and we had 'em in our hands.'

Twice he himself showed head and shoulders as he climbed recklessly to the front, and twice he ducked, as bullets whistled past him. And so, shifting restlessly from rock to rock, his rifle growing hot in his hands, old Shannon kept the posse at bay for around twenty minutes of precious time. His own horse was long out of sight, and he felt that his work had been accomplished.

His position had grown mortally dangerous, meantime. On the right the sheriff had pushed up into a flanking position, and on the left two others were able to rake him. Twice, leaden slugs splashed on the face of a rock nearby, then a hammer blow struck Shannon on the side of the head, and he rolled helplessly over upon his back.

There Lank Heney found him, eyes rapidly glazing, arms thrown wide. He leaned over the fallen man, then he kneeled by his side.

'It's Shannon!' he exclaimed. 'Man, man, how'd you happen to get mixed up in this game?'

But the hermit had fallen back into his familiar rôle. He only raised himself a little on one elbow and pointed down the shallow valley before them with a smile of triumph, as though to indicate that he was satisfied with the work that he had done in placing his two companions beyond the reach of the law. Then he fell back, one struggle convulsed him, his eyes closed.

'Ride on down the far valley!' shouted the sheriff to his men. 'We've still got a ghost of a show!'

But he kept at the side of the fallen man, waiting for the last moment, full of awe and wonder such as comes on the sternest, when a man lays down his life for a friend.

The closed eyes opened. A flash of life appeared in them, but they were looking far off beyond the face of Lank Heney.

'Death is not the worst evil, my dear,' said Shannon, and with that his eyes opened still wider, grew fixed, and the final tremor passed through his body.

Chapter Forty-Two

Sheriff Lank Heney, a man who never forgot, wrote down all that episode in red in his heart of hearts, more so since the mystery never was explained. The mysterious Shannon died, died with words upon his lips, but thereafter nothing whatever was learned about his past. The dashing young outlaw, Shawn, never was heard of again, and many felt that he must have lost his footing, in going along one of the narrow, snow-covered mountain trails and fallen to his death on the rocky floor of some cañon, half a mile below. Neither did the girl return, and for her Mr. Bowen made a brief but fervent appeal to all his fellow citizens of the range. However, at the end of a few days, he sent out word that he was convinced that further search was useless, that this matter was in wiser hands than his and that it would be folly for him to attempt to alter the ways of divinity.

What brought the whole matter again into the mind of the good sheriff was that, when hunting a slippery cattle thief through those same highlands at the knees of Mount Shannon, he came to the spot where Shannon had died and where they had given him burial among the boulders. He found the spot, but the heap of stones was vastly greater than the one that he and his men had made, and a big block of gray granite had been hewn roughly and with great, deeply bitten letters. The sheriff read the legend with attention:

HERE LIES SHANNON, THE BRAVEST, THE GENTLEST, AND THE BEST OF ALL PARTNERS. GOD GIVE HIM THE HAPPINESS THAT HE GAVE TO HIS FRIENDS!

Now when the sheriff read this notice, he bit his lip and narrowed his eyes, for a sudden thought smote him like a pain and haunted him long after.

However, it was several years after this that he was riding far north and came to a little-frequented corner of the range, for the vast mountains and the broken trails made the district difficult of access. And when he twisted his way through this region of cliffs and rough valleys, he came suddenly on a little paradise in the midst of the wilderness—a four-mile ravine, a quarter as wide as it was long, the floor covered with the richest of river detritus, and all that sweep of land skillfully put to use.

He saw it from above and marked the order of the place with an approving eye, then, having passed down the trail, he rode through sweet-smelling orchards, and fields of springing grain, and wide, rich pastures where blood horses walked, and fine cattle wandered.

All that man could wish for was being raised on that ground, as it appeared to the sheriff. He took smiling heed of it, and so he came to the house.

It was not overly large, but vastly comfortable. It stood near the bank of the creek, surrounded by a vast tangle of garden that was allowed to run half wild. Farther up the stream was the mill and the mill dam, and around the mill there appeared to be a tiny village. At least there were the signs of the carpenter, miller, blacksmith, storekeeper, and a crossroads seemed to indicate that people came down from some distance in the mountains to make their trading headquarters here.

The sheriff viewed these scenes with the greatest pleasure, for it is always a delightful thing to see prosperity, particularly on what seemed to him such a princely scale. And then he took note of three handsome youngsters tumbling in the garden, and beyond the garden a bit of fine pasture with a beautiful chestnut horse standing in it. It was the sight of the horse that gave him his clue, after all. He rode closer. He stared with hungry eyes. There was no doubt about it—that chestnut was Sky Pilot.

Then he turned sharply and regarded the children. At last he called to the oldest, a sweet-faced girl of seven, and, when she came running, he lifted her up beside him in the saddle.

'Now, honey,' he said, 'I want you to tell me something. You've got a fine mother and daddy, I take it.'

She nodded; she was not attracted by the manner of Lank Heney.

'You remember this. Say it to your mother and your daddy the first minute that you can find 'em . . . "Sheriff Heney has been here, and he wishes them well." Do you hear?'

'Yes.'

'Repeat it now.'

She obeyed.

'Aye,' said Lank Heney, 'you've got the very look of her. And before you're full grown, honey, you'll be at work breakin' hearts.'

With that, he rode slowly down the trail beside the creek, and the little girl scampered into the house. Presently a man ran out, saddle and bridle in hand. He called the chestnut, and Sky Pilot came to him a blast of storm wind, vaulting the fence in his haste. However, with the horse beside him, the man hesitated, and, looking long and earnestly after Heney as he disappeared down the road, at last seemed to feel that it was best to let the other go unhailed.

He turned thoughtfully back into the house, the door closed softly behind him, and all was as it had been before. But not quite. For a great shadow had been lifted from that happy valley on this day, never to return.